There was just o...
Dane Marchwood that sh...
wife he angrily accused her of being.

"If I must prove my love for you, then I will," she said softly, undoing her nightgown and allowing it to fall to the floor.

His gaze moved slowly over her, and then returned coldly to her face. "I take no man's leavings, madam."

She went to him and sank to her knees. "Please don't turn me away, Dane," she whispered.

She heard him exhale slowly. "What's this? Has someone brewed a potion to turn my ice-wife into a creature of flesh and blood?"

He didn't move away, though, and for a moment she thought his fingers touched her hair. He was close enough to touch, to caress. She longed to feel his warmth, and suddenly could no longer resist. She reached out slowly to put her trembling finger-tips against his thigh.

**She was seducing her own husband—but she still had to find out if this act of love was a lie....**

# SIGNET REGENCY ROMANCE
## Coming in July 1995

---

### *Anne Barbour*
My Cousin Jane

### *Elisabeth Fairchild*
Lord Endicott's Appetite

### *Elizabeth Jackson*
Rogue's Delight

---

# Magic at Midnight

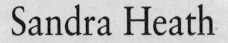

## Sandra Heath

A SIGNET BOOK

SIGNET
Published by the Penguin Group
Penguin Books USA Inc., 375 Hudson Street,
New York, New York 10014, U.S.A.
Penguin Books Ltd, 27 Wrights Lane,
London W8 5TZ, England
Penguin Books Australia Ltd, Ringwood,
Victoria, Australia
Penguin Books Canada Ltd, 10 Alcorn Avenue,
Toronto, Ontario, Canada M4V 3B2
Penguin Books (N.Z.) Ltd, 182–190 Wairau Road,
Auckland 10, New Zealand

Penguin Books Ltd, Registered Offices:
Harmondsworth, Middlesex, England

First published by Signet, an imprint of Dutton Signet,
a division of Penguin Books USA Inc.

First Printing, June, 1995
10  9  8  7  6  5  4  3  2  1

PUBLISHER'S NOTE
This is a work of fiction. Names, characters, places, and incidents either are the
product of the author's imagination or are used fictitiously, and any resemblance to
actual persons, living or dead, events, or locales is entirely coincidental.

# *One*

~

The hot New York afternoon gave no hint of the extraordinary events in store for Kathryn Vansomeren over the following weeks. There was no warning at all of the amazing emotional entanglement that would change her existence in every imaginable way.

It felt like any other summer afternoon, and her marriage was in the same mess it had been for the past year, ever since she lost the baby. No, if she was honest, it had been in a mess for longer than that. They were temperamentally unsuited, and should never have married in the first place. At least, that was how she felt; she didn't really know if Richard thought the same. They seldom communicated properly these days, which was something they did both know, but were refusing to face.

This was why the English vacation was so important. As far as she was concerned, it was far more than just a fortnight in Gloucestershire to trace his mother's family; it was a lifeline that might give her a chance to think positively about the mess her career was in, and might also save her marriage, which right now was in real danger of drowning.

Researching his ancestry was something Richard liked to do. Before they married, he'd gone to Holland to trace the Vansomerens; this year it was the turn of the English Larvilles. She'd once tried to find out about her own family, but it proved impossible. She was adopted, and the New York agency that dealt with all the paperwork had burned down a few weeks after her birth. Now there was no information to be found about who her real parents had been. Not that she really minded. She'd been adopted by the Hilliards, an Albany accountant and his wife, and she adored them both.

This particular Saturday afternoon brought things to a head where her marriage was concerned. It was early July, and the weather was hot as Kathryn read one of her favorite historical romances on the roof garden of their Manhattan penthouse. Money was no object for Richard, so theirs was a sought-after address. He was unusual; though young he was a rising star in one of the premier firms of architects in the city, and his family was very wealthy, so he could afford the best. In fact, it had to be said that in every area except his marriage, Richard Vansomeren had it made.

If the same could have been said for Kathryn's situation, it mightn't have been quite so bad, but her career was no longer as rewarding as it had once been, which meant she was unhappy both at home and at work—a lethal combination when it came to remaining sweet-tempered and level-headed at all times.

It was through work she and Richard had met. He'd been the project architect for the new offices commissioned by the local TV station she worked for as a junior reporter. She liked her job then, and it seemed like the sky might be the limit, but that was before her old boss retired and his successor arrived on the scene. Anyway, for some reason she couldn't remember now, she got picked to attend a site meeting one bitterly cold January morning.

She'd been wrapped up like an Eskimo, with only her eyes showing through a frame of fur. Not exactly haute couture, but at least she stayed warm. The last thing she needed when she was dressed so unflatteringly, was to come face-to-face with a tall, blond, blue-eyed god with a divine smile and a Mount Olympus tan. To make matters worse, she slipped on some ice and fell on her butt in front of him. God, what an entry. The leading lady made a real hash of her opening scene with the leading man of her dreams. Oh, yes, Richard was the sort of man she went for in a big way, but in those first few minutes it really seemed she'd blown it. But he looked past the fringe of ice-tipped fur and liked the hazel eyes peeping out at him. So much so, he asked her to dinner that night.

Things had gone from strength to strength after that, and it wasn't long before they'd become lovers. She wasn't very experienced, sleeping around had never been her thing, and she was afraid of disappointing him in bed, but eventually it was to be the other way around, and *he* would disappoint her. But, like the change for the worse in her career, that too was to come.

In those heady days of first romance, they'd been happier than they ever thought possible, and for a while she walked on air both at home and in the office. She was certainly floating around too much to realize what changes there'd be when Joe Carini retired and Diane Weinburger took over. From that moment on, Kathryn found herself being steadily and cleverly elbowed out, so instead of the sky being the limit, maybe her desk top might have to do instead. But she didn't really notice at first. What did a change of boss matter when one was in love?

Richard got sent to Hawaii for a week to set up a new project, and she'd been able to take time off to go too. It turned out to be a week in paradise, but paradise made one a little forgetful, and she overlooked her pill twice and came back pregnant.

She half-expected Richard to run a mile, or at the very least to offer to pay for a termination or something, but instead he'd been over the moon. Nothing less than marriage would do, and she'd been swept along on a wave of happiness. What more could any girl want? She thought she had a great career and a great guy, and that the future couldn't look rosier. And all in the space of a few months from that fateful January day when she'd gone down on her butt on the ice.

It was when she was in the middle of the worst morning sickness since Eve that she began to realize how bad things were becoming at the TV station. Diane Weinburger had just been waiting for an excuse to find fault, and a few late mornings caused by a difficult pregnancy were just what she needed. She began to pick away, undermining and underinforming, so Kathryn gradually ended up on the sidelines of everything. The choice assignments Joe would have seen she got from time to time, to bring out the qualities he knew she had, never came her way now. There was an element of personal vindictiveness too. It wasn't just Diane Weinburger versus another female colleague, it was Diane Weinberger versus Kathryn Vansomeren in particular. Kathryn got sent on all the stomach-turning jobs, which then got mysteriously omitted when the programs went out, and after a while her pregnancy was used as an excuse to exclude her. Diane would give one of her sweetly concerned smiles and murmur something about one having to take care at such times.

It was a downward slope, and Kathryn was sliding fast, but at least her marriage was solid and happy. At least, she thought it was, because there hadn't really been time yet to realize she and Richard had too many conflicting ideas about what they liked to do. Being in the middle of a lousy pregnancy didn't make her the life and soul of the party, and going out until all hours had never really appealed to her. Working full time meant she needed to rest in the evenings, but Richard still wanted to go out. There came a time when she had to insist on staying in, and at first he tried to stay in too. But he was bored. God, was he bored! He liked company, lots of it, and sitting alone in the penthouse with just her and the TV was like putting him in jail! He wanted her to give up work for the time being, pointing out, very reasonably, that they didn't need the money. But she wanted to cling to her independence. Being married meant being a partner, not a chattel, so she kept her job. He began grumbling then, and maybe he was right, for with hindsight it was plain there was something very wrong with the pregnancy.

The clashes over whether or not she should work, and whether or not it was really necessary for her to stay in every single night, showed her the honeymoon was well and truly over. It also showed that the everyday business of marriage wasn't simple. But there was still the baby, and that meant everything to Richard. He was looking forward to being a father—no, more than that, he was *longing* to be a father. Just like some women aren't happy unless they're surrounded by babies, Richard seemed like he wouldn't be complete until he had a child. Boy, girl, it didn't matter, just so long as it was his.

Then the worst happened, and she miscarried. It started when she was sent to cover a union dispute at a sewage treatment plant—yet another of Diane's malevolent assignments, which in the end didn't get broadcast anyway. Standing around for hours on end waiting for something to report had left her feeling decidedly unwell. Gradually she felt worse and worse, until she was doubled up in agony. For once, Diane couldn't have been more helpful, but afterward it became clear the situation simply provided her with another chance to prove how the station could function perfectly well without Kathryn Vansomeren's dubious input.

Nothing could save the baby, and as if that weren't bad enough, the doctors discovered that due to complications she was very unlikely to ever have another. It wasn't beyond the bounds of possibility, but highly improbable. She'd been devastated, but Richard had been distraught, and for several weeks it was his own loss that concerned him, not hers. When she'd been allowed home, he'd gone through the motions of looking after her, but she could sense his unspoken accusations. Losing the baby was *her* fault; if she hadn't selfishly insisted on keeping her career going . . . He didn't say it out loud, though, and for that at least she was thankful. She felt guilty enough already, and didn't need to be told that trying to do a high-powered job while in the middle of a difficult pregnancy wasn't the wisest thing in the world. But it was done now, and they had to pick up the pieces, if indeed there was much left to pick up.

Now it was like a cold weather front had gotten stuck right over their penthouse, when everyone else in New York was sweltering under the summer sun. The marriage was going downhill as fast as her career, and she knew that the crisis point for both of them had almost been reached. It didn't help that they seldom made love now, or that she'd succumbed to the temptation of a brief fling with a colleague, for that fling had opened her eyes to what sex really could be like. Harry Swenson was a practiced lothario, and she didn't really know why she'd let it happen, except she'd been at her most vulnerable and he knew when to pounce. But he sure as hell knew his stuff! Being with him reminded her of a commercial she'd seen on Irish TV during a weekend assignment in Dublin. Something about a particular brand of beer reaching the parts other beers couldn't. Harry definitely knew what parts to reach! He knew about parts Richard never dreamed existed, and she didn't know much about either.

After that she tried to tell herself that the physical side of marriage shouldn't be given too much importance, that she should concentrate on building up the rest of the crumbling estate of her particular portion of holy matrimony. The trouble was, Harry had opened her eyes too much, and sex suddenly mattered a lot more than it used to. She discovered she had a wanton side that longed for the sort of erotic gratification Richard couldn't or wouldn't give. She yearned for romance and excitement, to be swept off her feet and kept off them! She'd have liked more spontaneity where sex was concerned. If possible, she'd like it in the middle of the morning, on the floor, over the table, in the shower, in the car, and anywhere else the mood took her, but the distance between Richard and her seemed to widen by the day, and now it was several weeks since they'd made love at all.

From the pinnacle of happiness she'd known when they came back from Hawaii, everything had somehow gone wrong. And she had Diane Weinburger on her back as well. The woman wanted her out, and Kathryn had reached the point of wondering whether it was better to go before she was pushed. What satisfaction was there in a job that had deteriorated to this extent? And what satisfaction was there in a similarly deteriorated marriage? Should she get out of both before it was too late?

That was why the forthcoming English vacation was so important. What had started out as a chance for Richard to trace his roots had turned into something much more important. She knew they needed time together if they were to patch things up, and she needed time to think about her career. God, the more she dwelt on it all, the more stressed out she became. She needed a rest just to stay sane!

That was how things stood that baking hot summer afternoon when Richard came home from playing golf to tell her the vacation was off.

# *Two*

~

Hearing him arrive home, Kathryn put her book down and went inside, closing the glass doors on the city noise. She was slender and lithe, some said boyish, with bobbed chestnut hair and large hazel eyes, and she wore jeans and an old blue work shirt. Before he said so much as a word she knew something was wrong. The studied way he put his golf clubs down gave him away. He was thinking of how to tell her something she wasn't going to like.

Intuition told her what it was. "England's off, right?" she said.

He took a deep breath and nodded. "There's a problem with the Chicago project and I have to go see what can be done." He didn't look at her because he knew her eyes would be registering reproach on a grand scale.

"A problem? What sort of problem?" She tried to keep cool, even though anger was already bubbling inside.

"Someone fouled up with the dimensions so one of the elevator shafts doesn't fit."

"Is that all?"

His blue eyes were cold. "It mightn't seem much to you, but from where I stand it's pretty vital."

"Are you the one who fouled up?"

"No, it was Brand."

Brand Philips was one of the senior partners at his firm. She raised an eyebrow. "If it was him, why are you the one who has to go sort it out? Shouldn't he do it?"

"Yes, he should, but it's my project now."

"Since when?"

"Since the ninth hole, damn it. He told me at the ninth, okay?" He went to fix a Scotch and water.

"So, over a casual round of golf, he happens to mention this goof, and tells you to go clear up his mess?"

"It wasn't quite like that."

"But near enough," she replied dryly. Brand was always a little too quick to pass the buck. He was never there when problems he created cropped up, but always around when medals were handed out. Maybe that was how he had gotten to be a senior partner.

"Look, the thing needs clearing up quickly or we'll be into penalties for overrunning." He swirled the Scotch and drank half the glass.

"Why can't he do it?" she asked shrewdly, wondering what sort of get-out clause Brand had dreamed up this time.

"He can't." He avoided her eyes again.

"Why?"

He didn't reply.

"Come on, Richard. Why can't he go?"

"Because he'll be on vacation!" With an angry gesture, he finished the drink and poured another.

Kathryn gave an incredulous laugh. "Well, if that doesn't beat all! He must have his vacation, but ours can go to hell!"

He swirled his glass and took a more conciliatory stance. "We can go to England another time."

"Can we?" she replied dryly.

"You know we can. Oh, come on, Kathryn, what's the fuss? What does it matter if we go now or later?"

"The fuss is, we *need* to go now," she said quietly.

"It's only a goddamn vacation! Can't you be adult about it? Your career might be going down the tubes, but mine isn't!"

She was so upset she didn't trust herself to answer, and so turned to look out at the New York skyline. There were tears in her eyes. She didn't want it to be like this. There had been good times, and maybe they'd find them again. Two leisurely weeks in England would have been ideal, but now he'd pulled the rug from under, and her resentment was such she could feel herself trembling.

He spoke again. "Kathryn, you have to be reasonable about this. My career—"

She saw red. "Okay, you've made the point, your career's

still important, mine clearly isn't, so you go to Chicago if you want, and I'll go to England on my own." She hadn't even realized the words were on her lips, but the vacation meant too much to give it up because of Brand Philips's ineptitude! Maybe there was no chance now of using England to patch up the holes in their marriage, but she could sure as hell use it to give some real thought to her other problems!

He was startled as well. "On your own?" he repeated.

"Yes."

"You can't be serious."

"Why not?"

"What the heck interest is Gloucester to you?"

"It's the place where we've rented and paid for a luxury apartment for two weeks, that's what the interest is. Besides, as you pointed out so sensitively, my career's down the tubes, so I've got some thinking to do, and right now Gloucester seems blessedly far away from here!"

He ran his fingers through his hair. "I'm sorry I said that about your career. I didn't mean it."

"Oh, yes, you did."

"Look, I want this vacation too, so can't we put it off a while? Just until I get back from Chicago."

"How long will that be?"

He hesitated. "Well, Chicago might not take all that long," he admitted, "but after that I might have to go to Phoenix."

"Why?"

"There's a prestigious new project there, a leisure complex. But there's a question mark over it. Brand might be back for that."

"You can bet your life he will!" she observed sourly. "If it's prestigious, good old Brand will be there in the front line. Until he fouls up again, that is."

Richard glowered. "I only said I *might* have to go to Phoenix. It's not definite, but I can hardly go ahead with vacation plans until it's more clear."

"And how long do you reckon it will be before you know for sure?"

"If it goes ahead, two months at least."

"Two months! And how long after that before you might feel you can take two weeks for us?" Her tone couldn't have been more heavily ironic if she'd tried.

"You know how long new projects take to get off the ground."

"So we're talking maybe next year some time?"

"Possibly."

She was aghast. A minimum of six more months of this?

He glanced at her. "Look, it mightn't come to that. It might just be that I can come back from Chicago, and we can go."

"But it might not. I can't wait that long, Richard. I'm desperate to go now."

"Aren't you being a little selfish?"

"As is my wont, you mean?" she inquired acidly.

He fell silent.

She watched the way he kept swirling his glass. "Besides, what difference will it really make to you whether I'm here in New York or in England? Either way, you'll be in Chicago with your damned elevator shaft, or in Phoenix doing whatever it is you have to do there."

Her tone needled him. "I have a job to do, Kathryn!"

"Don't give me that. You're going to Chicago because it suits you, and you're hoping like hell to get that Phoenix project too. Anything to further your career."

"And that rankles with you right now, doesn't it?" he fired back.

"Yes. No. Oh, I don't know." She looked out at the skyline again. "All I do know is that I want you to come to England, like we planned."

"You know your trouble? You have an attitude problem!"

"If by that you mean I think this vacation is more important than getting Brand Philips out of his own hole, then yes, I have an attitude problem! Maybe you don't know, but I don't just have an attitude problem. I have a marriage problem too. Correction, *we* have a marriage problem. In case you hadn't noticed, things aren't hunky-dory around here anymore."

He gave a cold laugh. "Oh, I've noticed, all right. I've noticed that any difficulties we have are usually your doing. You've made it pretty damned clear lately that you resent my career, which I think is a little rich coming from someone who once put her career before everything else. If you hadn't lost the baby . . ." He didn't finish the sentence, but looked accusingly at her, his blue eyes bright with bitterness.

Was this the long-overdue explosion? The one that was far

too late in coming? She made herself meet his eyes. "Lost the baby? You make it sound like I mislaid it somewhere in the subway!"

"Do I? Well, that wasn't my intention," he said evenly.

The tone wasn't lost on her. "Then what was your intention?"

He averted his gaze, so she pressed him. "Come on, Richard, there's obviously something on your mind, so you might as well say it."

"All right, damn it, I will! Your selfishness caused that miscarriage. You were so darned determined to keep your stupid career going that you sacrificed our child! And for what? You haven't got any damned career worth mentioning anymore anyway!"

"It wasn't selfishness," she whispered.

"No, you preferred to call it independence! Well, screw your independence! I've no doubt that part of you is glad about what happened, for a top TV reporter can't be tied down by babies, can she? But then it all came to nothing anyway because Joe Carini retired and Diane Weinburger took over."

The accusing words hung in the air long after he'd said them, and for a moment she was too distressed to respond. She'd always know he blamed her for the miscarriage, but she hadn't realized he thought she didn't regret it. "Is . . . is that what you really think? That I was *glad* I lost the baby?" she asked haltingly.

He shifted uncomfortably. "How could I not think it?"

Tears leapt to her eyes as she fired her own reproaches back. "Did you ever bother to ask? You're so quick to accuse me of selfishness, but what of yours? When it all happened, you were so wrapped up in your own grief, you never gave a thought to how *I* felt! Well, for your information, I *did* want that baby, I wanted it more than anything else in the world."

He'd colored a little when she pointed out his lack of concern toward her at the time of the miscarriage, but guilt made him continue the attack. "I wish I could believe you, Kathryn, but somehow I can't help doubting."

"Then there's not a great deal more to be said, is there?" she observed quietly.

"Meaning what, exactly?"

"That we should seriously consider if there's anything left to save."

He cleared his throat. "Look, we're both overwrought. I've been working too hard, and I know your health has taken a long time to recover since the baby . . ."

It was an olive branch of sorts, and in spite of the bitterness of the altercation, she responded to the conciliatory tone. They might be racing toward the brink, but the brakes could still be applied. If only he'd come to England with her . . .

She pleaded again. "I'm begging you to come on this vacation, Richard. We desperately need to spend time alone together."

He drew a heavy breath. "I hear what you're saying, but I simply *must* go to Chicago. It really is important. You see, Brand's going to retire and he's considering putting me up for a partnership in his place."

"So, that's the carrot, is it?" she replied coldly.

His eyes flashed again. "Call it what you will, it's what matters to me. I want to be a partner."

She saw how useless it was. What room did such ambition leave for marriage? "Do what you want, Richard."

"Then you agree to postpone things?"

She shook her head. "No, I'm still going to England."

His temper snapped. "Then go, damn it!"

"I intend to." She walked from the room.

He was in Chicago when she left at the end of July. Right up to the moment her flight took off she hoped he'd change his mind and join her. He didn't.

She didn't know she'd never see him, her family, home, or friends again, that she was flying to a destiny so fantastic she'd never have believed it possible.

# Three

~

England was all she could have hoped for. Even the weather. She drove out of London in brilliant late July sunshine, and soon left the capital far behind as she made her way west toward Gloucester, choosing to go across country rather than follow the main routes. She liked the rolling green countryside, the quaint towns, and the slower pace. She even liked the narrow roads and the evil gears of her rented car, but in her present frame of mind she'd probably have liked anything that took her away from the twin battlegrounds of marriage and career. Right now, both Richard Vansomeren and Diane Weinburger seemed magnificently far away on the other side of the Atlantic.

She was determined to use the next two weeks to think carefully about the future. There was no point in having this time to herself if she was just going to pick up where she left off. Something had to give in her marriage, or she and Richard were headed straight for the divorce court. As for her fond wish of becoming a top TV reporter, well, she could kiss that good-bye as things stood now.

All this was going through her head as she drove, but as she reached the edge of the escarpment above the wide valley where Gloucester and neighboring Cheltenham were laid out before her, something happened that was so strange it made her temporarily forget all her problems.

The moment the panoramic view came into sight, she was struck by such a fierce feeling of *déjà vu* that she almost swerved her car into the path of an oncoming truck. With a scream she slammed on the brakes and the truck thundered past. It was a close call, and her heart pounded as she rested her forehead weakly against the steering wheel.

As she recovered a little, she looked at the view again. There was something so oddly familiar about the way the magnificent medieval tower of Gloucester cathedral rose from the late afternoon haze, that she shivered in spite of the summer heat. Then she shook her head. The prospect was clearly a famous one, for there was a special parking area, so she told herself she must have seen it in a travel magazine or something. But if she had, it wasn't recently, because she hadn't looked at any of the literature Richard had sent for. A wry smile touched her lips. If anyone should experience *déjà vu* here, it was Richard, not her. After all, it was his mother's family, the Larvilles, that came from these parts.

The "been here before" feeling lingered as she drove on down into the valley carved by the River Severn, and intensified the closer she went to the city. By the time she turned into the short cobbled street that led to the cathedral gates, the sensations were so strong she felt that at any moment she'd see someone she knew. But there was no one.

The rented apartment lay just off the street, and was reached by a narrow lane about fifty yards long between the cathedral gates and a picturesque half-timbered restaurant called the Monk's Retreat. The lane was wide enough to take a car, and ended in a rose-decked courtyard where derelict eighteenth-century cottages had been turned into luxurious tourist accommodations. The little development was right in the heart of the medieval part of the city, but at the same time was very private and secluded, and every apartment enjoyed a splendid view of the cathedral tower against the flawless blue sky.

There was a resident janitor to take care of things. He was a burly, comfortable man, with a broad smile and equally broad Gloucestershire accent. He came out the moment he heard her car in the yard.

"Would you be Mrs. Vansomeren?" he asked, buttoning his blue coat.

"Yes, I would, Mr. er . . . ?"

"Elmore. Jack Elmore. I'm the caretaker. Everyone calls me Jack."

"Right, Jack. I take it you got my message about my husband not coming?"

He nodded as he helped take her luggage from the trunk. "I trust you had a good journey?"

"Yes, excellent, thank you." The courtyard roses were sweet and heady in the warm air, and the fragrance seemed to stir hidden memories. It was another odd feeling, like the way she'd felt when she saw the view from the escarpment.

"This way, if you please." He led her to a corner door, beyond which a staircase led to the upper apartments. A thick plum-colored carpet softened their steps, and white-painted walls were hung with foxhunting prints. It was very quaint and "olde worlde," as was the six-room apartment which was to be her home for the next fortnight. The pretty floral chintz furnishings, polished brass and copper, low beams, and alcoves were just what one wanted of England, but all the modern comforts were provided too. The kitchen was very well equipped, and the refrigerator was filled with all the food Richard had meticulously listed when he'd first made the booking.

Jack put all her luggage in the main bedroom. "I hope you like your accommodation, miss, I mean, Mrs. Vansomeren. Begging your pardon, but may I just call you 'Miss'? It's my habit, and I keep slipping back into it."

"That's okay. And yes, I do like the rooms. To be honest, I feel quite at home." Well, certainly as if I've been here before, anyway!

"I'll take that as a compliment to my wife's homely touch, miss. Now then, we've stocked up everything on your husband's list, and things like bread and milk are delivered every day. If you want to eat out, you won't go wrong at the Monk's Retreat. It's run by my sister Daisy, so I can recommend the cooking! Nothing fancy and Frenchified, just plain English recipes. But if you prefer ready meals delivered to your door, I know the best places for dishes from Chinese, Indian, Greek, Italian, and so on."

"Thank you."

He took a sheaf of leaflets from his pocket. "These might be of interest. They tell you about most of the attractions in the area. The Victorian docks are well worth a visit at the moment."

"Docks?" She was taken aback, for Gloucester was inland.

He grinned. "I can tell you haven't done your homework."

"None at all."

"Gloucester's been a port since Roman times because it's at the first fordable point on the river, which is tidal and treacherous quite a way inland. It's got the second highest tide in the world, the highest is in Canada, I believe, so they built a dock basin and a canal to avoid the worst of the estuary."

Something strange happened again then. She suddenly felt she knew all about the docks and the canal, and yet this was the first she'd heard of them. It must be some effect of jet lag!

Jack went on. "The tall ships are in at the moment, some of them genuinely old, others built for the movies. You shouldn't miss seeing them. There's a carnival, too, with all sorts of entertainments. It's not quite Rio de Janeiro, but we try our best." He chuckled. "Well, I'll leave you then. Now don't forget, if there's anything you want, I'm your man."

"Thank you, Jack."

When he'd gone, she opened all the windows to let the scent of roses flood in. There was no great city roar, no automobile horns blaring, no distant sirens, just voices and the sound of footsteps on cobbles. It was a world away from New York. She gazed up at the cathedral, and knew she'd done the right thing coming here on her own. She felt relaxed already—in fact, she almost felt at home.

At home? She thought again how familiar everything seemed, then sighed. She was out of practice at traveling, Diane Weinburger had seen to that! The flight here had taken a long time, then there'd been a drive on the "wrong" side of the road in a car she didn't like. All she needed was a rest to be as good as new.

After taking a shower and selecting something from the refrigerator, she rang Chicago in the hope of speaking to Richard, but though the hotel paged him, he was nowhere to be found. To be truthful, she wasn't too displeased not to have caught him, for any conversation they had now was almost certain to end acrimoniously. So she left a message and then settled back to watch some TV, browse through the literature Jack had left, and generally while away what was left of the long summer evening.

It was twilight and she was just about to go to bed when Richard returned her call. As she feared, the conversation didn't go well. He left her in no doubt he didn't think much of her taking the vacation alone, then he hung up after again accusing her of selfishness. Slowly she put the receiver down. They couldn't even speak long-distance without snarling, and she was beginning to feel divorce was inevitable.

She gazed down at the phone. Right now she felt like calling him back to say where he could stick his resentment and chauvinism. And after that she'd like to call Diane Weinburger and tell her a few choice home truths. The temptation was almost too great to resist, but resist it she did. She'd come here to think *sensibly*, not to let her stress run berserk.

After such a hectic day, she expected to sleep like a log until morning, but something woke her just before midnight. She lay there in the darkness wondering what had disturbed her. The night was unexpectedly humid and uncomfortable, not what she'd expected of England. Maybe she shouldn't have closed the window before getting in bed.

She got up to open it again. Cooler air swept refreshingly over her naked skin, and the night perfume of the roses in the courtyard was almost intoxicating. The cathedral was floodlit, standing out in amber glory against the starry black sky. A group of people laughed and joked together as they left the Monk's Retreat, and she was watching them cross the road when they suddenly disappeared.

Disappeared? She stared blankly. One moment they'd been there, the next they'd simply vanished. But then, so had most of the street detail she'd seen so clearly only seconds before. Then she realized there were no bright street lamps anymore. Everything was in virtual darkness, even the cathedral. The medieval stonework that had been bathed in yellow-orange, was now merely a shadow against the heavens. What had happened? Had there been a power outage?

Instinctively she turned to try the TV, but it wasn't there; instead, there was a lighted candle on a table. The little flame swayed gently, illuminating a room that wasn't there either. At least, a room that shouldn't be there, but was. The bed she'd just gotten out of had changed into an ancient but good-quality four-poster that almost touched the low ceiling. There was no TV, video, or phone, not even a carpet, nothing modern at all, just the bed, two chairs, a table, and a dusty old fireplace that yawned blackly where a few moments before there had been a replica inglenook complete with traditional log effect.

It was a simple room, not the property of someone of

means, but at the same time not of someone impoverished. A
retired servant from a mansion, perhaps. Yes, that would explain
the four-poster, which had clearly once been a very superior
piece of furniture. . . .

Her mouth ran dry. She was looking into the past, at the cottage as it had been at the beginning of the nineteenth century.
Oh, God, first all the *déjà vu,* now she was hallucinating! She
choked back a cry, closed her eyes, and turned toward the window again. This wasn't happening. It couldn't be happening.
She'd count to ten, pinch herself, and then look again.

But when she'd done that, and hesitantly opened her eyes
once more, she found herself staring at her jeweled reflection
in the window glass. *Jeweled* reflection? She gasped, for a
glittering comb sparkled in her carefully arranged golden
curls. Her heart gave a sickening lurch. She didn't have a
comb like that, or long golden hair worn up in a style that reminded her of ancient Rome, but the woman who gazed back
at her had both, and was dressed in a high-waisted emerald
silk gown in a style that had been all the rage in the first quarter of the nineteenth century. English Regency. Yes, that was
it. Like a character from Jane Austen, or Georgette Heyer.

She gazed incredulously. Everything about her had changed.
Her boyish figure had become much more feminine and curvaceous, with a tiny waist and full breasts that were almost exposed by the low-cut neckline of her gown. She was still in her
mid-twenties, but now had an appealingly beautiful face, with
a pale but perfect complexion, and eloquent lips that trembled
a little nervously. She was clearly a woman of high fashion,
poised and confident. No, perhaps not poised *or* confident—in
fact, this new self was clearly uneasy, maybe even a little
frightened, and not just from the shock of what had happened.

Always one to seek a rational explanation, Kathryn's first
thought was that the reflection must be of someone standing
behind her, so she glanced sharply over her shoulder, but there
was no one there. Maybe it was a trick of the light, like in the
desert or most of the so-called UFO sightings. Yes, that could
be it. But when she looked at the reflection again, she knew it
was no mirage. What she was seeing was really there.

Her lips parted, and her heart almost stopped. There was no
doubt about it, she and the woman in the glass were one and
the same!

# *Four*

~

Kathryn could still see her own hazel eyes behind those of the green-eyed stranger, as if she were trapped inside. A terrified numbness settled over her. She was two people at once! But that was impossible, there *had* to be a logical explanation—the reporter in her told her so. She was dreaming! Yes, that was it, she'd never really awoken and left the bed. But as she continued to look at the glass, her own eyes faded, and there were only those of her new self—wide, clear, and expressive.

The initial confusion began to disperse, and new knowledge flooded in its wake. She suddenly knew the identity of this dream self! Her name was Rosalind, Lady Marchwood. More than that, she was married to Sir Dane Marchwood, one of Regency England's most feared gentlemen, and she'd gone back in time to perhaps the most famous Regency year of all, 1815, the year of Napoleon Bonaparte's final defeat at Waterloo. But Lady Marchwood felt little joy at the great victory. She was too frightened to be happy, because she was an adulterous wife, and her husband was a very dangerous man to cross.

But how could all this happen to a modern New Yorker? Kathryn's glance went to the table where a wedding ring shone in the glow of the candle. For an illusion, the flame seemed very real. She felt that if she reached out, she would feel its heat. And yet she was *sure* it was a dream. Yes, for what else could explain it?

Suddenly she realized there was someone else in this most vivid of dreams, for a man appeared behind her.

"Rosalind?" He touched her naked shoulder softly as he said her name. "You must leave Dane and come with me, somewhere he'll never find us. We were meant to be together, and all we have to do is go to my plantation in Jamaica. He doesn't even know I've purchased it." His voice was very English and refined, reminding her of Lawrence Olivier in the old black-and-white *Wuthering Heights* movie. He was twenty-seven or twenty-eight, of medium height, with tousled brown hair and warm dark eyes. His clothes were fashionable, a sage-green coat and cream cord breeches, with a pearl pin in his starched neckcloth, and he had about him a hint of the same anxiety that pervaded her.

Oddly, in spite of his dark coloring, he reminded her of Richard, although she couldn't have said why. She knew who he was. Thomas Denham, Rosalind's lover, the man she'd risked everything for, and the reason she'd set her wedding ring aside for a few stolen hours tonight.

She knew he was waiting for her to respond, but she didn't know what to say. In a situation as incredible as this, the cat had more than gotten her tongue!

Her silence perplexed him. "Did you hear me, Rosalind?"

"Yes. Of course." Her voice was no longer modern New York, but British and reserved. But it *was* her voice!

"Then why don't you answer?"

"I . . . I can't."

He turned her to face him. "Can't answer, or can't leave him? Rosalind, I will not believe it to be the latter, for you don't love him, how can you when you so eagerly break your vows with me? We've lain together this very night while he dines barely two hundred yards away with the bishop and other worthies. You wouldn't do that if you felt anything for him." Thomas searched her face in the candlelight. "Yours was an arranged match, pure and simple, and you should never have gone through with it. The two years since you went to the altar have been misery for you because he can't put his first wife's memory to rest. Every time he touches you, he still touches Elizabeth."

The first Lady Marchwood had died ten years ago giving birth to Dane's only son, Philip, who now attended Eton and was at present staying with friends for the summer vacation. Kathryn felt dizzy from the potent mixture of knowledge and confusion swirling through her. She knew so much about Rosalind, but was aware she hadn't completely taken on this new self. Inside she was still Kathryn Vansomeren. That was why she was sure it was all a dream. She must have read all this in one of the historical romances she couldn't get enough of, or maybe seen it in an old movie, and now her subconscious was recalling it in this weird dream.

Well, whatever it was, she had to go along with it, for it was real enough, or would be until she awoke. That meant getting a grip on herself, like deciding what she felt right now. The real Rosalind was deeply and irrevocably in love with Thomas Denham; Kathryn Vansomeren in Rosalind's clothing most certainly wasn't. The real Rosalind went in fear of Sir Dane Marchwood, but her dream alter ego was curiously intrigued about him. For the moment he was a shadow on the edge of her consciousness, and she couldn't bring him forward into the light, but hearing his name caused her a shiver of illicit excitement.

Thomas put his hand lovingly to her cheek. "Dane will still mourn Elizabeth ten years hence; to him you'll never be anything more than the wife he took to oblige his father's long-standing friendship with your father. You're his property, but to me you're everything in the world."

"I . . . I know." She was aware he was speaking sound common sense when he urged her to run away with him, but there were disconcerting gaps in her knowledge, as if her subconscious couldn't quite recall the entire plot of whatever book or movie this came from.

Thomas smiled. "Please give the answer that will make us both happy. Nothing binds you to him anymore, but a great deal binds you to me. After what you've told me tonight, it's plain we have to leave before things become obvious. We've played with fire and are about to be burned."

Now she definitely didn't know what he was talking about. He might know what was soon going to be obvious, but she certainly didn't! She almost wanted to laugh aloud in her frustration. Was this the place she'd skipped a chapter, or switched channels? Whatever the reason, she had no idea at all what Rosalind had just told him.

He took her face in his hands. "I know you're afraid, my darling, but I'll take care of you. Just say yes, and I'll make all the arrangements. We can take passage from Bristol for Jamaica within days. . . ."

She had to stall, she didn't know what else to do. "I . . . I'll give you my answer soon."

"How soon?" he pressed.

"I don't know. Just soon."

He looked swiftly into her eyes. "I don't understand why you're so hesitant. After what you've told me tonight, we *daren't* delay. To stay here now will be to deliberately court disaster. Dane isn't renowned for his sweet temper, and on the three occasions he's called men out, he's extinguished them all, including my brother. As for his valor on the battlefield, well, you and I both know how many times he's been mentioned in dispatches—he could never be accused of a lack of courage. I have little doubt that the army was the ideal setting for a man of his disposition, and I only wish he'd elected to stay where he was instead of resigning his commission in order to come home once and for all. You've admitted it's been a relief his army career has kept him away for most of your marriage; well, he won't be away from now on—he'll be here, demanding his conjugal rights."

Suddenly she was sure of her facts again. She knew all about Dane's decision to leave the army. She also knew that the two-year marriage had been wretched because Rosalind had always loved Thomas, but the part of her that was Kathryn Vansomeren felt a perverse desire to defend Sir Dane Marchwood. "Dane may be many things, but he isn't quite the black-hearted villain you paint."

Startled, Thomas released her. "Rosalind, I *know* him for a black-hearted villain! My brother William didn't do anything to warrant being called out at dawn. His only crime was to be a Denham."

"I concede that Dane doesn't like your family any more than they like him, but even so there must have been more to it than that. Not even he would call your brother out simply for being a Denham." She didn't know what had caused the fatal quarrel between Dane and William Denham, but this was because Rosalind didn't know either. No one knew why the challenge had been issued, not even Thomas. The only one alive to tell was Dane, and he'd never uttered a word.

Thomas found her attitude bewildering. "Why are you behaving like this? I admit that a simmering dislike had always existed between Dane and my family, but the only time it ever erupted into a public quarrel was over that miserable parcel of marshland on the boundary of Marchwood. Surely you aren't suggesting that was why Dane chose to call my brother out? No, of course you aren't, because the truth is that Dane takes pleasure in dueling, and the temptation of indulging that pleasure and eliminating a Denham at the same time was simply too great to resist. I warn you, if he finds out about us, he'll have a much better reason for calling me out than he ever had William!" Realizing he'd raised his voice slightly, he swiftly took her hands. "I'm sorry, but I'll never forgive Dane for William's death—none of my family will."

His touch disturbed her. The real Rosalind would have trembled with delight but Kathryn was unmoved, a fact he'd surely perceive at any moment. She began to pull away before he realized, but he slipped an arm around her waist and drew her close to press his parted lips over hers. It was a passionate kiss, meant to dispel what he saw as her inexplicable reluctance to take the wise way out of a deep scrape, but she found everything about him suddenly so eerily like Richard that she might almost have been with her blond, blue-eyed New York husband instead of this dark-eyed Englishman from an earlier century.

Suddenly the dream took on a much more sensuous tone. His mouth moved over hers, and she felt the flick of his tongue between her lips. He stroked her breast through the thin stuff of her gown, teasing her nipple between his fingertips. Part of her wanted to respond to the memory of happier days with Richard, but the greater part held back. He pressed her body tightly against his, and she could feel him becoming aroused. They'd already made love tonight but he was ready again, pressing eagerly toward her.

To her relief, another voice interrupted them, an elderly female voice, frail and heavily Gloucestershire, so not that of a lady. "Sir Dane will be here in a few minutes."

Kathryn turned quickly. An old woman had just entered the room. She was bent and gnarled, with a wizened face and hands like claws, and she walked with the aid of a stick. There was a knitted shawl around the shoulders of her simple gray linen gown, and she might have been taken for any old woman if it hadn't been for her eyes, which shone like those of a quick and clever raven. She was Rosalind's beloved old nurse, Alice

Longney, and the wisdom of ages seemed to wrap around her like a cloak.

Alice addressed Thomas. "You must go, Master Thomas, but not by the front way, for you may encounter him."

He nodded, and then looked at Kathryn again. "Please give me your answer now, my darling," he begged.

"I'll tell you at the ball tomorrow night; there'll be many opportunities for us to speak then," she replied. The ball entered her head as much without warning as everything else. It was to be held at the Royal Well ballroom in Cheltenham to celebrate the victory of Waterloo. She was back to the original book or movie storyline again; how else did she know about the ball? Or the Royal Well ballroom!

He gave her a curious look. "At the ball? But you know I'm not going."

For a moment she was blank, but then remembered he'd already told Rosalind he couldn't attend the ball because of a prior dinner engagement. Why had she made such a blunder? Hastily she tried to smooth the moment over. "Forgive me, I . . . I'm so worried about everything I can't think properly. I'll send word to you soon, I promise."

He searched her eyes. "Rosalind, there's no time to delay, not after what you've told me tonight. I wish to God you'd told me before, but there's still time. We dare not tarry if I'm to make the necessary arrangements to sail from Bristol. Every hour you delay means we run the risk of Dane's finding out, and I don't relish the prospect of being the second Denham to die at his hands."

Alice was increasingly anxious. "Please, sir, you must go now! If Sir Dane should actually catch you here . . . !" She couldn't bring herself to finish.

He took Kathryn by the arms and gazed urgently into her eyes. "If we remain, you may be sure it will mean shame and ruin for you, and death for me." Then he was gone, striding swiftly past Alice to the narrow landing.

His steps sounded on the staircase, a door closed, and there was silence. Almost immediately the sound of a carriage disturbed the night, and Kathryn saw it pull up at the end of the lane. It was a gleaming maroon vehicle drawn by four grays, and its lamps shone brightly through the darkness of the poorly lit street. The door was flung open, and two gentlemen stepped down.

Both were in their mid-thirties, and dressed in formal evening clothes. One was short, with red hair that shone in the light of the carriage lamp as he clapped his companion amiably on the shoulder and then walked swiftly away toward the cathedral. Kathryn knew him to be Dr. George Eden, who came from a wealthy local family and possessed an elegant town house facing the cathedral. He was a much respected man, and one of the few who could count Sir Dane Marchwood among his close friends. It was Dane from whom he'd just taken leave.

Her gaze moved to Rosalind's husband. He was tall and arrestingly handsome, with thick black hair and a penetrating glance she could perceive even from a distance. His lean, athletic physique was perfectly suited to the fashions of the day, and few things could have become him more than his close-fitting black velvet coat and superbly cut white silk breeches, except perhaps the dashing military uniform he'd so recently set aside forever. The jewel in his lace-edged neckcloth caught the lamplight as he turned to speak to his coachman, and Kathryn's heart tightened within her as she gazed at him, for the feelings that surged through her now were unlike anything she'd ever known before.

He walked toward the courtyard, and the closer he came the more clearly she could see his eyes. She knew they were gray, and that there was something in them that hinted at dark secrets, something immeasurably exciting. He was the perfect hero, with looks to melt the hardest female heart, and a commanding air she found both arousing and frightening. Each step he took brought desire and hazard nearer, and the blend was exhilarating. On the one hand she found him more sexually attractive than any man she'd ever seen before; on the other she could sense the alarm the real Rosalind would be feeling now on being so nearly caught with her lover. But the latter feeling was only fleeting, for Kathryn Vansomeren found him devastatingly desirable, a man in an entirely different league from the dull and rather ordinary Thomas Denham, and certainly a world away in every sense from someone like Richard, or even Harry Swenson, for whom she'd so briefly but tellingly thrown caution and common sense to the winds.

Everything about Sir Dane Marchwood drew her like a pin to a magnet.

He reached the courtyard and seemed to sense she was at the window, for he halted and toyed with the spill of lace at his cuff as he looked directly up at her. The hint of latent power surrounding him was like a beacon in the darkness, and when their eyes met, she couldn't look away. She was conscious of the electrifying spell of his gaze. It was as if he knew her thoughts, and therefore must know all about the affair with Thomas Denham.

But it was Alice who knew what she was thinking. "No, Kathryn, as yet he only suspects."

Kathryn glanced swiftly around. "You know my name?"

"Of course."

"Ah, but this is a dream, so you would, wouldn't you? I know this is all some old plot I've read or seen, and that it's all mixed up with the real me!" Kathryn declared this almost triumphantly, like she'd just scored a winning point.

"Some old plot? I don't understand you."

Kathryn was suddenly less sure of things. Something about the intensity of the old woman's eyes conjured thoughts of sorcery and ancient magic. No, that was stupid. This was still a dream, probably brought on by jet lag, stress, and British food! Why couldn't her subconscious light on a story she remembered properly? If she'd turned into someone like Jane Eyre or Scarlett O'Hara, she'd know what happened next!

Alice smiled. "Don't look for answers now, my dear, for the rest of tonight could bring you more passion, excitement, and gratification than you've ever known before. Sir Dane Marchwood is the lover you've always longed for, and he's within your reach because for this one night you are his wife."

"If I am, I'm supposed to want Thomas Denham," Kathryn pointed out swiftly.

"Then let me put it another way. For this one night, you are Kathryn Vansomeren in Lady Marchwood's body. Dane suspects his wife of infidelity, but he doesn't know for certain, and if you wish to enjoy his caresses, you must convince him of your faithfulness and love."

"Lie to him, you mean?" Kathryn replied flatly.

"No, my dear, for although Rosalind has betrayed her vows to him, you haven't."

Kathryn had to look away as Harry Swenson came to mind again.

Alice smiled. "Oh, I'm not talking about the fleeting affair before you came here."

"You know about that, too?" Kathryn gasped.

"Yes, and when I say that Rosalind has betrayed her vows to Dane but you haven't, that is precisely what I mean. You, my dear, have never betrayed Sir Dane Marchwood, and that's what matters."

"You're talking in riddles."

"Am I? It's very simple, Kathryn. Do you want to lie in Dane's arms tonight?" Alice asked quietly.

Kathryn glanced down into the courtyard. "Yes." What point was there in pretending? Just looking at him filled her with desire!

The nurse's walking stick tapped as she went to the table and picked up the wedding ring. "Then you must not be without this symbol of wedlock, Kathryn, for when he placed it on Rosalind's finger, he swore that it would only be removed if the marriage should be at an end."

Kathryn looked at the plain golden band, and then remembered something. "But he doesn't love Rosalind; he's still in love with his first wife."

"Elizabeth bequeathed a bitter legacy, my dear. Just be yourself in Rosalind's guise, that is all you need."

"A bitter legacy? But . . ."

"Ask no questions, Kathryn, for tonight is to be enjoyed to the full. Dawn will come only too soon."

Kathryn needed no further bidding, but gathered her skirts to hurry down to him.

# *Five*

~

An irresistible eagerness bubbled through Kathryn as she emerged into the courtyard. It didn't matter that she wasn't really married to Sir Dane Marchwood, only that she was with him now. She felt as if she were in the early throes of a reckless, wonderful new love, and if he'd extended his hand to her, she'd have taken it readily. But he didn't. His expression was impossible to gauge. If he was glad to see her, he gave no sign, and if he was displeased, he gave no sign of that either. His face was a mask.

"I trust you're ready to leave now, madam?" he inquired coolly.

His tone was as chill as the glint in his gray eyes. Oh, such a gray, like the sea in winter, or a mountain stream beneath a stormy sky. But she knew if that bleakness lifted and he smiled, her very soul would melt. Instead, his remoteness washed soberingly over her, causing her steps to falter. Alice must be wrong to insist that he only suspected about the affair with Thomas. Surely the coldness pervading him now signified his certain knowledge that his wife was being unfaithful? What other interpretation could there be?

She managed to reply. "Yes, I'm ready, sir."

"Then let us go." He offered her his arm, but the action wasn't conciliatory or even attentive, merely a rigid observance of etiquette.

Her fingers slid tentatively over the rich black velvet of his sleeve. He felt so strong and firm, so very exciting, that she knew if he were to take her in his arms and kiss her as Thomas Denham had done, she wouldn't draw back.

They walked down the lane to the waiting carriage, where

the coachman flung open the door and Dane assisted her to her seat. She could smell the leather upholstery, and, more unexpectedly, the fragrance of crushed rosemary leaves. Then she remembered, or at least, the part of her that was Rosalind remembered. She'd walked in the gardens at Marchwood castle earlier in the evening, and picked a sprig of rosemary which she'd dropped underfoot in the carriage when they'd driven to Gloucester. It was lying there now, releasing its perfume into the summer night.

When Dane had taken his seat opposite her, the coachman climbed up onto his perch and stirred the team into action. The street was too confined for such a vehicle to turn, so the carriage had to drive around the cathedral precincts, passing George Eden's fine town house before emerging into the street again and coming up to a smart trot through moonlit Gloucester.

It was a very different city from the one she'd seen earlier. The streets were narrow and cobbled, sometimes with buildings right in the middle of the carriageway, and the shops had bow windows with bottleglass panes. There were watchmen with lanterns and rattles, and galleried inns where stagecoaches came and went.

And were reminders too of the recent victory at Waterloo. Colorful bunting was threaded across the streets, and occasionally she saw window illuminations of England's savior, the Duke of Wellington. But beneath the joy of victory, life went on as before. Those who'd been poor remained so, and those who'd been villains, remained so too. She saw ragged figures sleeping in doorways, and others slipping secretively away into shadowy alleys. Beggars existed in every age, and the footpads of the past were only the muggers of the future.

The city she saw now might be alien to Kathryn Vansomeren, but Rosalind knew it well, and both women were blended together in the person who now sat opposite Sir Dane Marchwood. No, Kathryn knew she needed to qualify that somewhat fanciful thought. Old Gloucester was known to her because of whatever book or movie this dream was based on! That was the only reason she and Rosalind had become entwined like this.

She continued to gaze out, and there was one building in particular that caught her eye as the carriage passed. It was

Pendle's Bank, an ornate half-timbered building on the cross-road in the heart of the city. Jeremiah Pendle was a shrewd and prosperous, but ruthless man who was frequently seen at the door of the bank, a fat figure mopping his forehead with a red-spotted handkerchief. The banker was Thomas Denham's uncle, and therefore uncle of the late William Denham as well, which made him no friend of Dane's, but prominence in Gloucester society frequently thrust them together. She felt a little uneasy as she gazed at the bank, as if it signified something of great portent. But what?

Gloucester slipped away behind as the carriage drove south through the city gates on to the Bristol turnpike. Marchwood castle lay three miles ahead. It had been the home of Dane's family for over five hundred years, and for the past two years it had been Rosalind's home too. But for this one night, it was Kathryn Vansomeren's home as well. . . .

She glanced at him, wanting to reach out to establish some sort of harmony, a basis upon which to gain his trust, but his cold demeanor forbade any such advance. The chill that shut her out also served as a reminder that in Regency England, he was one of the most hazardous men to fall foul of, as the three duels he'd fought and won bore witness. But formidable as his reputation was, the effect he had upon her was nothing short of overwhelming.

She studied him from beneath lowered lashes, wondering what it would be like to lie naked in his arms. He was handsome and almost mesmerizing in the moonlight. His very name whispered through her like a half-forgotten song, caressing her being. It seemed foolish to say he was her soulmate, but that was how she felt. He was the part of her that Richard had never become, and she wanted him in a way she'd never wanted her absent husband.

She pulled herself up sharply then. What was the matter with her? She was thinking about him as if he were real! He wasn't real, he was the product of her frustrated subconscious! She could have dreamed up a Mr. Rochester or a Rhett Butler; instead, she'd dredged Sir Dane Marchwood from some long-forgotten novel or other. What point was there in analyzing her innermost thoughts and reasons? She wasn't with her therapist, she was in the middle of a wonderful dream, and all she had to do was enjoy it all she could! Enjoy *him* all she could. . . .

He spoke suddenly. "I trust your ministering to the sick was well received?"

Hastily she collected herself. "Alice was glad to see me, if that's what you mean." God, how weird it was to have an English voice!

He gave the thinnest of smiles. "Of course, that's what I mean. What other interpretation could there be?"

But although that was what he said, everything in his tone suggested he didn't believe she'd come here tonight to visit her ailing old nurse. Again she found herself fearing Alice was wrong, and he *did* know about Thomas, but even as the thought entered her head, she realized it was wrong. He didn't know; he merely had a strong suspicion. She spoke again, and the words seemed to enter her head from nowhere. "Concerning Alice, it would please me greatly if she could return to my employ. She finds retirement dull."

"Isn't she a little old to take up her duties again?"

"Old maybe, but she pines. It does her no good to live on her own. Besides, I wouldn't expect her to do much, just be there."

He shrugged. "As you wish. You know you have no need to ask my permission for such a thing."

"Nevertheless, I wish to ask you."

He raised a wry eyebrow. "Then you have my consent."

"Thank you."

He searched her face in the darkness. "What is this, madam? Since my return I've received little from you but moods and excuses—to say you've seemed dismayed to see me again would be to put it far too mildly—but now, quite suddenly, you wish to placate me. Why?"

Since his return. Her thoughts raced as she plucked out the facts she needed. They'd seen little of each other during their marriage, but for the past year had been parted completely by his service overseas with Wellington, firstly in the Spanish Peninsula, and then at Waterloo itself. But all that was behind him now.

He studied her. "I await your reply, madam. Or is your silence all the answer I need?"

She decided to catch him off guard by taking a different tack. "I love you, Dane."

He gave a startled laugh. "You love me? Dear God, what manner of gull do you take me for, Rosalind?"

"It's the truth!" she cried.

"Oh, how smoothly you play the innocent," he murmured.

"I'm not playing the innocent, I *am* the innocent. Dane, I don't want things to continue like this. You're my husband and I want to be your wife in every way, if you'll let me."

He looked incredulously at her. "If you mean to astound me, madam, you succeed."

"I know I haven't been quite myself since you returned, but—"

"Not quite yourself? What a masterly understatement! At the very least I'd hoped for a friendly welcome, but you were hardly the joyous wife, were you?" He sat forward suddenly and seized her wrist. "Who is he, Rosalind?" he breathed.

Alarm lanced through her. "I . . . I don't understand . . ."

"Enough of this play-acting. I want your lover's name. Is it Denham? Has he been warming your bed during my absence?"

His fingers were like steel bands digging into her flesh. "You're hurting me!" she cried as tears sprang to her eyes.

"This is nothing to the pain you're causing me, Rosalind. I want an answer, and I want it now. Who is your lover?"

"I haven't got one!" She could say it truthfully, for as Alice pointed out, Kathryn Vansomeren hadn't betrayed Sir Dane Marchwood.

His eyes burned with distrust. "Would that I could believe you, but I can't. I suspect Denham, although what in God's name you see in that mewling stay-at-home carpet knight I can't begin to guess. He was born a coward, and will remain so for the rest of his worthless life, just as his spineless brother was before him. But the past and Denham's lily liver won't prevent me from calling him out if I find he's touched you. Do I make myself clear?"

"Please let me go, Dane!"

"You're my wife, Rosalind, and I won't wear horns because of your foolish infatuation with that milksop." He thrust her away.

"I'm not infatuated with him. You *must* believe me, Dane!" Yes, he had to believe her, or tonight wouldn't happen as she wanted.

"Why should I believe you when I know you've always wanted Denham?"

"That isn't so!" Her eyes were bright with reproach. "Besides, how can you accuse me when your own conduct doesn't bear close scrutiny?"

His gaze swung instantly toward her. "My conduct? What is that supposed to mean?"

"It means you didn't love me when we married, and you still don't. Elizabeth will always be everything to you, and she leaves no room in your heart for me."

"I forbid you to speak of her," he said coldly.

"I haven't made a cuckold of you, Dane, but you make a deceived wife of me every time you think of her. She'll always come first, won't she?"

"I said you weren't to speak of her!" he snapped, his eyes darkening.

He frightened her a little, and she drew back slightly, remembering what Alice had said about Elizabeth's bitter legacy. "Then let's not speak of Thomas either," she said.

He was silent for a moment, as if struggling to quell the anger she'd raised by introducing his first wife into the conversation. Then he looked at her again. "If I'm the only one, why have you been so distant and lackluster between the sheets since my return?" he asked dryly. "Oh, I accept that you've never been a creature of great sensuality and passion, but your enthusiasm is now conspicuous for its complete absence. I'm not a monster, Rosalind, I will not take my conjugal rights by force, but I do expect an explanation. If you no longer feel anything for me, you must say so, but if the reason is another man, then woe betide you both, especially him. I swear he'll soon draw his last breath, whoever he is."

Her voice was a tremulous whisper. "There isn't anyone, Dane. Upon my honor, I swear there isn't." Somehow she met his eyes.

He gazed intently at her in the moonlight and then sat back again. "We shall see," he murmured.

"I'm yours and only yours," she said softly.

He averted his gaze to the silhouetted hedgerows as the carriage left the main turnpike and struck west toward Marchwood village and the castle. "If that is so, madam, I trust you still intend to observe your wifely duties by accompanying me to Cheltenham tomorrow night. Or are you now considering another sudden indisposition?"

The Waterloo ball. "Yes, of course I'm still accompanying you. Mrs. Fowler is just putting the final touches to the new gown I've ordered for the occasion." God, the insignificant details she'd somehow absorbed from that darned plot! She even recalled the name of the dressmaker. It was crazy!

"It would be more suitable if you used a London couturiere rather than a mere Gloucester seamstress."

"Hardly a seamstress. Mrs. Fowler is excellent; the Duchess of Beaufort patronizes her occasionally, and so does Lady Berkeley."

"I daresay what you say is true, but I'm not fool enough to be taken in by the praise you heap on her. The truth is that a local dressmaker gives ample opportunity for assignations."

She had to look away, for he was right. That was indeed why Rosalind used the obligingly discreet Mrs. Fowler.

The sound of the carriage wheels changed. From drumming over hard-packed stones they rolled over uneven cobbles as the vehicle entered Marchwood village. Everything was quiet, except for the local alehouse, where she heard men singing a bawdy ballad in the taproom. Suddenly she saw the dark medieval towers of the castle looming above the rooftops. They rose among tall trees only yards from the main street, and then vanished from view as the carriage turned sharply off the road on to the gravel drive that led to the beautifully restored drawbridge and gatehouse. For a second or so there was the hollow rumble of hooves and wheels on ancient wood, and then the carriage swept into the wide courtyard where she knew from the Rosalind in her that the doomed Plantagenet king, Richard II, had bestowed a knighthood upon the first Sir Dane Marchwood.

The castle seemed to fold around Kathryn as Dane helped her alight. She could hear the night breeze whispering around the battlements and rustling through the ivy on the walls. Everything was silver from the moon, even Dane's eyes as they met hers for a moment.

"We've played husband and wife long enough today, madam. I bid you good night," he said abruptly, then released her hand and walked swiftly away toward the immense stone porch that guarded the main doorway in the corner of the courtyard.

She gazed after him and knew that the promised pleasure could only commence if she melted the ice within him. She closed her eyes and raised her face toward the moon. Dream or not, it was *her* dream, and she intended to indulge in it to the full.

She only had until dawn, for in the words of one of her favorite heroines from fiction, tomorrow was another day.

# Six

~

She followed Dane into the castle, but as she passed beneath the porch into the wide passageway beyond, there was no sign of him. She guessed he'd gone to his apartment, which adjoined hers, or rather Rosalind's, and so she made her way in that direction.

It was strange how she knew the layout of the castle. From the moment she entered, she was completely familiar with everything about the ancient fortress. She was also aware of exactly how to conduct herself, so that when she encountered a footman, she inclined her head just sufficiently and then swept on by in a whisper of emerald silk. It was almost amusing to know how completely she fooled him, but then why should he think of her as anyone other than the real Lady Marchwood? How could a lowly footman from early nineteenth century England possibly detect that beneath her ladyship's jeweled exterior there was a New Yorker from the future? Indeed, when she caught a glimpse of herself in a wall mirror, she found it hard to believe herself! But then dreams were like this, weren't they? The impossible and unlikely happened all the time. She'd once dreamed she walked naked down Fifth Avenue in broad daylight, so why not this?

Her route took her to the candlelit great hall, from where a grand staircase led up to the private apartments. She paused in the center of the vast chamber, and looked around. History seemed almost tangible in a place like this, where feudal barons had dispensed rough justice, and banquets had been held in honor of kings. But the grimness of the distant past had gone now, and Marchwood had become a gracious aristocratic residence, where medieval weaponry and suits of armor were decorative, not martial.

There was a minstrels' gallery and a dais, and a beautiful carved screen that still bore traces of its fifteenth-century paintwork. The lower walls were paneled in dark oak, above which the stonework had recently been covered with plaster and painted white, and everything was lit by the candles encircling half a dozen wheel-rim chandeliers suspended from a hammerbeam roof. A long table ranged down the center of the stone-flagged floor, and on its highly polished surface there was a vase of beautifully arranged flowers from the castle gardens.

More flowers brightened the hearth of one of the two enormous stone fireplaces that stood on opposite walls, but the second fireplace had been virtually dismantled and was in the process of being rebuilt because some of the Tudor stonework had been damaged. Fresh, newly carved slabs stood in readiness, and the masons' implements were neatly stacked against the wall. The dust and fragments of stone left by the day's work had been carefully brushed into a pile to be cleared away by the maids when they commenced their tasks just after sunrise.

She continued toward the staircase, but at the half-landing where the stairs divided, she paused again, this time to look at the wall paneling. A dark square marked the place where a painting had recently been removed in readiness for a new portrait of Dane by the fashionable artist, Sir Thomas Lawrence. The portrait had been commenced before Dane left for the Peninsular War, and would be delivered any day now.

Gathering her skirts, she went on up the staircase. Her steps took her unerringly along a wide candlelit passage with windows overlooking the courtyard. At last she reached the door of her private apartment, and paused again, her glance moving along to the door of Dane's rooms a little further on. The fact that he and his wife occupied separate apartments had never signified anything, for the rooms were connected by a set of folding doors. Tonight she meant to go through those folding doors. . . .

She entered her rooms, and found Rosalind's maid waiting. Josie Lloyd's slight figure and dark coloring gave her Welsh

ancestry away almost as much as her surname. She'd been in
Rosalind's service for five years now, and knew all about the
affair with Thomas. When Rosalind wished to send messages
to her lover, it was the maid who took them. Like Alice and
the dressmaker, Mrs. Fowler, Josie was the illicit lovers' ac-
complice. All three assisted in the tangle that was making a
cuckold of Sir Dane Marchwood.

Josie curtsied. "My lady."

"Josie." Kathryn glanced around the rooms. She was in the
little blue-and-white drawing room. The blue velvet curtains
were drawn at the window, which she knew faced over the terraced gardens and the meadows of the little River March to the
south of the castle, and candlelight shone softly over elegant
but feminine chairs and sofas upholstered in floral tapestry.
Through a doorway she could see the lemon and gray bedroom
Rosalind used when she slept alone, and just visible through
an archway beyond that was the dressing room.

Like everything else in the castle, Kathryn was immediately
acquainted with the rooms and their contents. She knew what
was in every drawer and trinket box, and what gowns and
other accessories were to be found in the dressing room
wardrobes. But it wasn't her own apartment that interested
her; she was more concerned with what lay on the other side
of the folding doors.

She turned to the maid. "Has Sir Dane gone to his apartment?"

"Yes, my lady, I heard him enter a minute or so before you
came in." Josie took a lighted candle through to the dressing
room, and soon Kathryn heard the chink of porcelain as warm
water was poured from a large jug into a bowl. The thought of
being attended by a maid was very odd, but Kathryn knew she
must proceed as Rosalind would, so after a minute or so she
followed Josie into the dressing room.

The maid unhooked the delicate emerald silk gown, and for
the first time Kathryn realized she wasn't wearing any undergarments. It simply hadn't occurred to her before, but the moment the gown slithered to the floor, she found herself
standing completely naked. She was startled. Rosalind didn't
even wear the proverbial stays? How very shocking of her. Or
was it? She seemed to recall having read something about Regency ladies damping their gowns to make them cling to their

legs, but even so, it seemed a little daring to go out with only a gown to spare one's modesty. Unless, of course, Rosalind had gone out that night prepared for her assignation with Thomas. . . . Yes, that was more likely the truth. How convenient and time-saving to slip out of a gown and get down to business with only Thomas knowing about the absence of whalebone.

She washed her face and hands, but as she did she became aware that there was something very important about Rosalind that was being withheld from her. She sensed it more than actually knew it, and the feeling was unsettling. Just as had happened earlier in the evening, when she didn't know what vital thing Rosalind had told Thomas, she was conscious of another mysterious blank in her knowledge, although this one came unbidden and unprompted. What was it? Another skipped chapter or switched channel?

Josie brought a lace-trimmed cream silk nightgown and slipped it over Kathryn's head, but as the maid began to tie the little pink ribbons at the throat, Kathryn shook her head. "I'll finish things myself now, Josie. You may go."

"But your hair, my lady . . ."

"I'll attend to it." Kathryn knew the real Rosalind wouldn't do her own hair, but every minute now was prolonging the wait before she could go through those folding doors to Dane.

Clearly taken aback, Josie curtsied. "Very well, my lady. Good night."

"Good night, Josie."

The maid went to the doorway, but then hesitated. "About tomorrow night, my lady. Do you still wish to wear the plowman's gauze gown if Mrs. Fowler doesn't complete the new one in time?"

"Yes."

"My lady." Josie withdrew.

Kathryn reached up swiftly to pull out the jeweled comb and countless hairpins keeping her coiffure firmly in place. How on earth Rosalind managed to make passionate love without disturbing so much as a curl, she simply didn't know. Unless, of course, hairdressing was one of Alice's many accomplishments. Yes, it probably was.

Slowly she picked up a tortoiseshell-backed hairbrush and began to draw it gently through the long golden curls to which she was so unused. Her own bobbed style was so much easier to manage, she thought a little wistfully, but when she looked in the dressing table mirror and saw the sort of hair many Hollywood stars would kill for, the wistfulness evaporated. Maybe she should think of growing her real hair as long as this. She continued to study her new self, taking in the pale but beautiful face, and the enchanting wide green gaze. "Kathryn Vansomeren, you've become quite an eyeful," she murmured approvingly.

The clock in the bedroom behind her struck two, and she put the hairbrush down and got up. It was now or never. She went to the folding doors, but then her nerve began to fail her. What if she couldn't pull this off? What if the real plot went a way she didn't like? Maybe there was a mistress her subconscious hadn't remembered! No, that couldn't be so, or Alice wouldn't have promised what she did.

She lowered her eyes for a moment. Alice might have promised, but it all depended on Kathryn Vansomeren, who suddenly wasn't quite as confident as she needed to be. During her fling with Harry, he'd done all the seducing, but now it was her turn. Playing the seductress was something she'd only thought about, a fantasy she'd toyed with in the hours of quiet frustration when Richard slept beside her. Was she really capable of putting those secret ideas into practice? Could she go through these doors now and use virtually untested erotic wiles successfully upon a man like Sir Dane Marchwood?

Her dwindling courage began to ebb away fast, but then she remembered the electrifying effect Dane had had upon her. With him she knew the fantasy could become reality. Her resolve swept back again and she drew the doors aside to walk through.

# Seven

~

The apartment beyond was in darkness, except for the moonlight in the bedroom, where she saw him standing naked by the open window looking out at the night. If he knew she was there, he gave no intimation.

Her gaze lingered upon him, taking in the perfection of his broad shoulders, slender waist, tight buttocks, and well-shaped muscular thighs. It was the sort of body that would look as good in modern designer jeans as in the best tailoring from Regency Bond Street, and he was the sort of man who'd been irresistible to women since time began. Dark, dangerous, devastating Sir Dane Marchwood.

She wanted to say his name, but although her lips moved, no sound came out. Then she knew he was aware of her presence, for he spoke without turning. "I believe you've made a mistake, madam, for this is my apartment, not yours."

"It's no mistake."

"Then you come to me as the lamb to the sacrifice, to allay my suspicions." He turned at last, and the moonlight caught a golden chain and pendant around his neck.

Now she saw all of him, the contemptuous twist of his lips, the dark hair on his chest and loins, and his potent masculinity, soft and slumbering now, but when aroused . . . A powerful excitement began to flow through her, quickening her pulse and heartbeats, and tightening her breasts so her nipples stood out. She was conscious of a dull ache deep within, the ache of desire. God, she'd never realized just how erotically susceptible she was. Every sense was alive to him, the blood flowing warm and eager through her veins. There was no modesty in the way she felt. She wanted to be one with him, to feel that magnificent virility thrust in to the hilt. But though she thought all this, she made no response to what he said, and her silence was misinterpreted.

"So you *are* the sacrificial lamb," he murmured sarcastically, going to a small table and pouring himself a glass of cognac from the decanter standing there.

For a split second she was reminded of Richard, and the Scotch he drank the day they'd quarreled about the vacation. But it was only a split second, and then Richard Vansomeren was lost in the mists of the future as she gazed at Dane. He wasn't self-conscious about his nakedness; in fact, it was almost as if he used it to mock her, for he made no move to put on a robe or conceal his loins.

She met his eyes. "Dane, I've come to you tonight because I want you," she said at last. God, how true that was right now.

"Perhaps I don't want you, madam, or hadn't that occurred to you?"

"Of course it's occurred to me, and if you don't, then I cannot blame you."

"No, you certainly can't," he said coldly.

She was conscious of the pendant around his neck. She knew it was a miniature of his first wife, beautiful flame-haired Elizabeth. She of the mysterious bitter legacy. Kathryn went closer to him. "I want to make amends, Dane," she said.

"Amends? I doubt you can, madam, for nothing can wash away the stain of adultery."

"I haven't committed adultery, Dane, but can you honestly say you've been equally faithful to me?" she countered.

He paused. "Would you believe me if I said yes?"

"Of course."

He gave a short laugh. "My God, how desperate you are to creep back into my good books. Why, Rosalind?"

"Because I love you."

"Forgive me if I take that with a pinch of salt. There's still the small matter of the lover my intuition tells me exists."

"I keep telling you I haven't a lover."

"That isn't how it appears to me, so go back to your apartment, Rosalind," he said wearily.

She remained where she was. "If I must prove my love for you, then I will," she said softly, undoing her nightgown and allowing it to fall to the floor.

His gaze moved slowly over her, but then returned coldly to her face. "I take no man's leavings, madam."

"If I'm any man's leavings, sir, that man is you."

Anger flashed into his eyes. "Don't insult me with this charade, Rosalind. We both know you never wanted this match, and that during my absence you've been she-catting in another man's bed!" Suddenly he flung his glass across the room at the fireplace, where it shattered into a thousand pieces.

She flinched at his fury. "No, Dane, it's not true!"

"Oh, yes it is, madam."

She went to him and sank to her knees with her head bowed. "Please don't turn me away, Dane," she whispered.

She heard him exhale slowly. "What's this? Has that old harridan been brewing potions for you?" he asked softly. "Has she concocted something to turn my ice-wife into a creature of flesh and blood?"

He didn't move away and for a moment she thought his fingers touched her hair. He was close enough to touch, to caress . . . She longed to feel his warmth, and suddenly could no longer resist. Looking up, she reached out slowly to put her trembling fingertips against his thigh. The contact seared through her like a flame as she slid her fingers tentatively over his flesh. If this was a dream, it was headier than reality. . . .

Still he didn't move away, and so she knelt up to embrace him, her arms encircling his hips. All her sensual fantasies blossomed into vibrant life now; she was a temptress intent upon making him want her. Erotic sensations quivered through her. Even these first moments transcended everything she'd known before. She was conscious of a sexual excitement that was almost too intense to bear, and a soft sigh escaped her as she lowered her lips to the forest of hair at his loins. His masculinity brushed against her, still unaroused as yet, but only, she knew suddenly, because he was resisting.

His unwillingness to succumb heightened her desire. She wanted to feel him hardening against her, wanted to make him surrender to temptation. Slowly, she lowered her lips still more, this time to the velvet shaft itself. The scent of him filled her nostrils, potent and stimulating, and at last she felt him stir beneath her lips, becoming longer and harder as need began to pulse through him.

Her nipples brushed against his thighs, and more delicious

sensation shivered through her veins. Still embracing his hips, she caressed his back and buttocks, then, almost weak with a sensuous craving, she moved her lips luxuriously against his shaft, now pounding like hot steel as it sprang from his groin. How virile and hard he was, and how exciting. For a heart-stopping moment she took the tip in her mouth, sliding her tongue over it and savoring the intense erotic pleasure of such an intimate caress.

The seconds hung, as if time itself had ceased, and she was lost in a wild torrent of sexual sensations that seemed to tingle over her entire being. She knelt before him as if in subjection, but he was at her mercy now. With her lips and tongue she stormed his masculinity, until he could resist no more and with a low groan dragged her to her feet and into his arms.

His lips crushed hers as he pressed her against him. Her breasts felt tender as her nipples rubbed against his flesh, and he eased his shaft between her legs. His fingers twisted in the hair at the nape of her neck and his tongue moved against hers as the kiss deepened.

She'd been kissed before, by Richard and by Harry, but it had never felt like this. Surely he would soon take her to the velvet-hung bed that stood in the flood of moonlight streaming through the window. Oh, how she longed to lie beneath this man.

He drew away suddenly and took her face in his hands, his eyes bright with desire as he looked at her. "Rosalind, if this is some trickery, I will never forgive you. . . ."

In that moment she saw his raw vulnerability, and it affected her as much as everything else about him. Surely the real Rosalind was the only woman on earth who could remain immune to his fascination? Fate—or the author—played him a diabolical hand when it dealt him such a wife. . . . she smiled. "No trickery, my love. I just know now how much I love and need you," she whispered, sliding her needful fingers down to enclose his erection for a moment.

He carried her to the bed, where she lay with her golden hair in confusion against the coverlet. She reached up to him. "Now," she breathed.

He joined her, putting his lips to one of her breasts and drawing the taut nipple deep into his mouth. More exquisite sensations gripped her and she held him close. She ached for him to penetrate the fastnesses that for so long had craved full satisfaction, but he held back. She felt the pendant cold against her, as if Elizabeth's ghost was trying to come between them, but not even a beloved shade could dampen his ardor now.

Kiss succeeded kiss as their caresses became more intimate and arousing. She was caught up in an oblivion of sexual delight. God, this man knew things even Harry Swenson hadn't heard of, but where Harry had shown her the way, Sir Dane Marchwood took her effortlessly to heaven's door. He didn't enter, though, but skillfully prolonged her agony of desire. He was lord of his art, the lover of her most abandoned and shameless dreams, and she knew that when the final moment came she would soar to the ultimate heights of ecstasy.

At last he moved on top of her, and her legs parted longingly. She felt his shaft touch her, lingering tantalizingly at the entrance before he pushed each inch slowly and exquisitely inside. She gasped with pleasure as she felt his entirety fill her for a few moments before he pulled out again to repeat the movement.

Tears stung her eyes as the pleasure intensified. His strokes began to quicken, and his eyes were closed. He whispered a name, but she couldn't hear what it was.

She exulted in every thrust he gave, and her very consciousness seemed in peril as at last an explosion of emotion carried them both toward the brink. She heard his shuddering breath and felt him tremble against her, but her own body quivered with gratification as she clung to him, her lips pressed to the damp saltiness of his shoulder. The pendant shone in the moonlight, and she closed her eyes to shut it out. Please don't let it be Elizabeth's name he'd whispered. Please . . .

At last he sank against her, but they remained one, joined in that most exquisite of ways. Gradually he softened inside her, but as his lips found hers again, she knew they'd make love many more times before dawn lightened the sky.

This was a night she wanted never to end. But it was only a dream. Only a dream . . .

# Eight

Kathryn was asleep in Dane's arms. Dawn lightened the sky, and Marchwood was ghostly in a summer mist when Alice came quietly to the bedside.

"It's time to go now, my dear," the old woman whispered.

Kathryn's eyes flew open. For a moment she didn't know where she was, but then memory returned. Dane. She reached out toward him, but suddenly there was the loud and incongruous beat of rock music. Marchwood and its lord had gone, and instead she was waking in the Gloucester apartment. The music came from the alarm radio by the bed.

Shocked and dismayed, she could only lie there. She didn't want to be here, she wanted to stay in her dreams with Dane! The harsh music jangled her nerves, and she reached out to silence it, then lay back again. She felt oddly dazed, like she was just regaining consciousness after an operation.

Then she glanced toward the dawn shining palely through the open window. The cathedral rose above a low mist, and she could hear the birds beginning the morning chorus. Modern sounds drifted in vaguely through the air as Gloucester began to stir for a new day, and with them came cold common sense. It had only been a dream, none of it had really happened, so what point was there in resenting having awoken? Okay, so it had been a humdinger of a dream, but that still didn't make it fact. It was just a very lucid dream.

She gave a rueful smile. If she was honest with herself, the whole thing had been brought on by wishful thinking. A lover like Sir Dane Marchwood was what every red-blooded girl wanted, so in her sleep her subconscious had rooted around in the memory banks and unearthed an old book or movie with the perfect hero.

The chink of bottles sounded outside, and curiosity got the

better of her, so she got up to see what it was. A milkman was making his daily delivery at Jack Elmore's door and whistled as he walked along the alley.

She shivered, for the misty air was cool and she was naked. She put her hands to her breasts, remembering the silk nightgown she'd left on the floor in Dane's bedchamber. Then she frowned at herself. She didn't leave any nightgown anywhere, because there hadn't been a Sir Dane Marchwood. She'd dreamed him, plain and simple. That was the end of it!

She made some coffee and went to sit on the windowsill in her robe. The sun was up now and the mist had gone. Seagulls called across the rooftops outside, reminding her that Gloucester wasn't all that far from the Severn estuary. She sipped the coffee and gazed along the lane to the street. Without warning a crystal-clear flashback swept over her, and suddenly she saw Dane walking through the darkness from his carriage. The illusion was so strong she gasped and closed her eyes. When she opened them again the lane was empty.

She put her coffee down. This was crazy. Was she sickening for something? Was that it? Or maybe the dream had been brought on by indigestion! Yes, maybe the food she'd eaten last evening had lain a little heavy, or something. Maybe it still was this morning. Maybe. Somehow she didn't think so. But then her glance fell on the literature the janitor had given her the night before. There, on top was a leaflet about Marchwood Castle.

Shaken, she stared at it, and then gave a self-conscious laugh. Of course! She'd flicked through so much tourist information the previous night she didn't even remember reading this one, but the fact that she had was all the explanation she needed for the dream. This was probably the last thing she'd read before going to bed, and when she'd fallen asleep it had gotten mixed up with her sexual frustrations and an old movie plot!

She leaned across to pick up the leaflet. On the front was a view of the castle from across the meadows, showing an incongruous blend of beautiful terraced gardens and gray stone fortifications. Another view, this time from the village, showed how the battlements and towers rose above the surrounding trees and rooftops. There was a skimpy map on the back, with the castle in the center and lines radiating all around to show how far away the nearest towns and other attractions were. The text wasn't very detailed, just a vague outline of the castle's history, but it did mention a Sir Dane Marchwood who'd been knighted in the courtyard by King Richard II in the fourteenth century. And there was a sentence about some cannon from the field of Waterloo. So here she had two of the elements of her dream, Sir Dane Marchwood and Waterloo. There was a clear link between her nighttime adventures and this stupid piece of paper!

Relieved to have some sort of rational explanation, she glanced through the leaflet again. Well, one thing was certain, her curiosity was aroused. Until this moment she hadn't decided where to go on her first full day here, but now there was no contest. Marchwood Castle was open to the public, and she intended to take a look.

The decision made, she took a shower and dressed in jeans and a blue check shirt. But just as she was about to leave, she noticed something odd. The tourist literature was in an unusually tidy pile. Unusual for her, that is. As she recalled, the night before she'd left everything scattered over the table, she certainly hadn't bothered to arrange it neatly. Something wasn't right.

Slowly she looked around the apartment, and next noticed her supper dishes. She'd left them in the washer and forgotten to switch it on; someone had put that right, and now the dishes were not only washed, but had been removed from the washer and put on the shelf!

Her unease increased as she continued to look around the apartment. When she dressed, she hadn't taken much of a look in the closet, she'd just grabbed the first things that came to hand, but now she saw that everything was far too carefully arranged. On arriving, she'd just unpacked any old how and put everything away with minimum regard to creases, so this excessive tidiness certainly wasn't her doing. She saw the reflection of the dressing table in the closet mirror, and turned sharply to look at the cosmetics placed so neatly on the polished surface. If she'd bothered to do her face this morning, she's surely have noticed them, but instead she'd just used some moisturizer. She felt suddenly cold inside. Someone had definitely been here while she slept!

She went through into the drawing room again, and for the

first time saw her jewelry box on top of the TV. She'd left it in a suitcase in the bedroom, but someone had found it! She gasped. Oh, no! How much had been taken? She hurried to see, but to her astonishment, everything was still there. She couldn't understand it, for some of the pieces were expensive and worth stealing. Why go to the trouble of breaking in if the only purpose was to tidy up and then inspect jewelry without taking it? If indeed theft had been the intention.

Her first thought was to call the police, but even as she picked up the phone she knew how stupid her story would sound. Well, officer, it was like this. Someone poked around in my apartment, washed a few plates, cleaned up a little, rifled through my jewelry and make-up, and then took off without stealing anything. She could imagine how plausible *that* would sound! Deciding there was no point in reporting anything, she put the receiver down again.

Then she noticed the telephone answering machine was blinking to show there was a message. God, she must have slept like the proverbial log not to have heard either the intruder or the phone ringing.

She pressed the button and Richard's voice came through clearly. "Hi. I guess you're asleep now. I just called back to say again how great it was to get that second call from you. I've hated the quarreling too, and can't bear to know you're so far away. If you really mean it when you say you'll cut the vacation short and come home right away, I just want you to know there's nothing would make me happier. I wish to God I'd told Brand to go play with his own shaft, but I didn't, so I'm stuck with it. Well, kind of stuck. Now I've taken a look, I'm sure the problem's probably not as bad as he thought. A little judicious dimension-tweaking here and there might just do it, and if I'm right, I won't have to stay here more than a few days. As for Phoenix, well, you were right, Brand intends to preen his incompetent feathers on that one. Still, he *is* retiring, and I'm the favored son right now. Aside from that, I could be back in New York by the weekend, and if you could be back there too . . . Need I say more? I love you, Kathryn, and want to forget all about the past few months. I don't care now if we can't have a family, I just want you. I know I've been a selfish pain for far too long now, and being apart, even for this short time, has proved you're more important than anything else. Just come home, sweetheart. Love you."

Kathryn stared at the machine. What was he talking about? What second call? As for calling her sweetheart and all that stuff about cutting the vacation short and starting anew, all she knew was her last call to him had ended with her thinking seriously about divorce! Was he being facetious? She rewound the machine and listened to the message again. No, he wasn't that good an actor. He meant what he said.

She felt uncomfortable. First there was all that "been here before" business yesterday, then the dream, followed by finding out someone had been in the apartment while she slept. Now this. Just what was going on here? Talk about dreaming an old movie plot, she was beginning to feel she was still in one. A Hitchcock movie!

For a moment or so she hesitated about going out, but then decided what the heck. Maybe Jack the Janitor went sleepwalking and liked to try on women's things! And maybe she'd been a little tidier than she remembered; after all, she had been very tired last night, so tired she didn't even recall reading about Marchwood Castle. She couldn't explain away Richard's message, though.

More than a little rattled, she deliberated about what to do. She still didn't see the point of informing the police, they'd be certain to think she was imagining things, and there wasn't much point calling Richard now. It was the middle of the night in Chicago, and when he was away from home he always told hotels not to put calls through to him unless they were urgent. She couldn't exactly pretend this was urgent, so she'd wait until later before calling. Besides, she wasn't in the mood to dwell on all this now. She wanted to go see that darned castle.

Armed with the road atlas she'd bought at Heathrow, she drove south out of Gloucester. It was the same route she'd taken in her dream, but that could be explained because when she'd fallen asleep she'd already seen the map on the back of the Marchwood leaflet.

It felt good driving out of the city on such a beautiful summer morning, while all the rush hour traffic poured in. Rush hour traffic? Compared to New York this was about as busy as a Kansas back road! Still, she didn't doubt the people of

Gloucester thought it just as much the pits as anything Manhattan had to offer on a bad day.

Soon she was in open countryside, but it wasn't long before she saw the sign for Marchwood, and left the main highway to follow the minor road to the village. As the first houses swept into view ahead she braked to stare at the castle, because the *déjà vu* she'd felt on first seeing Gloucester was as nothing to the feeling she had now. Maybe the scene had been moonlit in her dream, but everything was exactly as she remembered. Marchwood hadn't changed much over the centuries; the castle still loomed above the trees, and the village nestled in its protective lee.

Suddenly she felt stupid. Of course it all seemed familiar, it was one of the views on the leaflet! One thing was different from her dream, though, and that was the large parking lot provided for visitors. Last night she and Dane had driven through the village and then over the old drawbridge, but these days the village was spared the endless flood of visitors. Now cars were left on this new lot, and a new footpath led between the trees toward the side of the castle rather than the front.

She drove on. There were few visitors so early in the morning, and since her rented car had no air-conditioning, she chose a shady place beneath a wide-spreading tree and then walked a little nervously toward the small hut where entry tickets were sold.

Her appearance at the window startled the plump woman seated inside with her knitting. "Good heavens, you're bright and early."

"Yes, I guess I am," Kathryn replied.

"American?"

"Yes."

"Well, we've put on some grand weather today. You'll be able to go back and tell all your friends it's not true it rains here all the time," the woman said with a smile as she took Kathryn's coins and dispensed a ticket. "Just follow the path; everything's sign-posted."

"Thank you."

Gravel crunched beneath Kathryn's feet as she walked through the trees to the castle. Marchwood parish church stood behind a ivy-clad wall to her right, and to her left was part of the old moat, grass-filled and barely discernible. She passed the castle stables and coachhouses, now converted into a gift shop and restaurant, and then she emerged onto a wide area where the original approach road passed beneath the immense gatehouse into the castle.

This was where the Waterloo cannon were on display, and at the far side she could see ornamental steps leading down to the terraced gardens. Beyond the garden were the marshy meadows where the little River March, a tributary of the much larger Severn, wound its way across the estate, and then vanished into more woodland toward the estuary. It was from somewhere on those meadows that the view of the castle had been taken for the leaflet.

But it was at the drawbridge and ancient gateway she stared now, remembering how the wheels of Dane's carriage had rumbled on the wood before sweeping into the great inner courtyard. A cool finger ran slowly down her spine. This was exactly as she remembered it from the night before, and it wasn't a scene depicted on the leaflet. So how could she have possibly seen it so clearly in her dream?

# Nine

~

Kathryn felt quite rattled. All this was beginning to get just a little too creepy for comfort, and far from wanting to go on into the castle, she suddenly wanted to cut and run. No, that wouldn't do, for if she high-tailed it at this juncture she'd never forgive herself for being such a wimp. All she needed was a few minutes to sit and think.

She glanced toward the restaurant in the old stables, and quickly retraced her steps toward it. It was old-fashioned inside, with a self-serve counter, and tables and chairs that didn't match. It smelled of coffee and confectionery, and the radio played bland music. The coffee looked undrinkable, so she got the tea, which didn't look much better, but before sitting down she noticed an elderly woman seated at a corner table. Dressed in a neat brown suit and white frilled blouse, she was studying a newspaper crossword. The badge on her lapel announced her to be one of the castle guides.

After a moment's hesitation, Kathryn approached her. "Excuse me, may I have a word with you?"

The woman looked up. "Why, yes, of course."

"I see you're one of the guides, and wondered if I might ask you a few things?"

"About the castle? Feel free to ask anything you wish." With a charming smile, the woman indicated one of the chairs at the table.

Kathryn sat down and then toyed nervously with her cup and saucer.

The woman looked inquiringly at her. "What is it you wish to know?"

"It concerns the castle's history."

"Ah. Your ancestors came from these parts?"

"No. Well, my husband's family came from Gloucester, but that's not relevant. I'm actually interested in the Marchwood family at the time of Waterloo, or thereabouts."

"Waterloo. Now let me see, that would be Sir Philip's time—no, I tell a lie, it was his father Sir Dane's time! Yes, of course, what am I thinking. Sir Dane fought at Waterloo itself; he captured the cannon and brought them back here."

Kathryn's pulse quickened, and her mouth was suddenly dry. There really had been a Sir Dane at the time of Waterloo? The leaflet didn't mention *that!* She cleared her throat. "I, er . . . Dane is an unusual name, does it run in the Marchwood family?" she asked.

"Not really. There was another one in the fourteenth century, but that's all as far as I know. Maybe some minor members of the family were called it, but I wouldn't really know about that. As far as Marchwood castle is concerned, there were only two."

Kathryn didn't know what to say next.

The guide sipped her coffee. "The Waterloo Sir Dane was a very dashing and dangerous fellow, much given to pistols at dawn. He fought four duels and won them all, killing his opponent on each occasion."

Kathryn began to feel sick inside. Four duels? In her dream there had only been three.

The guide went on. "But the last one left a stain on his reputation. He always used his own set of dueling pistols, and on this occasion was alleged to have tampered with the one his opponent used in order to ensure victory, and since this adversary was the younger brother of one of his previous victims, you can imagine how shocked local society was by his apparent lack of honor."

Kathryn was numb. The fourth opponent had been the brother of one of the previous ones? Who else could it be but Thomas Denham? But the leaflet hadn't mentioned Thomas Denham, so how could she explain *his* appearance in her dream? Come to that, how could she explain knowing about the three original duels?

The woman didn't notice her stunned reaction. "Still, it was probably no more than Sir Dane deserved, for he played the devil once too often. Getting away with three duels was amazing, but to emerge victorious from a fourth was tantamount to a miracle. There had to be a penalty, albeit a relatively minor inconvenience to someone like him. Although, on reflection, I suppose having one's honor called into question was probably a serious business in those days." The woman drew a long breath. "Devil or not, he was very handsome. From his portrait, I'd say he'd give any present-day heartthrob a run for his money. The original tall, dark, and handsome, that was Sir Dane."

Kathryn had to ask about the last duel. "Who was his final opponent?" she asked, knowing in her heart what the answer would be.

"A gentleman by the name of Thomas Denham, of Denham Hall, just to the north of Gloucester. The duel was on Lammas Day, 1815. That's August the first," the guide added in explanation. "The whole business was most unfortunate, for Thomas's elder brother William had fallen foul of Sir Dane ten years previously. There was talk of a vendetta, or whatever word would have been used at that time. The Denhams were once an important local family, but have died out now, and the hall was pulled down about fifteen years ago to make way for a new road. Anyway, I'm wandering from the point. The story goes that Sir Dane accused Thomas of a liaison with his wife, Rosalind."

Shocked to the core now, Kathryn stared at her. There had been a Rosalind too? *All* the people she'd dreamed about last night had actually lived? She struggled to keep a grip on herself. It could still be because she'd read a book or seen a movie. She gave the woman a weak smile. "Tell me, has the story ever been turned into a novel? Or a movie?"

The guide laughed. "Oh, dear me, no; we're small fry here at Marchwood. The history of the castle has been written, of course, but that's all. Sir Dane's tale would make an excellent book, though, and if it were filmed, he would make a marvelously handsome hero." She sat back thoughtfully. "Actually, I suppose Rosalind would be the perfect heroine as well, for she was said to have been very beautiful. According to the records she had golden hair and green eyes, but the only portrait of her was destroyed in a fire about fifty years ago. She's a rather enigmatic figure, and must have been perverse, for how could any woman prefer the rather dull Mr. Denham to such a tempestuous and infinitely more exciting husband like Sir Dane? I really don't understand. Anyway, Sir Dane was succeeded by Sir Philip, his son by his first wife, Elizabeth. The Marchwood line eventually came to an end in 1990, and the castle has been the property of the nation ever since."

Kathryn didn't know what to think now. All her fancy theories about leaflets, books, and movies didn't hold water anymore, which meant she had to think of some other way to explain what happened in her sleep last night. She still felt okay, so it wasn't a fever or anything like that, nor was she on any medication that might produce such a vivid dream, and surely jet lag couldn't be the culprit. So what else was there? Her lips parted as something new struck her. Reincarnation? Was that it? Was she the reembodiment of Rosalind, Lady Marchwood? No, she couldn't be, she didn't even believe in such things!

"Are you all right, my dear?" the guide asked concernedly.

"Mm?"

"You look a little pale. I was wondering if you felt unwell."

"Er, no. Forgive me."

"Well, there isn't a great deal more I can tell you about Sir Dane. Is there anything else you wish to know about the family at that time?"

Kathryn felt she already had more than enough to chew on. She gave a quick smile. "Not really, except . . ."

"Yes?"

"You mentioned a portrait of Sir Dane?"

"Yes. Actually, you must have passed it while you went around the castle. It's on the staircase in the great hall. You can't miss it."

Kathryn thought back to the previous night. The space on the half-landing had been cleared for a new portrait by Sir Thomas Lawrence. "Er, no, I haven't actually been on the tour yet."

"You haven't? Oh, I thought you must have done. People usually come in here for refreshment *after* their dose of history." The woman smiled.

"I . . . I wanted a cup of tea," Kathryn explained lamely.

"Well, the dismal beverage they serve in here isn't exactly Fortnum and Mason. You'd have been better off sticking to coffee."

Kathryn managed a smile. "Perhaps I'll leave it then." She got up. "I think I'll go on my tour now."

"You do that, my dear, and remember to take note of Sir Dane's portrait. I'm sure you'll agree that whatever was said of him, he was a wickedly handsome fellow."

"I will. Thank you for your time."

"Not at all."

Kathryn went out into the sunshine again, and this time her steps were more determined. Somewhere there was a rational explanation for what happened last night, and she meant to find out what it was. As she passed beneath the gatehouse into the wide courtyard, the castle seemed to fold over her just like it had the night before. The first tour of the day was beginning to form, and she tagged along as a male guide conducted them inside.

The great hall was just the same, even to the repairs being done to one of the fireplaces. Kathryn paused. Repairs? In her dream, or whatever it was, similar repairs were in progress to the same fireplace. Then the stonemason's old-fashioned implements had been neatly piled against the wall, but now much more modern equipment was scattered around, and the area had been roped off for safety. There was an electric saw and drill, as well as various other stone-cutting tools, and the fireplace had been almost entirely dismantled.

The male guide observed her interest. "Ah, yes, madam, the fireplace is rather a sorry sight at the moment. I fear that the last time it was repaired, the mortar wasn't quite what it should have been. Anyway, when it's done this time, it will stand for centuries more."

"When was it last done?"

"Er, the early eighteen hundreds. 1815, I believe. Yes, it was, for the then lord of Marchwood ordered a Napoleonic cannon to be carved into the lintel, to commemorate his presence at Waterloo. He captured some cannon on the battlefield, you know. They stand by the gatehouse now."

"Yes, I know," she murmured. God, this was getting more and more bewildering. Last night she'd crossed this very hall and seen those original repairs in progress. She *had* to be Rosalind's reincarnation, what other answer was there?

The tour continued. Footsteps echoed on the stone flags, and the guide's voice reverberated around the hammerbeam roof as he began to describe various points of interest in the hall. But Kathryn no longer listened to what he said, for her attention was drawn inexorably to the staircase, and the portrait on the half-landing.

She went slowly toward it, drinking in every feature of her beloved Dane. Sir Thomas Lawrence richly deserved his status as Regency England's finest portrait artist, for the likeness was so accurate it might almost have been a photograph. It so captured the essence of its subject that Dane seemed to breathe as he gazed at her from the canvas. He was the epitome of the dashing Regency gentleman, in an indigo coat and tight-fitting white trousers that vanished into gleaming top boots. A lacy neckcloth blossomed at his throat, and more lace pushed through his partially buttoned gray-and-white striped waistcoat. A faint smile played on his lips, and his eyes seemed to mock her a little, as if he were amused at her expense.

She was transfixed. She'd somehow spent last night making passionate love with this long-dead Englishman. . . . Her body tingled as she thought of those wonderfully erotic hours, and fresh desire awakened in her. God, how she wished she were with him again! How she wished he were standing behind her now, and that at any moment she'd feel his arms around her waist and his lips against the tender skin where her neck and shoulder met. Oh, the delicious thrill she'd feel if that were to happen. . . .

The great hall was suddenly quiet, but then a man spoke coldly. "The portrait was delivered an hour ago, and, I fancy, looks well enough, but I hardly dare ask what you think of Lawrence's little daub. No doubt your opinion on this will be as baffling as everything else about you at the moment."

She turned with a gasp, for it was Dane.

# Ten

~

She was in Regency clothes again, this time a pink muslin gown embroidered with white daisies. Her golden hair was piled up on her head, with heavy ringlets tumbling down to the nape of her neck, and her white silk shawl trailed carelessly along the floor. She wasn't asleep now, so it couldn't be a dream, and she no longer thought an old movie or book had anything to do with it. Was this what happened in reincarnation? Was the modern person plagued by strangely real memories without warning any time of night or day?

For a split second the unanswered questions gripped her, but then she dashed them aside. If she was honest, right now she no longer cared about explanations. Night or day, asleep or not, her wish to be with Dane again had been granted, and happiness sang through her as she looked down to where he stood at the foot of the staircase.

He wore a bottle-green riding coat and skintight gray breeches, and his neckcloth and the top fastenings of his shirt were undone, affording her a fleeting glimpse of the golden chain. His hair was windswept and he'd tossed his top hat and gloves on the long table in the center of the hall behind him. But as she saw the dark shadow in his eyes, her happiness began to subside. He was angry with her. Had they quarreled?

She knew he'd just returned from a ride, a wild ride to give vent to the fury coursing almost visibly through, but that was all she knew. Everything else that had happened in the hours since dawn was being withheld from her. One thing was only too clear, though, and that was that the warm, passionate man of the previous night was now cold and mistrustful again. At least . . . A new thought struck her. She was only presuming he'd returned to being cold and mistrustful. Maybe this memory was from *before* last night! Who's to say things like this happened in chronological order? They might dodge about haphazardly for all she knew.

"Another enigmatic silence?" he observed sarcastically as he came up the staircase to where she stood.

"You startled me. I . . . I didn't realize you were there," she explained weakly, trying to collect herself.

"Clearly my approach went undetected because you were so rapt by my likeness." His tone was heavy with irony.

"Yes, I was."

"Oh, come, Rosalind, let's not start all that again. I don't pretend to know why you sought to seduce me last night, I only know it was clearly a fleeting aberration."

"No, it wasn't." Well, at least she now knew this was happening *after* last night's events. So why had he changed? What had occurred in the few hours since she'd last been with him?

"Oh, yes, it was, Rosalind."

"I don't understand, Dane. Why have you changed so?"

They both became aware of a discreet tap-tapping sound from across the hall, and he turned irritably toward it. A stonemason and his apprentice were at work on the fireplace, applying hammer and chisel carefully to an intricate corner of stone. They were endeavoring to appear as if they weren't aware of the scene on the staircase, but clearly they could hear every word.

Dane called sharply across to them. "Leave us!"

Without a word, the two put down their tools and hurried away. The moment they'd gone, Dane returned his attention to her. "Why have *I* changed? By God, madam, I have to admire your nerve. You step brazenly from my bed to send a *billet doux* to your lover, and now look me in the eyes again as if you wish to step back into that same bed!"

*Billet doux?* She stared at him. "I . . . I don't know what you're talking about, Dane. How can I send something to a lover I don't have?"

But as she spoke, the information she so desperately sought came flooding into her head. Thomas had sent Rosalind a note informing her he'd be able to attend the Cheltenham ball that night after all. Dane didn't know about this, but had somehow found out about the response Rosalind dispatched with Josie, asking Thomas to meet her at midnight on the bridge by the Well Walk. The walk was a famous two hundred yard avenue of elm and lime trees that led from the edge of Cheltenham to the Royal Spa, where the ball was being held.

The knowledge tumbled so dizzily through her that it was all she could do to remain outwardly composed. For a few moments she thought it was the end of the marital road for unfaithful Rosalind, but then knew that although Dane had found out about the reply to Thomas's note, he still didn't know what either message contained. Rosalind had gotten away with it by the skin of her teeth!

Oh, surely all this *had* to be caused by reincarnation! What other possible explanation could there be? She knew everything the real Rosalind had done—well, nearly everything—and knowledge like that had to come from memories hidden deep in modern-day Kathryn Vansomeren. She wasn't inventing anything; these were actual events. And she knew about things that were yet to happen in 1815. Like the fourth duel. On Lammas Day, August first, Dane was going to kill Thomas Denham. August first was the day after tomorrow! Right now Rosalind only had a temporary reprieve, for her infidelity was about to be exposed no matter what.

Something of her unease must have shown after all, for Dane's eyes sharpened. "You seem rattled, madam; could it be you aren't quite as audacious as I first thought?"

"Dane, I'm not rattled or audacious, I'm upset, and, after last night, I'm also deeply hurt you should think ill of me again this morning." She felt driven to persist with the pretense. Everything Alice had said last night had come true. By persuading him of her love and fidelity, she'd been granted a few hours of exquisite pleasure and happiness. Such happiness was addictive, as was the man himself. . . .

"I don't merely *think* ill, Rosalind, I know it. You dispatched your maid with a note you had the gall to scribble in the very room where I was supposedly still asleep! But I wasn't asleep, I watched you write it and give it to Josie. I then had her followed to the Gloucester carrier, to whom she gave both the note and a coin for his trouble. Would that I'd gone so far as to instruct my man to retrieve the note at all costs, but I didn't. Not that it makes any difference, for the fact remains that it was clearly for Denham."

He was right on every count! Rosalind had done all he said. Kathryn's thoughts were in chaos again, for she didn't know how to explain it away.

Suddenly he seized her arms and shook her slightly. "Admit that it was for Denham, damn you!"

Inspiration came from thin air. "Dane, you're entirely wrong about this. It wasn't a love letter, but an instruction for Mrs. Fowler."

He looked blankly at her. "The dressmaker?"

"Yes. The last time I visited her I told her to put silver lace on my new ballgown, but when I awoke this morning I suddenly knew it would look better without it, and since she'll be delivering the gown in time for Cheltenham tonight, I thought it best to send a message without delay. I often use the carrier like that because he's very reliable." Encouraged by the uncertainty that crept into his eyes, she moved closer and linked her arms around his neck. "Oh, Dane, it was an innocent note, truly it was."

"You think you can so easily gull me?" He disengaged her arms.

"I'm not trying to gull you, I'm telling the truth."

"If it was a message for the dressmaker, why were you so secretive?"

She met his gaze a little accusingly. "I thought you were asleep. Would you have me wake you up simply to tell you I'd decided I didn't want silver lace on my ballgown? I can well imagine your response to *that!*" She smiled then. "Maybe you'd prefer me to do that in future? When I next choose to change pink ribbons to peach, I'll be sure to seek you out particularly."

He searched her eyes. "Either you're telling the truth, or you're the most accomplished liar since Ananias," he murmured.

"Shall I send for Mrs. Fowler?" she offered.

"No, there's no need."

"Does that mean you believe me?"

He met her gaze. "Yes," he said after a moment.

She didn't dare give in to relief. Not yet. "Are you quite sure?"

He smiled a little then. "Of course."

Relief had its way. She linked her arms around his neck

again, and looked earnestly into his eyes. "I don't know what's been the matter with me lately, Dane. I know I've been contrary, but I'm trying not to be now. I do love you so, surely you knew that last night?" Touching him excited her. He felt so warm and strong, and the scent of southernwood clinging to his clothes was oddly arousing, like an expensive modern aftershave.

He put his arms around her slender waist. "Rosalind, you must understand how confused I am where you're concerned. I knew you wanted me last night, but not necessarily that you loved me. As you say, contrariness has been your mark of late."

Again she was conscious of his vulnerability, and of the powerful effect it had upon her. Everything about him touched a chord in her. She only had to be near him for her whole being to tingle with awareness, and already she felt closer to him than she'd ever felt to Richard. She'd known this man for less than twenty-four hours, but it was as if she'd drawn her first breath at his side.

"Trust me, Dane," she whispered.

"Trust must be earned, Rosalind," he said softly.

"Then I will earn it." She pressed close, moving her hips seductively against his, and her reward was the way his hands moved down from her waist to enclose her buttocks and hold her to him.

Confidence suddenly carried her away. She was the siren now, luring him into the delights of the flesh. Seduction was uppermost in her mind again; she wanted him to make love to her again as he had during the night, and she was determined to have her way. She raised her lips to meet his, and sank shudderingly against him as he returned the kiss.

Her breath caught as she felt his potency swell swiftly against her, and her body yielded to his masculine contours. Her lips parted as she drew his tongue into her mouth. His hold tightened and he pushed her against the wall, caressing her breasts as he kissed her again. Desire began to pound irresistibly through them both. He moved a hand to her thigh, caressing her through the daisy-sprinkled muslin as he pressed his hips forward. His arousal pounded against her, and waves of pleasure began to carry her away. Just feeling his hardness was sufficient to raise her to a peak of ecstasy, and he willingly gave her enjoyment without demanding his own release.

As the intense gratification ebbed sweetly away, she clung weakly to him. Her cheeks were flushed, and she closed her eyes as she rested her forehead against his shoulder. Her heart was beating swiftly, and her skin felt damp and relaxed.

He put his hand to her chin and raised her lips to his again, brushing them softly with a tender kiss. "I must wait yet, my darling, but I swear I'll soon take my own measure of delight."

"We can go upstairs now," she whispered, slipping her arms around his waist. In a moment of sharp insight, she knew she loved him. It wasn't a passing fancy, but a strong, vibrant emotion that struck from her very soul. She, Kathryn Vansomeren, was in love with Sir Dane Marchwood, a long-dead English nobleman! Long dead? No, he was very much alive, and in her arms now, but the day after tomorrow he'd discover how Rosalind deceived him, and he'd face her lover at dawn.

Her arms tightened protectively around his waist. It was Thomas Denham who was going to die, but it was this man she wished to shield from hurt. She wanted to be the wife he needed, the faithful, loving, passionate wife he believed her to be right now. "Please come upstairs now," she pleaded again.

"Madam, when I take you upstairs, it will be for an hour or so, not a hasty few minutes before Jeremiah Pendle arrives."

Her thoughts scattered as loving desire was replaced with sudden guardedness. The banker? But why would he come here? He was no friend of Dane's, not since William Denham's death. "You expect Pendle?" she asked.

"You know I do. It's something about the tolls due to the Canal Company on the *Lady Marchwood*. No doubt he intends to see I pay well over the odds, but I'll see him in Hades first."

The *Lady Marchwood*. Kathryn dug into her store of knowledge. Like many men of consequence in Gloucester, Dane owned a number of merchant ships, and the *Lady Marchwood* was an ocean-going schooner recently completed in a Gloucester yard. The following day, Lammas Eve, she was to set off on her maiden voyage to bring timber from the Baltic. She was only the second deep-sea vessel to be built in the basin, and her departure would be an occasion of great celebration. All ships built and launched in Gloucester came under the auspices of the Canal Company, which owned the dock basin, and Jeremiah Pendle was a prominent member of the board. Dane was probably right, if the banker could swindle more tolls out of him than necessary, he would.

But the more Kathryn thought about Pendle, the more uneasy she felt. He was definitely Dane's enemy, and instinct told her he posed a threat of some sort. In what way though?

Dane smiled regretfully. "I don't particularly want to see him, but he's sent word it's important. Then, when he's gone, I'm afraid I have urgent estate matters to attend to, so madam, pray take pity on your poor frustrated husband and help turn his thoughts to less carnal matters." He drew her away from the wall and made her face the portrait again. "Well? Has Lawrence done me justice?"

"Oh, he has. I vow you look very dashing."

"I fear he hasn't quite caught the nobility of my forehead and regal perfection of my nose."

"Or the tongue in your cheek, sirrah." She glanced smilingly at him again.

"That too." He laughed, and then looked intently at her. "I welcome this change in you, whatever has caused it."

"So do I." Kathryn marveled that the real Rosalind could ever find Thomas Denham more appealing than this man.

His gaze became a little disconcerted. "Sometimes I could almost swear . . ." He didn't finish.

"Almost swear what?"

"That I'm married to two different women."

She managed a light laugh. "What's this, sirrah? Are you a bigamist?"

"If I am, I vow I much prefer the second wife to the first," he murmured, studying her eyes for a long moment. "The light in here must be strange, for . . ."

"Yes?"

"Oh, nothing." He kissed her nose, and then cupped her face in his hands. "Maybe I married twins, one warm and passionate, the other cool and *dis*passionate."

"Maybe you did, sir." Right now, you definitely did, she thought, for that was certainly the context in which this whole weird business might be interpreted. She slipped her arms around his waist again. "Well, this is the warm and passionate twin, and she wishes to be between the sheets with you again as soon as possible. Promise that the moment the odious Pendle has gone, you'll postpone your estate business long enough to come to me." Please let me stay in this time for long enough . . .

His gray eyes were warm, and he stroked her cheeks with his thumbs. "Methinks you're a forward jade, Lady Marchwood."

"Oh, disgracefully forward, sir," she murmured. His caresses affected her, and her voice was husky with desire.

"Persist like this and I won't be able to contain myself from tumbling you here on the staircase after all. One can imagine Pendle's shock if he were to be shown in and find us thus engaged," he declared, releasing her and moving determinedly away from temptation.

The sensuous spell began to unravel, and she drew a long breath as she composed herself. Then her store of borrowed knowledge surged to the fore again. "Dane, why do you deal with Pendle again? After all the things he said when William Denham died—"

"I deal with him because I must, and he was entitled to say them," he interrupted.

"Entitled to vow revenge?"

"Grief affects us greatly, and William Denham was his favorite nephew."

She looked curiously at him. "Why did you fight that duel? You've never explained properly."

"Nor do I intend to. Suffice it that I was more than justified, as Denham himself knew full well. It was between him and me, no one else."

"If you were justified, why didn't you give your reasons? Pendle wasn't the only one to think ill of you because of that duel."

"Do you think ill of me?"

"No, for I know you wouldn't have called him out without good cause." She spoke the truth, for with all her heart she believed in Sir Dane Marchwood. His reputation didn't matter to her; it was the man himself who meant everything.

He seemed amused. "But I'm renowned for dueling—indeed, everyone knows I exult in such things and avidly seek provocation," he remarked dryly.

"I know better."

"Rosalind, I killed William Denham long before I knew you, and I refuse to explain the cause of the quarrel, so how can you defend me with any real conviction?"

"Because I know you would never behave shamefully."

"Perhaps I already have, toward you at any rate," he murmured, looking away.

"What do you mean?"

"It's of no consequence." He gave her a quick smile and touched her cheek reassuringly.

She caught his hand. "Dane, there's something I wish to ask."

"What is it?"

"Is the *Lady Marchwood* named for me?" She hadn't even realized the question was there, but she did know that it was Kathryn Vansomeren who needed the answer, not Rosalind.

Almost imperceptibly he drew back. "What an odd question."

"Is it?" She looked at the chain at his throat. "After all, there was another Lady Marchwood, was there not?" she murmured.

"I don't wish to discuss this, Rosalind." A change came over him; he was suddenly chill and distant.

"It's important to me, Dane."

"Elizabeth has been dead for ten years now, and—"

"And you still grieve for her," she interrupted.

"I loved her." His tone couldn't have been more clipped.

"She's not here now, Dane, I am, and I need to know you love me."

"Words mean nothing."

"You wear her likeness," she pressed.

"Leave it, Rosalind."

"Dane . . ."

"I said leave it."

Before she could say anything more there was the sound of a curricle arriving in the courtyard outside.

He glanced toward the sound. "Pendle's here."

The unease of earlier swept over her again, but more strongly now. The banker was a real threat of some kind! A keen sixth sense told her to be on her guard. "I . . . I hope you won't mind if I stay while you see him?"

"Stay? But you won't be remotely interested in what he has to say."

"On the contrary, I'm quite intrigued."

He shrugged. "As you wish. I intend to receive him in the drawing room, so we'll adjourn there." He offered her his arm, and together they went up the staircase.

# *Eleven*

~

The drawing room was hung with fine Brussels tapestries, and had particularly elegant gilt furniture. Its ceiling was beamed and its walls the original stone of the medieval castle. The arched door was paneled and carved, and the deeply embrasured windows overlooked the courtyard on one side, the terraced gardens and meadows on the other. One of the windows above the terrace stood open, and the breeze rustled the ivy growing against the wall. The sound made Kathryn shiver unexpectedly as she glanced around the rest of the room.

Brightly colored Chinese vases stood on either side of the fireplace, and over the mantel there was a panoramic painting of the Battle of Minden, at which Dane's grandfather had fought with conspicuous gallantry. There was an impressive cabinet standing in a corner near the door. Its lower half comprised bow-fronted drawers, but its upper portion was of glass-fronted shelves set out with a collection of ivory and amber figurines. More figurines stood on a marble-topped table nearby, and with them a velvet-lined leather case containing two exquisite dueling pistols. The name of the German gunsmith who made them was embossed on the case: *Siegfried Meyer, Paternoster Row, London.*

The richly decorated handguns were of unusual design, containing concealed chambers from which nine balls could be fired in succession. They were costly weapons, and had once been owned by Dane's father, who'd had one tucked in the breast of his coat when, riding home one night across notorious Hounslow Heath, a highwayman fired at him, and his life had been saved when the shot struck the pistol stock and was deflected. From that moment on the pistol had been regarded

as lucky, and Dane had decided against having the damaged
stock repaired. He'd used the weapon successfully at each of
the duels he'd fought.

She noticed the case as soon as they entered the room, and
recalled that the guide had told her these were the weapons
used at the duel in which Thomas died. Thomas clearly
wouldn't use the "lucky" pistol, which meant that it was the
other gun that was supposed to have been tampered with. Dane
wouldn't do such a thing; he simply wasn't capable of dis-
honor. Maybe he was fiery, courageous, and dangerous as an
opponent, but he would always observe the rules of conduct.

Dane followed her gaze. "Damn, I forgot them," he said,
going to close the case. "I sent them to Meyer to be over-
hauled, and they arrived back this morning. I'll put them away,
for there's little point in reminding Pendle of his nephew's
demise." She knew he was telling the truth about the London
gunsmith, and about the pistols having arrived back at Marchwood that morning, so the reason for their being out like this
was perfectly plausible. Plausible? What sort of word was that
to use? It suggested some kind of clever deceit on his part. Besides, he still didn't know for certain about Rosalind and
Thomas, so why would he start meddling with the guns at this
juncture? No, she was just letting her thoughts and fears run-
away with her.

The banker was shown up the grand staircase, and Dane
quickly closed the pistol case and took it to the cabinet where
it was always kept in one of the drawers. He was just placing it
inside when Jeremiah Pendle was shown in. She felt as if winter entered the room with him, and she shivered, just as she
had on hearing the ivy rustling a few minutes earlier.

The banker was sweating profusely after the drive from
Gloucester and the climb up the staircase, and, as always, was
mopping his forehead with his customary red-spotted handkerchief. His carefully powdered wig was slightly askew, and his
immense girth was corseted into a pale blue coat and beige
breeches. He appeared preoccupied with his physical discomfort, but Kathryn couldn't help noticing how sharply his clever
little eyes flickered toward the case in the second before Dane
closed the drawer. She wondered what the banker's thoughts
were in that moment, for he knew they were the weapons used

when William Denham died. But whatever his feelings, he hid them behind a sleekly false smile.

He bowed. "Good morning, Sir Dane. My lady."

Dane inclined his head to him. "Good morning, sir. Well, I understand there's something you wish to discuss with me about the *Lady Marchwood* tolls? I trust there's no problem?"

"A little, er, difficulty, Sir Dane, that is all. You expressed concern that you'd already paid toll on most of the timber used to make the *Lady Marchwood*, and said you did not think it right the Canal Company should exact more for her actual building and launching."

"Correct."

"And I agree with your argument. On your behalf I've been endeavoring to persuade the board to waive the charges, or at least reduce them. I fear I haven't succeeded." The spotted handkerchief waved slightly as the man made a regretful gesture.

Everything about him grated upon Kathryn like a fingernail being drawn down glass, and she no more believed he'd tried to plead Dane's case than she believed his smiles and expressions of regret. He hated Dane more than anyone else in the world, and it was a hatred she found almost tangible.

Suddenly she couldn't bear to be in the same room with him, and turned to Dane. "I . . . I think I'll leave you to discuss this. I have things to do."

He smiled, not surprised she was apparently bored after all. "*A bientôt, cherie,*" he murmured, raising her hand to his lips.

Her fingers closed earnestly over his as she replied in a soft whisper Pendle couldn't hear. "Beware of him, Dane, for Old Nick himself would make a less dangerous foe."

"Fear not, for I have his measure."

"I pray so." She squeezed his fingers slightly. "Promise to come to me when he's gone."

"You're reprehensibly persistent, madam."

"Nothing ventured, nothing gained."

He smiled. "In this you have certainly gained. Of course I'll come to you."

A warmth entered her cheeks and she turned to leave, but as she did so, the wind rustled the ivy once more. Again she shivered, her gaze drawn reluctantly toward the window and then to the banker. Their eyes met, and she felt his malevolence so strongly she couldn't bear it, but had to hurry out in order to break all contact.

In Dane's apartment, she stood looking at the view over the terraced gardens, and the meadows and woodland beyond. She could hear the low murmur of voices as Dane and Pendle spoke in the drawing room, which was only a little further along from where she stood, and her thoughts returned to the banker. She'd never before been particularly intuitive, and certainly never had anything approaching a sixth sense, but warning bells were ringing loudly where Jeremiah Pendle was concerned.

The minutes passed, and at last the tone of the conversation in the drawing room changed as Pendle began to take his leave. Dane would come to her soon now. She glanced at the bed. Please let them make love for a long time now; don't let fate snatch her to the future before she again sampled the erotic passion of last night.

Slowly she began to undress, taking infinite delight in the way her dainty Regency gown fell softly around her ankles. She already knew this time that there were no undergarments, she'd realized *that* on the staircase! For whatever reason, Rosalind was evidently a lady who abhorred whalebone and stays, and Kathryn was very thankful. The thought of being trussed up in hot summer weather like this was quite awful.

When she was naked, the light breeze drifting through the window was cool and sensuous on her skin. Fleetingly she thought again about the incredible events of the past hours, and of how she felt as if she'd known Dane for much longer. If she was indeed Rosalind's reincarnation, then of course she felt she knew him. But as the thought struck her, so did the paradox it posed. Rosalind might have been Dane's wife, but it was Thomas Denham she loved, so why did Kathryn Vansomeren—as Rosalind—cleave so passionately to Dane?

There was no time to think more, for his steps approached. He came in and his glance moved over her with lazy appreciation. "I see you are impatient, madam," he murmured, closing the door and leaning back against it.

"Very impatient, sir."

His eyes met hers. "Would that you had always been like this, Rosalind," he murmured.

"If I've been a less than loving wife until now, I regret it with all my heart."

He smiled and held out a hand. "Then come to me."

She needed no second bidding, and ran to him. With a laugh he caught her close, lifted her into his arms and carried her to the bed. He put her down gently on the silk coverlet, and then drew his fingertips softly across her excited nipples as he looked intently into her eyes. "Tell me you are a changeling, and I will believe you, for the woman I look upon now is the perfection I've always longed for. When I took you as my wife, I knew you didn't love me, but I hoped that love would grow in time. Now, at last, it has."

The way he stroked her breasts sent frissons of pleasure through her. She put a hand to his thigh, sliding it slowly up until she felt his iron-hard erection, outlined so clearly by the tightness of his breeches. "Let's consummate that love now," she whispered, closing her hand needfully over his virility, and gently massaging the end.

He closed his eyes, his breath escaping on a shuddering sigh, then he halted her caresses by putting his hand over hers. He smiled lazily down at her. "I've yet to make love with my breeches still buttoned, madam, and I don't intend to begin now. Besides, your body is an altar at which I intend to worship with every reverence."

When he was naked, he bent over her to press his lips to her breasts. His kisses moved down to her abdomen, and then ever more tenderly to the dark hairs at her groin. Then he lay down with her, his knowing fingers sliding expertly between her legs. "Two can play this game, my love," he whispered as her breath caught on a gasp of pleasure.

Then he stopped her gasps with a kiss, and the lovemaking began in earnest. He was ardent but leisurely, taking her to the edge of ecstasy and lingering over the moment as if forever. Her pleasure mattered as much as his, and he took care to carry her along with him. Their bodies were warm and damp, their union complete in every way. If she was the altar, then his worship was divine, and the resulting rapture was sublime.

But a shadow lay across the bed, a shadow perhaps only she could see. He still wore Elizabeth's likeness, and it seemed to Kathryn that his first wife had a mocking smile on her lips, as if she knew her successor could never completely have his heart.

He stayed for two hours that passed all too quickly, but at last he felt unable to postpone his pressing estate business any longer. She lay there watching as he dressed. Her body was warm and relaxed, her desire pacified, but as she looked at his strong slender form, she knew she could never have enough of him. It wasn't purely sexual, though, for it went far beyond that. There was something about Sir Dane Marchwood that reached past all her defenses, something that told her again and again that he was her other half. She'd felt it when first she saw him, and now the conviction was even stronger because she loved him. If she'd really been the woman he married, she knew they would have been wonderfully happy together. Already there were times when they anticipated each other's thoughts and words, when they laughed at something foolish to anyone else but themselves, and when they glanced at each other at the same precise moment. They were a perfect match in every conceivable way. Except they weren't a match at all, for she was here on borrowed time.

She wished she understood why all this was happening to her, but when she was with him, she didn't really care why, only that it went on and on without end. But it would end, for at dawn on Lammas Day, he and Thomas Denham would face each other because of her—no, because of Rosalind—and that would only happen because Dane found out once and for all that his suspicions were well founded. What hope would there be then for Kathryn Vansomeren to retain his love? Even presuming she could still come back to this former self. . . .

Tears sprang to her eyes and she sat up, reaching out impulsively to him. "Hold me, please . . ."

His fingers were firm and reassuring as he caught her hands. "What is it, sweetheart? What's wrong?" he asked concernedly.

"I love you with all my heart, you must always believe that," she whispered.

She wanted him to say the same in return, but he didn't. He moved closer to her, though, cradling her head against his waist and twining his hand in her hair. She wrapped her arms around his hips and closed her eyes as tears welled down her cheeks.

He tilted her face anxiously. "Tell me why you're so sad. If it's something I've said or done . . ."

She strove to collect herself, wanting desperately to tell him the truth, but knowing she couldn't. "It's nothing, I . . . I'm being foolish."

"But if there's something wrong . . ."

"No. Nothing's wrong."

"Are you sure?"

She gazed up into his eyes. "Quite sure."

He released her then. "I must go now, for I have a veritable plethora of pressing matters to attend to, from bickering between tenants about closed sluice gates, to stolen cheeses, a deliberately damaged wagon, and, would you believe, a potentially violent dispute about rustled hens! A landlord's load is varied indeed, but while I'm engaged upon all this excitement, you must rest. You must be the belle of tonight's ball." He smiled and bent to kiss her nose, then he left.

She watched the door close behind him. Which twin could attend the ball with him tonight? Warm, passionate Kathryn? Or cold, unloving Rosalind? She prayed it would be the former, for she longed to go to such a glittering occasion as Lady Marchwood, but she feared she would have returned to her own time again by then.

Something made her get up and dress. She wanted to lie back and savor the warmth of the sheets where he'd lain, but was prevented by a strange urge to return to the great hall. Her golden hair was tangled and untidy, so she went through to her own apartment to use a brush and select a ribbon from the drawer.

Looking neat again, she went to the top of the grand staircase, where the first person she saw was Alice.

# Twelve

~

The old nurse was standing on the half-landing, almost as if waiting for her, and looked up with a smile.

"Ah, there you are, my dear. Did I not promise you more passion than you'd ever known before?"

The stonemason and his apprentice were at work on the fireplace again, but were so engrossed in the intricacies of a corner that they didn't even glance around.

Kathryn went slowly down to the landing, and faced the nurse. "Yes, you promised me."

"And is he not everything you could ever want in a man?"

"Yes, he is." There was something Kathryn had to know. "Am I Rosalind's reincarnation?" she asked bluntly.

"If by that you mean has she been born again in you, the answer is no. You are two very separate persons, with nothing to link you except circumstance. When the moment is right, I will explain everything. In the meantime I must return you to your own time again."

"No! Please! I want to ask so much. I . . . I know the day after tomorrow Thomas Denham is going to die at a duel with Dane."

Alice hesitated and lowered her glance for a moment. "Yes, it would seem that on Lammas Day he will breathe his last."

"Can't you stop it happening?"

"No. Dane will find out about Rosalind and Thomas, nothing can prevent that."

Kathryn was desperate to find out all she could before she suddenly found herself in the future again. "What's all this really about, Alice? I've gone through all the possibilities, from

books and movies, to hallucinations on account of jet lag, and
ending up with reincarnation, but—"

"I don't understand. Movies? Jet lag?" The old woman
looked mystified.

"Oh, there's no time to explain, all you have to do is tell me
what's going on."

"It concerns a quest for happiness, my dear, and commenced with two people, but has now spread to four. You are
one of them, and have the chance to bring about the change
that will bring joy to all four. You are the key, Kathryn; only
through you can the door to joy be opened."

What mumbo jumbo, Kathryn thought, but then she looked
into the old woman's bright eyes and changed her mind. There
was clearly much more to this than seemed possible right now.
Her thoughts hurtled swiftly on. Okay, so let's assume it's all
genuine. Alice talked of four people being involved. The other
three were clearly Rosalind, Thomas, and Dane, but Thomas
didn't have a future, he was set to die on Lammas Day. She
spoke at last. "Maybe I'm being stupid, but what good is this
going to do Thomas Denham? You've just said nothing can
stop the duel, so presumably Dane's going to kill him no matter what?"

"Yes."

"Then I fail to see—"

"Trust me, Kathryn."

"That's a lot to ask under the circumstances."

"I know, but you have a lot to gain."

"Do I?"

Alice nodded. "If fate is kind, yes."

"So there's a catch," Kathryn observed dryly.

"Nothing is certain in this life. Or any other life."

"Except that Dane is about to kill Thomas Denham because
of Rosalind."

Alice didn't reply.

Kathryn eyed her. "You're Rosalind's nurse, and so know
her very well indeed, right?"

"Yes."

"And you've been helping her conduct this affair with
Thomas. Oh, don't deny it, for she met him in your cottage!"

"I wasn't going to deny it, Kathryn."

"Okay, so you admit you're in on all she does?"

Alice nodded.

"And she's supposed to be deeply in love with Thomas?"

"She is."

Kathryn shook her head firmly. "She can't be."

"Why do you say that?"

"Well, if you know all about the duel and Thomas's death, so does she, and if she loved him like you say, she'd do all she could to stop the duel happening. In short, she'd give Thomas up to save his life. I'd give Dane up; there's no way I'd carry on seeing him if it meant his death."

Alice smiled. "If only it were that simple, my dear; but Rosalind is powerless to change events here in this time. She, Dane, and Thomas are bound by their stars, but you are different."

"How?"

"You have powers, oh, maybe not as strongly as mine, but you do have them. That is how I know you across the years. I have the sight."

"The sight? Second sight, you mean? Being able to see into the future?" Kathryn paused. "Well, I can tell you right now, *I* don't have the sight. I've never even had a premonition!"

Alice studied her intently. "Are you sure of that? Your powers are there, my dear, they just have yet to be fully realized. My gifts are fading now, soon they will be gone, but I am using the strength I have left to try to bring happiness to four people to whom it is due. Maybe I'm reaching beyond my capabilities, maybe it's far too audacious a plan to ever succeed, but I believe it can be done."

Kathryn was dumbfounded. Whatever she'd expected, it hadn't been this. She tried to keep a hold on her wits. "What exactly are my powers supposed to be?" she asked after a moment.

"Among them you may count intuition, my dear. We all have it to a certain extent, but in you it is very strong indeed, and you may always rely upon it."

"Alice, I—"

"Don't ask me more now, Kathryn, for it's time to return you to your own time. If you wish to attend the ball tonight, and thus see Dane one more time before tomorrow, when at the *Lady Marchwood's* departure on her maiden voyage he will find out about Rosalind and Thomas, you must be in

Cheltenham at ten o'clock this evening. Be at the Royal Well. It's easy to find because it's the reason for Cheltenham's fame." Alice put a hand on her arm. "Now look at Dane's portrait again, my dear, and think well on how much you love him. And remember, trust your intuition."

Kathryn started to obey, but then looked swiftly back at the nurse. Instead of the old woman from the past, she saw the guide she'd spoken to in the castle restaurant.

The woman was concerned. "I didn't mean to startle you, my dear, it's just that I spoke three times and you didn't answer. Are you sure you're all right, my dear?"

Kathryn's heart pounded. She was her modern self again! She looked past the woman at the great hall. Another tour was just beginning, and the stonemason and apprentice of the past had vanished. How long had she been standing here? Had the outer shell of Kathryn Vansomeren been gazing at Dane's portrait for well over two hours, while her inner self went back in time to become Rosalind?

She summoned a weak smile. "I . . . I'm quite all right. I was so engrossed in the portrait I just didn't hear you."

"Well, I saw you drive away earlier, but when you came back again a few moments ago, I knew you were smitten with Marchwood, and with Sir Dane in particular, if I'm not mistaken."

She'd driven away and come back? Kathryn tried not to show she didn't know what the woman was talking about.

The guide looked at the portrait. "I told you he was handsome."

"A girl could give way to wicked fantasies," Kathryn replied, recovering sufficiently to try to joke.

The woman laughed. "A girl could indeed," she agreed.

There was much Kathryn needed to find out, and the Marchwood archives seemed the best bet. "Is it possible to see the castle records? Maybe there's a library or something?"

"I'm afraid not. Everything was sent to the public library in Gloucester. Do you know Gloucester at all?"

"I'm staying there."

"Anyone will be able to direct you to the library in Brunswick Road. When you get there you'll see a sign directing you to the Gloucester Collection on the upper floor. It's all reference, so you won't be able to take anything home with you, but you can examine most things at your leisure on the premises."

"Thank you, I'll do that. I want to find out more about the duel," Kathryn explained, glancing again at Dane's portrait.

The guide smiled. "Well, I'm afraid there isn't a trustworthy account in existence. The only so-called authority is the diary of a prominent local citizen of the time, a man named Jeremiah Pendle, and he's biased to say the least."

Kathryn's lips parted. "Jeremiah Pendle? The banker?"

"You've heard of him? Yes, the same, and as odious a slug as ever lived. If it weren't for him, Sir Dane's reputation might never have suffered, for the diary contains the only description of the duel, and therefore the only reference to the business of the pistol's being tampered with. Pendle died of a heart attack the night after the duel, but as far as I'm concerned, it's a pity he didn't do so a day before. I would much have preferred Sir Dane's character not to have been sullied by charges of dishonorable and shameful conduct, even if he might indeed have done the despicable deed."

Jeremiah Pendle! Kathryn remembered how instinctively she'd disliked and distrusted the banker. Alice had told her she could rely on her intuition, and in this it had certainly served her well! Now it told her that something very untoward indeed had gone on at the duel. What, though? Had the pistol been meddled with? Or was that taken for gospel because it was in Pendle's diary?

The guide smiled at her. "I can see you're eager to find out all you can."

"Yes. I'll go back to Gloucester right now."

"Good luck."

Kathryn smiled and then hurried from the courtyard. Her steps were lighter than they'd been when she'd arrived. She'd been with Dane again, and knew she'd see him tonight as well. What Alice had told her still didn't really make sense, but she'd go along with it anyway. All that stuff about audacious plans, happiness, and mystic powers was a bit deep—or crazy—but was the only explanation on offer right now.

She still couldn't see the logic of including Thomas Denham in any quest for happiness, because come hell or high water, he was going to die at dawn the day after tomorrow. As for Dane and Rosalind, there didn't seem much hope there either. Tomorrow, Lammas Eve, he was going to find out about his wife's affair.

She drove quickly back to the Gloucester apartments, where Jack was tending the climbing roses. He was listening to classical music on his portable radio and gave a start when the car suddenly appeared. Then he grinned and turned the radio down a little. "I was miles away, miss."

"I didn't mean to make you jump." She glanced uncertainly at the radio, for there seemed an odd sort of stereo echo, as if someone else was tuned in to the same station.

Jack didn't notice anything amiss. "I should keep my wits about me, but I can't resist a little bit of Beethoven or Mozart. Nothing better to soothe the savage breast, eh?"

"I guess so. Anyway, I won't keep you. If you could just tell me how to get to the library?"

"Certainly, miss." He told her exactly how to get there. "It's about a quarter of a mile from here," he added.

"Okay. Thanks."

"Any time, miss. Any time."

At the end of the lane from the apartments, she examined the menu outside the Monk's Retreat. Maybe she'd eat there this evening. Jack promised good plain food, so she should try it. The British weren't renowned for their cuisine, but some of it must be okay.

She walked on toward the crossroad in the center of the city, and suddenly saw Jeremiah Pendle's bank. At least, it was the same building, but it was now a stylish modern bar called Jeremiah's Cellars. There were tables and chairs outside, and its impressive half-timbered facade spilled over with hanging baskets of flowers. Music and laughter echoed into the street, which she couldn't help thinking was singularly inappropriate for anyplace boasting a connection with a sour apple like Jeremiah Pendle.

She walked quickly past, for in spite of the modern trappings, she still felt the banker's presence. If he suddenly appeared in the doorway now, mopping his forehead with that damned spotted handkerchief, she wouldn't be at all surprised.

The library was a gray Victorian building without a great deal to commend it. Richard wouldn't care for it much, she thought as she went into the vestibule. The reference section was on the second floor, and the noise of the street faded behind as she went on. Signs directed her to the Gloucester Collection, which was housed in a tall-windowed room at the end of a long corridor. It was very quiet. Several people were seated at tables with notepads and piles of old books assembled before them, and the only sound was made by someone using a copying machine in a corner. The electric whir was out of place in such Dickensian surroundings.

A woman librarian was seated at a large desk close to the door. She was matronly, with gray hair tugged back into a tight bun, and she smiled pleasantly as Kathryn approached.

"May I help you?"

"Yes, I hope so. I've been told this is the place to come to find out about events in the Gloucester area at the end of July, beginning of August, 1815."

"It certainly is." The woman got up. "What is it you're particularly interested in?"

Kathryn didn't have to think long. "The Waterloo ball in Cheltenham, the maiden voyage of the *Lady Marchwood* from Gloucester docks, the duel between Sir Dane Marchwood and Thomas Denham, and the death of Jeremiah Pendle. Oh, and his diary, of course."

"Well, we can accommodate you. We have a recent edition of the Pendle diary, so you won't have to struggle with Jeremiah's old-fashioned handwriting, and everything else will be on microfilm of the *Gloucester Journal* newspaper. I'm afraid all the old print can be very hard on the eyes, they didn't believe in wasting space in those days, but if you're prepared to plow through . . . ?"

"I am."

"Follow me. You're in luck, there's a machine free. Usually they have to be booked in advance." She led Kathryn through into a small darkened side room, where large-screened consoles were placed at desks around the walls. The screens were difficult to read, hence the dark room, and the only unoccupied machine was in the darkest corner of all. The woman switched the screen on and then went into another adjoining room to find the appropriate microfilm.

She placed it on the machine and showed Kathryn how to wind it to and fro. "It's all very antiquated, I'm afraid, but at least it's simple to operate. Now then, everything's arranged in months, so I'll start you off at the beginning of July. Ah, there it is. I'll leave you to it, then. If you need me, I'll be at my desk."

"Thanks."

Alone by the console, Kathryn gazed at the screen. Small print? The woman hadn't been joking! Thank God the screen enlarged it a little, otherwise she'd need a magnifying glass. Right, she'd take things in chronological order, which meant starting with the Waterloo ball. She wound the microfilm to the end of the month and began to scan the columns.

# Thirteen

~

The microfilmed pages were so tightly packed that finding anything seemed impossible, but suddenly Kathryn saw what she was looking for. It was tucked away at the foot of a column, between a report on a horrid murder and robbery, and an item about the sad loss of one of His Majesty's frigates during a storm off Iceland.

"At the Royal Well in Cheltenham the noble victory of Waterloo was celebrated with the greatest festivity at a grand ball attended by all the nobility and gentry of the country. At one time the number of carriages seen approaching the venue exceeded seventy. Among those present were the Duke and Duchess of Beaufort, the Marquesses of Worcester and Lorne, the Earls and Countesses of . . ."

Kathryn hurried through the list, and at last saw the names she sought. Sir Dane and Lady Marchwood. And there, much further down the list, Mr. Thomas Denham. She also saw another name she knew, Dr. George Eden, the trusted, well-respected man who was one of the few people Dane thought worthy of close friendship. She half expected to see Jeremiah Pendle's name as well, but it wasn't included. She read on.

"The ball was opened by the Duke and Duchess of Beaufort. Country dances and reels were elegantly interspersed with minuets, ländlers, polonaises, and that newest addition to fashionable and superior occasions, the waltz, which was executed with particular distinction by Sir Dane and Lady Marchwood."

Kathryn raised an eyebrow. Executed with particular distinction? What exactly did that mean? She continued.

"There was a supper of such magnificence that it was advantageously compared with anything Mr. Gunter could supply.

Favorite airs were played during the repast. After supper the company repaired outside to witness a great number of beautiful fireworks, consisting of rockets, brilliant suns and stars, wheels, and emblematical devices displayed in radiant fire, the whole concluding with a grand discharge of rockets, fireballs, Indian trees, serpents, etc. The guests began to disperse at daylight, and the occasion was universally acknowledged to be the most suitable and laudable for such a momentous time in our history."

It had sure been quite a Regency wingding, Kathryn thought, sitting back as she finished. Update it a little, and it could be a modern embassy reception, or something at the White House.

She began to scan the screen again, this time searching for a report on the *Lady Marchwood*. The ship had set off on her maiden voyage on the day after the ball, so anything about it must follow fairly quickly. She found it almost straightaway.

"This day was the deep-sea vessel, the *Lady Marchwood*, seen off in splendid style as she departed on her first voyage to bring timber from the Baltic. Watched by Sir Dane and Lady Marchwood, and to the acclaim and cheers of a large gathering of notable persons, the ship was hauled through the lock from the dock basin, and on entering the river was turned by means of ropes in order to sail downstream on the full tide. A band played sea shanties, and the general populace was entertained by a fair which went on until midnight. The vessel is expected to return to Gloucester in one month's time."

The report ended there, and the column ran on without break into something about a large importation of prime Westphalia hams being sold at Portsmouth. Prime Westphalia hams? It hardly seemed possible that such an inconsequential fact was considered important enough to put into print! On second thoughts, though, maybe it wasn't all that inconsequential. In the days before refrigeration, the arrival of such a commodity was probably of considerable significance.

Putting the hams from her thoughts, she looked again at the report on the *Lady Marchwood*. There was no mention of anything untoward, and certainly no mention of Dane's challenging Thomas Denham to a duel. Thomas's name didn't even crop up. Maybe she'd find a few lines about the duel itself. . . .

She wound the film on, but almost immediately saw Jeremiah Pendle's name. "The Death of Mr. Jeremiah Pendle. It is with great regret that we report the demise of one of Gloucester's foremost citizens. Mr. Jeremiah Pendle passed away this morning after suffering a tremendous seizure of the heart. He was found at his desk in his premises at the Cross, and is believed to have been stricken by the unfortunate death yesterday of his nephew, Mr. Thomas Denham, who was misguided enough to enter into a dawn meeting with Sir D——e M———d. Mr. Pendle leaves no immediate heir, and his estate therefore devolves upon the only remaining member of the Denham family, a gentleman farmer believed to be at present residing in Norwich."

As before, the column then ran on into another item, this time the prices of ewes at Gloucester market. She wound swiftly ahead, searching for anything else about the duel, but it wasn't mentioned again.

The librarian came in to see how she was managing. "Have you found all you wanted?" she asked.

"Yes, I think so. The duel doesn't get much of a mention, though. Sir Dane Marchwood's name isn't even printed properly, just the first and last letters of each word."

"That was frequently the case in those days. Most publications are littered with disguised but excruciatingly obvious names. I can only suppose it was to get around the then libel laws. As to no proper report on the duel itself, there wouldn't be. Duels were illegal, you see, and to make a lengthy report might lead to the authorities suspecting participation of some sort by the newspapers or their proprietors. Jails weren't terribly savory places then. Anyway, I've looked out the copy of Pendle's diary. It's strange, but the events you're looking up appear to be very popular all of a sudden. The microfilm and diary have been logged out once already this morning, usually they don't get looked at from one month to the next. Anyway, the final few pages are all you'll really be concerned with, because the duel was the last thing Pendle wrote about before he died. Actually, I've just had another read myself, it really is a curious and intriguing story."

Kathryn looked at it with distaste. The reporter in her always loathed distorted writing, and she knew before she started that Pendle's account would be very slanted indeed. Still, if it was the only record of the duel, she had no choice but to read it. Unless, of course . . . She looked up hopefully at the librarian. "I'm told this is the only authority on the duel, but perhaps there's another one? Surely *someone* else wrote about it?"

The woman shook her head. "Everyone in Gloucester knew about it, of course, for the challenge was rather publicly issued the day before, but if anyone wrote about it, their version has never come to light. The only people present at the actual duel were the duelists themselves, and their seconds, Jeremiah Pendle himself, and a local doctor, George Eden. Pendle was apparently the only one to put pen to paper. The real so-called lowdown only got out when Pendle died and a distant member of the Denham family got the inheritance. The diary was found and the new heir wanted to bring Sir Dane to book for Thomas Denham's murder, but for this he needed Dr. Eden's evidence, and the doctor had gone to America. So it didn't come to a trial, but there was whispering ever after. Not that Sir Dane was the sort of man to care what was said of him; he'd as likely tell the Devil to go to hell."

Kathryn smiled at that. "Yes, he would," she murmured.

"Anyway, I'll leave you to it."

"Thank you." Kathryn took a deep breath and opened the book a few pages from the end.

"Lammastide. This is yet another sad and harsh day, for once again has black-hearted Sir Dane Marchwood robbed me of a nephew. Oh, that such a devil incarnate should live and breathe, while my nephews must sleep forever beneath the earth. The truth must out, so that Marchwood is brought to account for his fiendish crimes. His villainy today leads me to conclude that similar villainy prevailed ten years ago, when he laid waste the fine life of William Denham, who was as noble and laudable a gentleman as ever existed.

"But I rush ahead of myself, for the tale must start at daybreak, when I accompanied Thomas to the oak grove on Marchwood estate, where at the allotted time Sir Dane arrived for the confrontation. His second, Dr. Eden, was also there.

"The pistols used for the duel were Sir Dane's, for Thomas, being a law-abiding citizen of the realm, possessed no such infamous weapons. Sir Dane himself presented one of the pistols to his opponent, saying that it was the very weapon he had used to kill William and two other victims, and that he did not wish to be accused of unfair advantage by using such a fortunate firearm. Oh, ignoble soul, for the pistol he thus foisted upon Thomas offered no protection to the user or threat to the opponent, having been rendered useless by clever means.

"Dr. Eden called the commands, and the two adversaries commenced to walk apart. At the command to turn and fire, Thomas's pistol failed to discharge. Sir Dane, with cold pleasure, took steady aim and fired directly into his helpless foe's heart. Thomas fell dead.

"Sir Dane might as well have fired into my heart as well, for as surely as if the shot had entered my feeble frame, I can feel my life ebbing. With Thomas has died my will to live, and my heart will surely soon beat its last.

"There was no mistaking Sir Dane's lack of fear, or his knowledge that he had time to make certain of his accuracy. He knew the pistol would not operate because he had interfered with it. Was this same infamy practiced ten years ago to eliminate William? Did Sir Dane also dispatch his other unfortunate victims by the same despicable means? I vow he is no gentleman, and has no claim to honor. Let Beelzebub soon claim his evil soul, and have no mercy upon him. That I should lose one beloved nephew to his rapacious thirst for blood would be cross enough to bear, but to lose two is burden beyond endurance. And to think that Thomas died because of a harlot, for by what other name can one speak of Lady Marchwood? She promised my nephew her unswerving love, and when she tired of the liaison, deliberately lured him into hazard with a Judas kiss. She knew what her husband would do, and felt no pity for the man whose love led to the forfeiture of his life. I curse the Marchwoods, may they suffer plague and pestilence for what remains of their wicked lives.

"God rest my nephews' souls. And God rest mine, for I know I am not long for this world."

Kathryn found her hands were trembling as she closed the book. Pendle's vitriolic hatred for Dane had almost reached out of the pages, but where did fact end and fiction begin? Just how much did the diary follow actuality? God, if ever she needed her so-called infallible intuition, it was now. It would be interesting to meet Dr. George Eden, whose name she now knew figured among the guests at the ball. Maybe she'd look him up when she was there tonight. The casual way she thought it brought her up with a start. When she was there tonight? She'd just read an ancient newspaper report about a ball in 1815, a ball she was actually going to attend in a few hours' time. It was weird, almost too weird to contemplate.

Putting the ball from her mind for the moment, she decided to read the account again, just to be certain of what Pendle said, then she closed down the microfilm console, and took the film and book out to the librarian. "Thank you, I've finished now."

"I hope it was informative?"

"Very, but I certainly don't believe that was how it happened."

"Ah, there has been debate in plenty ever since, but few people are inclined to take Sir Dane's side. You see, with his track record of dueling, and the astonishing way he managed to dispatch every opponent, people were inclined to think there wouldn't be smoke without fire. Oh, before you go, would you please sign the book over there? We're supposed to keep a record."

"Okay. Thanks again."

"Not at all."

Jack was watering the roses when she returned to the apartments, and he was still listening to his radio, for she could hear it as she reached the courtyard. But when she got to him, she was startled to see he was now using earphones and a Walkman. God, he must be stone deaf to have it so loud she could hear it from a distance when *he* had the earphones on!

Seeing her, he switched off the hose and removed the earphones. "My wife said I'd get water on the other radio, and made me use this newfangled thing instead," he explained, but then a look of puzzlement crossed his face, for the music continued as loudly as before. "That's odd," he said, glancing at her. "I . . . I heard your radio playing earlier and thought you must already be back from the library."

She smiled. "No, I'm just back now, and anyway, classical music isn't my thing, I'm more into blues guitar."

"Well, your radio's tuned in to the same concert I'm listening to," he pointed out, gazing up at her open window, from which the unmistakable sound of a Mozart symphony carried clearly into the afternoon air.

She looked up as well, and her heart began to sink. She

hadn't had the radio on at all, not since the bedside alarm first thing, and that hadn't been for more than a minute! Besides which, it had been tuned to a rock station, not anything high-brow. Then she remembered the strange stereo effect she'd noticed when she spoke to him on returning from Marchwood. Her radio must have been playing then as well!

Jack saw her unease. "Is something wrong, miss?"

"Does anyone else have the keys to my apartment?"

"Only me, miss. Why do you ask?"

"Oh, it's probably nothing." No, damn it, it wasn't nothing! Someone had been in her apartment the night before, and now this. She felt distinctly rattled. Maybe it was her famous intuition again! "Look, Jack, I'm sure someone was in my apartment last night, but I decided not to do anything because nothing was taken and I thought I'd look a bit stupid, but now I'm beginning to wonder if . . ." She looked up at the open window again. "I haven't had my radio on, and if I did, it wouldn't be to that sort of concert."

"Right, well I reckon I'd better take a look, just to be on the safe side." He shoved the earphones in his pocket, took off his gardening gloves, and moved toward the door.

"I'm coming too," she said determinedly. If anyone was there, she wanted to confront the person.

"As you wish, but keep behind me." He preceded her up the staircase, and the music got louder all the time. He knocked loudly at the door, and Kathryn held her breath, expecting the music to be abruptly switched off, but that didn't happen. In fact, nothing happened, and after a moment they used her keys to go in.

The apartment appeared deserted, but someone had definitely been there, because it was the living room radio that was playing, and she knew she definitely hadn't touched it. She switched it off, and then looked uneasily around. Just like before, the few dishes she'd used had been washed and put away. And this time the TV and radio magazine lay open on the settee, together with an empty chocolate wrapper. Whoever it was liked dark chocolate and almonds!

"Someone's been here," she said emphatically, pointing at the wrapper. "That's not mine."

Jack looked swiftly at her. "I'll make sure they aren't still around, then if you check if anything's missing, we'll call the police."

"Okay." She remained by the door while he went carefully from room to room. Then he returned. "Whoever it was has gone now, miss. It's safe for you to take a look at your belongings."

The first thing she thought of was her jewelry, but nothing had gone. And all her clothes were as she'd left them. Like last night, it seemed someone had just come in, stayed a while, then left. What was going on?

"Is anything missing, miss?" Jack asked as she returned.

"No."

"Well, reckon we'd best report it to the coppers anyway."

"Is that a good idea?" she asked doubtfully.

"I don't follow."

"What's to tell them? Nothing's been taken, and what will they think if I say someone washed the dishes, played a little Mozart, and ate some chocolate? It's crazy! They'll think *I'm* crazy. Maybe I am," she added, thinking about the unbelievable events of the past hours.

"Lord knows what they'll think, but I feel they should be told. Whoever's coming in might be some headcase. There's a prison down by the docks, though I don't think anyone's escaped in the last day or so. It's always on TV if that happens."

"Look, I don't want to look a fool, and that's what will happen if we report this. Maybe if you could just have the lock changed? If anyone's got another set of keys, they'll be useless then." She didn't want any hassle, not when she had other more important things on her mind. If some creep found it funny to play house in her apartment, a new lock should put a stop to it. Apart from that, something inside told her not to take this any further. It felt like intuition again, and that was enough for her.

But Jack wasn't happy about not telling the police. "I don't know, miss . . ."

"Please, Jack. I'll pay for another lock," she offered hopefully.

He still wasn't happy, but gave in. "All right, but you must promise that if anything else happens, anything at all, you'll tell me and we'll report it."

"Okay, I promise."

He glanced around again. "A rum do, and no mistake," he muttered, then left.

She closed the door thankfully, but as she turned her gaze was drawn to something she hadn't noticed before. A piece of paper lay on the floor beneath the windowsill, and she could see something written on it.

Curiously she picked it up, and then her heart almost stopped, for in an elegant old-fashioned hand, someone had written the name Rosalind over and over again.

Stunned with sudden realization, she could only stare at it. Why hadn't she guessed before? Why hadn't her wonderful new intuition told her that if she was going back in time, the real Rosalind might be coming here to the present? They'd been changing places! Suddenly a great deal was explained. The second call to Richard, the washed dishes, the jewelry box, make-up, radio, and so on, were all Rosalind's doing!

Trying to think, Kathryn sat down at the windowsill. Alice had spoken of Rosalind's great love for Thomas Denham, and her quest for happiness, but how could that equate with coming here into the future? Why make conciliatory overtures to Richard? Why tell him she wanted to start again and was going home this weekend? It was as if Rosalind were undoing the damage to Kathryn Vansomeren's marriage, just as she was doing to Rosalind's own marriage in the past. But why? *Why?*

She stared toward the cathedral. There was no point racking her brains over it; her much vaunted intuition told her she wouldn't get further with the information she had so far. But she trusted Alice, and would go along with everything as it took place.

And tonight she'd go to Cheltenham to see what happened next.

# Fourteen

∼

Kathryn whiled away the rest of the day as best she could. She caught up on a little sleep during the afternoon, and then had a meal at the Monk's Retreat. Jack's sister Daisy was easy enough to pick out, for she was just like him, and he was right about the food, it was plain but good. Fortified by a tasty steak and french fries, with several glasses of unexpectedly good local wine, she took a shower, changed, and then made the half hour drive to Cheltenham.

Contrary to Alice's assurances about the Royal Well's being easy to find, it proved quite a task to pinpoint the exact location. She'd asked Jack if he knew where it was, and he'd immediately declared it to be the present-day bus station, a claim that seemed to be confirmed by the street map he produced. So that was where she made for.

She left the car in a nearby street, where trees cast leafy shadows over fine Victorian mansions. It was a warm summer evening, and still not quite dark. The sunset was a fading glow on the far western horizon, and a faint breeze stirred through the trees. There was some traffic, and people strolled the sidewalk as she made her way to the bus station, which consisted of little more than long covered shelters that would accord the minimum protection for those unfortunate enough to have to wait in the rain or winter. It seemed British bus companies didn't exactly woo their passengers, more shrugged at them and said "Take it or leave it."

To one side of the station were the somewhat unedifying rear elevations of the buildings in the nearby Promenade, a beautiful flower-decked street where some of the best shops were located, and to the other was an elegant crescent of Regency construction. Like its much more grand counterpart in Bath, it was called the Royal Crescent, but there the similarity ended, for where the Bath crescent was sweeping and magnificent on its hillside, that at Cheltenham was hemmed in, and spoiled as a consequence.

There was a small pub on the corner, with people seated outside, and occasionally she heard bursts of laughter. A car radio blared out as a young guy in a sportscar drove ostentatiously past and then pulled away from the junction with a squeal of tires as he tried to impress his girlfriend. It all seemed perfectly normal, just as a late summer evening should be in a town like this. She felt it shouldn't be quite so ordinary, that there should be something in the air to presage what was about to happen to her. But there was nothing.

It was about ten to ten as she began to pace up and down the sidewalk at the rear of the Promenade, but the sheer normality of everything was oddly disturbing. Something wasn't right here. She knew Jack and the map insisted this was where she should be, but instinct told her it wasn't. Instinct? No, her famous intuition, more like. But the minutes were ticking away. What should she do? If ten o'clock arrived and this was the wrong location, would she fail to go back to 1815?

She glanced swiftly around, and then her glance fell hopefully on one of the men outside the corner pub. He was about forty, tall and thin, with a ginger beard, a long nose, spectacles, and an overanxious expression, but, most important of all, he wore a dog collar. Priests always knew about their local area, so she'd ask him if this was indeed the Royal Well. Crossing her fingers that he was from Cheltenham, she hurried along the sidewalk.

A juke box was playing in the pub, and the chatter of voices was really quite loud as she reached him, so she had to raise her voice slightly to attract his attention. "Er, excuse me, Father, may I have a word with you?"

"I . . . I beg your pardon?" His owlish, rather watery blue eyes swung inquiringly toward her.

"A word?"

"Er, yes, of course. Shall we move away a little? One can't hear oneself think here." He put his beer down and ushered her back along the sidewalk until they were able to speak without being deafened. "How may I help you?"

"I was wondering, are you from around here?"

"Cheltenham? Yes."

"Can you tell me if this is the Royal Well?"

He seemed surprised. "Why, yes. At least . . ."

"At least what?"

"It's what's known as the Royal Well now, but isn't the original well, of course. That doesn't exist anymore. I take it you're interested in the mineral spring where King George III took the waters and made Cheltenham fashionable at the end of the eighteenth century?"

"Yes, I suppose I am," Kathryn replied, remembering what Alice said.

"You're a little late, I fear. They've built the Ladies College over it." He pointed across a busy nearby road toward some discreet Victorian gray stone buildings that reminded her of the library in Gloucester. The college was one of the most exclusive girls' schools in England, and its premises stretched for quite a way up an incline toward the area named on the map as Montpellier. Skirted on both sides visible to her by roads, the college certainly didn't seem to offer much hope of pinpointing the exact location of the old well.

The priest grinned. "It's the best I can do for you, I'm afraid. Where we're standing is what is known as the Royal Well now, the Ladies college is where the Royal Well used to be."

She glanced at her watch. Five minutes to go. There had to be more she could find out. She looked swiftly at him. "There was a ballroom at one time, wasn't there?"

"Yes, it was called the Long Room. It was at the actual well, which I suppose must have been about two hundred yards from here. The Chelt flows under our feet, you know."

"The Chelt?"

"The river, or, I suppose by your standards, it's little more than a stream. Hardly the Mississippi, eh?" He laughed.

She made herself laugh too, but was finding it hard to hide her impatience. "So the ballroom would have been about two hundred yards up there? Which side of the road?"

He glanced curiously at her. "The right. Look, I don't know what your interest is, but if you hope to find traces of it, you're going to be disappointed. They didn't even bother to preserve the Well Walk, which was considered the finest double avenue of elms and limes in England. It led from a rustic footbridge over the Chelt, right up to the well itself, and was quite a fashion parade at the height of its fame."

The footbridge over the Chelt was where Rosalind was to meet Thomas at midnight! Kathryn almost wanted to shiver. She looked up the hillside toward the far end of the college. "So if I wanted to be more or less where the Long Room was, I'd have to be somewhere up that road over there?"

"Yes, although I couldn't be exact."

"Thank you, you've been very helpful."

"I have?"

He would have said more, but already she was hurrying away. She dodged between the traffic and then almost ran up the sidewalk alongside the college. It was quieter here, and thankfully there was hardly anyone around. She looked back down the road and saw the priest had rejoined his companions by the pub. He glanced up toward her, and she quickly looked to the front again. He probably thought she was some sort of history freak. The irony of such a notion made her smile then, for she was indeed a history freak! And how!

A church clock began to strike ten, and her pulse quickened expectantly. How would it happen this time? Would she just turn and see Dane again? Maybe it wouldn't happen at all! She walked restlessly up and down, counting the chimes and praying she'd suddenly find herself back in 1815.

The last note died away and she closed her eyes tightly, but nothing seemed to change. Beyond the pounding of her heart she could still hear all the same sounds, the traffic at the foot of the hill, a few voices, and the general hum of a large town late on a summer evening. And she could hear music. A polonaise.

A polonaise? She wouldn't know a polonaise if it jumped up and bit her! But that was exactly what she could hear now, she was certain of it. She glanced toward the brilliantly lit doorway of the building next to her. There were chandeliers inside, and elegant ladies and gentlemen in silk, satin, and velvet. Ladies and gentlemen in Regency fashions! She'd gone back in time without even realizing it! Relief coursed gladly through her. She was where she wanted to be!

She looked swiftly around. The Royal Well itself was housed in a low brick structure flanked on either side by two much larger buildings, one containing superior shops, the other the ballroom, or Long Room, outside which she stood. The entrance overflowed with flowers and was lavishly illuminated with variegated lamps that cast dainty pools of colored light over the arriving guests.

She examined her gown of magnolia silk stitched with tiny pearl beads. It was the loveliest thing she'd ever worn, better even than the wildly expensive Paris original she'd worn the day she married Richard. Her golden hair was sprinkled with jewels and piled up on her head, a fan and little drawstring bag were looped over her wrist, and her arms were encased in long white gloves. From top to toe she was Rosalind again, and it felt good.

The jewels in her hair sparkled in the light from the entrance. She'd just alighted from the Marchwood carriage, and was waiting while Dane spoke to the coachman about something. She gazed at him, but then felt a finger of anxiety. What had happened during the past few hours? Was he going to be as cold now as he had been by the portrait earlier? But then the anxiety evaporated, for as he turned toward her, he smiled, and her whole being turned to jelly. God, what an effect this man had on her!

He was dressed in formal evening black, just as he had been the first time she saw him. His immaculately tailored velvet coat was deliberately cut too tight, so the buttons had to be left undone in order to reveal his white satin waistcoat and the intricate lace trimming on the front of his shirt. More lace protruded from his cuff and adorned his neckcloth, which also sported a solitaire diamond of enviable proportions. He wore white silk breeches that outlined his long, firm thighs, and there was a tricorn hat tucked beneath his arm. As he came to take her hand and draw it over his sleeve, she smelt the clean fragrance of southernwood clinging to his clothes.

For a moment his hand rested over hers. "Are you ready?"

"Of course."

He smiled, and they went up the steps into the glittering vestibule, where the chatter of refined conversation filled the warm air. She immediately recognized some of the aristocrats she'd seen mentioned in the *Gloucester Journal* at the library, or rather the part of her that was Rosalind recognized them.

The Duke and Duchess of Beaufort, and their son, the Marquess of Worcester, were talking to the Countess of Berkeley, and all three turned to acknowledge Sir Dane and Lady Marchwood. Kathryn felt almost like laughing out loud. Oh, if only they knew the truth! What would these fine Regency folk have said then? The forty-nine-year-old duke was a kindly man who was widely respected for his public benefactions, but he didn't like formal occasions such as this, as he made quite clear to his poor duchess, who tonight was rather fussily dressed in frilled and sequinned sapphire satin. But their son and heir, a twenty-three-year-old dandy, was both a wit and a ladies' man. Splendid in the dashing uniform of the Tenth Hussars, he clearly thought himself God's gift to the fair sex, bestowing inviting glances upon every female who caught his attention. Married for less than a year to a niece of the Duke of Wellington, he was known to be still associating with one of the most famous and notorious courtesans in London, as well as keeping several mistresses in Gloucestershire, and as he gave her a lazily appreciative look, Kathryn knew it was only Dane's alarming reputation that prevented him from trying his chances with herself as well. Vanity he had, but not to the point of recklessness. Unlike the outwardly more staid Thomas, who seemed far less likely to take such a risk, but nevertheless continued to take it time after time!

Where was Thomas now, she wondered, and glanced uneasily around. He was bound to be here somewhere, and she suddenly realized she wasn't prepared for the moment she saw him. How should she react? The real Rosalind would clearly give him secretly flirtatious glances, and will the time away until midnight, when they'd both slip out separately to keep their tryst on the footbridge at the other end of the Well Walk.

But that wasn't what Kathryn Vansomeren intended to do! Without warning, a stubborn determination surged over her. Midnight could come and go, but she wasn't going to leave the ballroom! Thomas Denham could go whistle for tonight's planned illicit assignation.

However, Kathryn reckoned without the relentless march of fate. No matter how much she might determine to the contrary, she was going to keep the meeting on the bridge.

# *Fifteen*

~

The glittering green and gold ballroom was already a crush, even though many guests had yet to arrive. The polonaise was flowing, and an ocean of people danced, the ladies' plumes waving and jewels flashing as they moved. The murmur of refined conversation vied with the music, and from time to time she heard toasts being drunk to Britain's hero of the hour, the Duke of Wellington.

When the polonaise drew to a close and the master-of-ceremonies announced a ländler, Dane turned to Kathryn. "My dance, I believe, my lady," he murmured, leading her out onto the floor.

The ländler was a slow and delicate measure from southern Germany, and involved couples dancing with their arms entwined. Until the advent of the waltz it had been considered the most intimate, and therefore slightly shocking, dance acceptable in fashionable ballrooms, and it had always been one of Dane's favorites. The music began and he smiled into her eyes as they danced.

Oh, it felt so good to be with him like this. It really was like a dream come true. She was reminded of the balls her favorite fictional heroines had attended: Scarlett O'Hara dancing so shockingly in her widow's weeds, Elizabeth Bennett overhearing Mr. Darcy's disparaging remarks, and shy governess Jane Eyre being persuaded to dance with Mr. Rochester. What woman who'd read the book or seen the movie hadn't secretly pictured herself in the leading role? Well, now it was Kathryn Vansomeren treading a measure with notorious, devilishly handsome Sir Dane Marchwood. God, if her friends could see her now!

She danced on air, conscious of the beauty and elegance of her gown, and of her faultless grace. She knew every twist and turn, and took infinite pleasure in the complicated sequences. She glowed from head to toe, and knew it. For these few wonderful minutes she was the personification of happiness, and all because she was with Dane. But it was going to end. The hours were slipping relentlessly away toward Lammas Day.

After the ländler, they observed the unwritten rules by changing partners for the next dance, a cotillion. For this she was led out by no less a person than the Duke of Beaufort himself, while Dane escorted the young Marchioness of Worcester, who was very pretty in midnight silk and lace. After that, an hour seemed to pass in no time at all, taken up by a succession of dances with different partners. Kathryn's knowledge of Regency measures was seemingly endless, from minuets, cotillions, and polonaises, to allemandes, ländlers, country dances, and the wonderful waltz, which had only been permitted in polite circles since Lord Palmerston and Countess Lieven, wife of the Russian ambassador, had daringly introduced it at Almack's the year before.

Of Thomas Denham there still seemed no sign, but Kathryn could sense that he was nearby. He was being very careful indeed to keep well and truly away from her while Dane was there, and for that she was very thankful. Seeing Rosalind's lover would spoil tonight, which so far had been a heaven for the new Lady Marchwood.

The magnificent supper Kathryn had read of in the *Gloucester Journal* proved to be every bit as recherché as the admiring reporter had claimed. Gunter's of London's Berkeley Square might with justification claim to be the finest caterers in the capital, but the food provided at Cheltenham's Waterloo Ball was more than a match. There was lobster and salmon, York ham and pâté de foie gras, chicken and cold roast beef, with a sumptuous array of salads and savories, to say nothing of the jellies, Italian creams, and trifles. Fruit, both in and out of season, abounded, from peaches and nectarines, to strawberries and pineapples, and to go with all this was a seemingly endless supply of iced champagne.

It wasn't long after the supper that Dane was claimed for a minuet, and for the first time Kathryn elected not to dance as well. She found a seat on one of the sofas arranged in tiers around the edge of the crowded floor, and watched as the dance began. Her thoughts were of the duel, and whether or not she might be able to do something to prevent it. She hadn't been there long when a man spoke at her elbow. It was George Eden.

"What's this? Lady Marchwood reduced to watching a minuet from the sidelines without treading the measure herself? An unheard state of affairs, I do declare. I prescribe a tonic, and without delay."

She'd forgotten all about him, and yet he was to be Dane's second at the duel. She gave a quick smile. "And what tonic might that be, Master Physician?"

"Why, another dance, of course," he replied with a broad grin.

He wasn't quite as short as he had seemed when alighting from the carriage the night everything began, but his hair was more carrot-colored, and his eyes unexpectedly shortsighted. His smile was warmly amiable, though, and she liked him straightaway. "Come now, sir, I happen to know you loathe dancing," she said.

"Well, I admit I'm not the world's most renowned hoofer, but I can wend my way around the floor with some semblance of grace."

"You'll be relieved to know I'm content to just watch, but please sit with me a while."

He did as she asked, and then studied her concernedly. "Is something wrong?" he asked suddenly, searching her eyes. "You seemed a little, er, preoccupied a moment ago."

"I'm quite all right, truly." But she resorted to her fan.

He observed the fact, and then glanced out onto the dance floor. "No doubt you were keeping a wary eye on the Fast Lady of France," he murmured.

"Who?"

"Dane's partner for this dance."

"Is that what they call her?"

"Not without cause. She's only been in England since Waterloo, but has apparently been doing all she can to conquer the conquerors. I'm told there are wagers at White's Club as to her final tally, but I shouldn't concern yourself, for Dane's name won't figure on the list. He has become that most dull of things, a faithful husband."

"Has he?" She thought of Elizabeth.

"Yes. Surely you don't doubt it?"

She didn't know why, but suddenly she wished to confide in him. "I don't want to doubt it, but what else can I do when he never tells me he loves me?" she replied quietly.

"Do you need to be told? Surely his actions say all that's necessary?"

"Actions don't always speak louder than words. I'm afraid I'm one of those foolish female creatures who needs verbal reassurance." She looked away, toying with the dainty wrist chain of her fan.

"Would it help if I told you he's confessed to me that he loves you?"

Her eyes swung back to him. "Has he really said that? Or are you—"

"I'm not the sort to tell white lies," he interrupted quietly, putting his hand briefly over hers. "I was with him for a few minutes a little earlier, and we watched you dancing that allemande. Dane told me how much he loved you, and you may count upon it that he meant what he said."

She lowered her glance to hide her confusion. It was what she wanted to hear, but at the same time she didn't really know what interpretation to put on it. Was it the new Rosalind that Dane loved? Or the old one, the unfaithful one whose heart had always secretly belonged to Thomas Denham? And then there was Elizabeth . . . Oh, God, she was in such inner turmoil she didn't know what to think. Except that she wanted Sir Dane Marchwood to love *her*, Kathryn Vansomeren.

The doctor was surveying the ballroom. "I believe this will be my last Cheltenham ball," he said suddenly.

"Oh? Why is that?" But she remembered what the librarian had told her about his sudden departure for America not long after the duel.

"I have an opportunity to go to Boston. That's over in Massachusetts, not here in England," he added quickly.

She smiled too. "And you mean to go?"

"I think so. It's short notice, but the offer is very advantageous, and I've always had a secret desire to visit America. If I decide to go, I will be taking my leave of you and Dane within a month."

"Gloucester's loss will be Boston's gain," she murmured.

The minuet was drawing to a close, and the doctor prepared to leave her.

She thought of the duel again, and as he got up from the sofa she spoke quickly. "May I ask you something?"

"Certainly."

"You know Dane to be an honorable man, don't you?"

He looked at her in surprise. "What an odd question. Yes, of course. Oh, I know he has a certain reputation for being dangerous and hotheaded, but the truth is different. I don't profess to know the reason for all his duels, but I do know I have complete faith in his integrity." He searched her face again. "Something *is* wrong, isn't it, my dear?"

"No. No, of course not."

The orchestra played the final note of the minuet, and he looked at her again. "You may rely upon my discretion if you wish to discuss something. You know that, don't you?"

"Yes, I do."

It was true. He meant every word he'd said. Suddenly she got up and hugged him. "We'll miss you when you go to Boston."

He laughed at her exuberance, but then corrected her. "I haven't finally decided yet."

"Oh, I think you have," she said more seriously. He was going to Boston; it was a historically recorded fact.

She watched him wend his way toward the supper room, and then something made her look up at the large longcase clock next to the orchestra. It was five to midnight, and she knew she had to keep the tryst on the footbridge. She didn't want to, but something compelled her. So much for hoping she might be able to prevent things happening! Clearly Rosalind really had met Thomas on the bridge tonight, and that meant Kathryn Vansomeren had to as well. It was another historically recorded fact.

She looked around for Dane, and saw that he'd been drawn into conversation by a small group of gentlemen, including the Duke of Beaufort. He didn't see her gather her skirts to hurry out of the building into the cool shadows of the summer night.

Carriages were still arriving, although she couldn't imagine how more guests could possibly squeeze into the ball. She glanced around to try to get her bearings. She could see the Well Walk. The double avenue of elms and limes rustled softly in the light breeze. Lanterns shone between the branches, and people strolled to and fro quite close to the upper end, but further down the avenue, toward Cheltenham, there was hardly anyone to be seen. The town had retreated across a meadow, and was visible as some twinkling lights in the distance as she began to walk down toward the little rustic bridge at the far end of the avenue.

She heard the splash of the Chelt as she neared the bridge, which was adorned with a slender wrought iron arch from which a suspended oil lamp cast a poor light over the footway. She wished she'd been able to resist coming here. What was she going to say to Thomas? She couldn't be Rosalind; there was too much Kathryn Vansomeren in her for that.

She was still deliberating as she reached the bridge, but almost immediately she heard a step behind her. She turned, and saw Thomas. He wore a purple velvet evening coat and white silk breeches, and the gold pin in his neckcloth shone a little as he came to take her in his arms and press his lips passionately over hers.

# *Sixteen*

❧

For a moment she was immobile with shock, for she hadn't expected him to embrace her without saying anything first. She didn't experience any of the fire and excitement such intimacy would have aroused if it were Dane. Instead, she was again reminded of Richard. Everything about this man was like a reflection of her modern New York husband.

Her immobility ended as his hand moved to caress her left breast through the soft silk of her gown. She didn't want such intimacy from him, he was the wrong man! She pulled sharply from his arms and glanced nervously toward the Royal Well buildings. "Th . . . this is very foolhardy."

His brown eyes were warm. "There's no one here except us."

"Can we be sure?"

"Everyone we know is either at the ball already or still to arrive."

"I still feel uneasy about meeting you like this."

"We've done it before," he reminded her.

"And have been lucky to get away with it." You're not going to be lucky tomorrow if you persist, and the day after that you're going to be dead! She suddenly felt an overpowering urge to warn him about the duel, but the words wouldn't come. Something stifled them on her lips, and she knew it was because nothing could prevent what was to happen on Lammas Day.

He smiled. "Well, right or wrong, you're here now, so let's make the most of these few minutes together." His voice was soft as he reached out to pull her toward him again.

She resisted. "No, Thomas."

Her reaction took him by surprise. "What is it?"

"I . . . I shouldn't have come here."

"But you did, and we both know why. Rosalind, it's too late to change things now. What's done is done, and we have to decide about our future."

What future? You don't have one! The words screamed silently through her, but again didn't reach her lips. She had to do something, though; she couldn't just stand idly by and let things roll inexorably toward dawn on Lammas Day. "Thomas, I shouldn't have kept this assignation because I don't love you anymore. I love Dane, and want to stay with him."

To her astonishment, these words came out, but then she supposed they had nothing to do with actually trying to prevent the inevitable. They were just incredibly hurtful as far as Thomas was concerned, apart from the fact that they made not one jot of difference to the relentless march of events.

He was incredulous. "You love Dane?" he repeated.

"Yes."

"Rosalind, I don't know what's brought this on, but I do know I don't believe you. You're trying to protect me, aren't you? Why? Has Dane found out about us?"

"No, but he suspects. Thomas, please believe me, I really don't love you anymore."

"You can't possibly stay with him! It's madness!" he cried.

"It's what I want."

"But, you're carrying my child!"

She was thunderstruck. Child? Rosalind was *pregnant?* So *that* was what he'd been told last night just before the first transition took place! God, how obvious! They'd played with fire and been burned, and things would become obvious before long. Of course they would, for pregnancy didn't remain invisible for long!

Thoughts tumbled wildly through her. The real Rosalind might be carrying a child, but Kathryn Vansomeren wasn't, and she was sure Rosalind's body wasn't pregnant now she was in it. She remembered how she'd felt when she first knew she was expecting Richard's child. It was a weird feeling, like she wasn't really there, and it had persisted right up to the day she lost the baby. She didn't feel like that now, and intuition told her the body she was in now definitely wasn't pregnant. So what did that mean? Had Rosalind's un-born child traveled with her into the future? Did Kathryn Van-someren's body become pregnant when Rosalind took it over?

It was an incredible thought, and should have been deeply painful, but Kathryn felt oddly detached, as if she were delib-erating over a problem that concerned two people who had no connection whatsoever with her.

Thomas took her arms to shake her slightly. "Answer me, Rosalind!"

She struggled to find a response. "I . . . I'm going to tell Dane and beg his forgiveness," she said at last, but it sounded lame and unconvincing, and she knew it.

He released her swiftly, and ran his fingers agitatedly through his hair. "His *forgiveness?* Dear God, have you taken leave of your senses?" He shook her again. "What is this, Ros-alind? One moment you run gladly into my arms and whisper everlasting love, the next you tell me you not only want to stay with him, you're also going to tell him you're carrying a child that cannot possibly be his. It lacks all logic! Your condition has made you irrational."

"It has nothing to do with my condition."

"There's no other explanation."

"Please let me go, for my mind is made up."

"I don't accept your decision!" He didn't loose his hold.

"You have to accept it. It's finished between us, Thomas. I'm Dane's wife and I intend to stay that way."

"Stay that way? When you expect my child? Dane won't have you! For God's sake, Rosalind, you have to see sense on this!"

She could see the desperation in his eyes, and hated herself for hurting him so, but it was all she could think of doing. If she could just instill a little doubt in his mind, if he could be made to think she'd never go to him, maybe she could turn fate on its head after all, no matter what Alice might say. So she pressed on. "I don't love you, Thomas! I love Dane, and I always will!"

"No!" His face contorted distractedly, and his voice choked on a sob. "No, I won't believe you!"

"Let me go!" She wrenched herself away and gathered her skirts to flee from the bridge and along the lantern-lit walk.

"Rosalind!" His distraught voice followed her, and she

could feel his anguish reaching out after her. Tears stung her
eyes, but she didn't look back. She'd placated her conscience
by doing what she could; now she needed to find Dane, to feel
his arms around her again. No, what she really needed was to
be able to confess all this to him! But she couldn't, it was almost too incredible for her, and so was bound to be to him.
The tears welled down her cheeks as the thoughts spilled de-
jectedly through her, and she felt dangerously close to flinging
herself hysterically into Dane's arms and blurting out everything.

But common sense returned as she neared the line of carriages. She couldn't do anything as rash as that; besides, she
probably wouldn't be able to! She'd already tried altering the
course of things, and it hadn't gotten her very far. No, better to
compose herself and behave rationally—well, as rationally as
possible under the circumstances.

Knowing her present tearful state would cause a stir, she
paused beneath one of the trees to smooth her gown and pat
her hair. Having applied the brakes to her wild impulse to tell
all, she soon brought her reckless impulses under control, but
when she glanced toward the bridge again a few moments
later, she saw Thomas hurrying up the walk. Renewed dismay
washed through her, and she gathered her skirts to run on past
the line of carriages to the brightly lit ballroom.

The warmth inside the building was almost stifling after the
cool air outside, and as she reached the edge of the dance
floor, Kathryn looked anxiously around. She desperately
wanted to be with Dane now, but where was he? He wasn't
with the Duke of Beaufort's party now, nor could she see him
on the dance floor. She might never find him in a press like
this! The whole of Gloucestershire seemed to have attended,
for every sofa was now occupied, every corner filled with people talking, and every inch of space around the edge of the
dance floor taken up with guests who were either watching the
minuet now in progress, or threading their way toward someone they knew.

At last she saw Dane. He was dancing after all, and his partner was a pretty brunette woman in peach gauze and plumes,
who smiled flirtatiously at him from beneath fluttering lashes.
Every glance told of availability should Sir Dane Marchwood
wish to take advantage.

In spite of her anxiety after the meeting with Thomas, Kathryn was stung with jealousy, and had to look away for a moment. She was angry with herself for reacting like a stupid teenager. A man like Dane was bound to get "come hither" looks by the score! Quelling the feeling, she looked at him again, and without warning he met her eyes. Suddenly it was as if they were alone. All sound seemed to die away as his glance caressed her across the crowded room. He smiled, and her jealousy faded into oblivion.

"I love you," she whispered, knowing he'd read her lips.

She willed him to whisper the same words back, but his attention was drawn back to the dance.

It seemed an age before the minuet ended and he escorted his partner to her friends by the entrance of the supper room. The flirtatious woman tried to detain him, but he resisted and returned to his wife, leaving the lady to gaze wistfully after him.

Kathryn's heart quickened as he raised her gloved palm to his lips. "So, sir, I turn my back for a moment and in those minutes I find you being reeled in on a hook," she said teasingly.

"I'm too wily a fish for that," he replied, gazing into her eyes and smiling. "Where have you been?"

"I . . . I went out in the fresh air for a while."

"You felt unwell?"

"I was just a little hot, that's all."

His glance moved beyond her and darkened a little. Without him saying a word she knew he'd seen Thomas. She spoke quickly. "Perhaps you'll honor me with the next dance?"

He met her eyes again. "Did you know Denham was here tonight?"

She managed a light laugh. "No, I didn't, but I must say I'm not surprised. The entire county's here."

"I'm not concerned about the entire county, just him."

"Dane, I swear your fears are unfounded. I'm not in love with Thomas Denham; no other man has meant anything to me since I met you." Oh, how true that was.

The master-of-ceremonies announced a waltz, and she took Dane's arm. "Please don't talk of disagreeable things, my lord. Let's waltz instead," she pleaded.

To her relief, the smile returned to his lips. "The wicked waltz?"

"The wickeder, the better," she murmured, suddenly remembering the newspaper report she'd read at the library. What had it said? Something about Sir Dane and Lady March-wood dancing the waltz with particular distinction?

"You're incorrigible, madam," he said softly, bending his head to kiss her on the cheek.

She pretended to tap his sleeve reprovingly. "La, sir, is it done for a man to kiss his wife in public?"

"Hardly, but then you are no ordinary wife, my lady."

"I trust not, sir."

He searched her face. "Would that I understood you of late, but I fear I don't. Every time I think I have your measure, you confound me."

"A lady should retain a certain mystery, sir."

"She should indeed." He put his fingers to her cheek.

"I adore you, Sir Dane Marchwood," she whispered, again yearning for him to say the same to her, but again he didn't. Instead, he took her hand and led her onto the floor where the dancers were gathering for the waltz.

She lowered her glance. Twice in the space of only minutes she'd confessed her love for him, and twice he'd failed to reciprocate. George Eden had tried to reassure her, and Dane certainly appeared loving, but he didn't *tell* her, and she needed to hear him say it.

Was Elizabeth the reason for his reticence? She was suddenly so conscious of the chain around his neck that it was almost as if she could see it beneath his rich clothing. She wished she knew what bitter legacy his first wife had left him, but Elizabeth remained enigmatic behind a cloak of impenetrable mist.

The waltz began, and he whirled her around the floor. His hand was warm against her waist, and his fingers curled over hers in a way that made her aware of everything about him. Their bodies didn't touch as they danced, but she felt as if they did. He held her eyes, and again it was as if they were alone in the room. She wanted him to kiss her passionately on the lips in front of everyone, and, as if he knew her thoughts, he suddenly pulled her closer. She raised her lips instinctively to meet his.

They continued to dance with their lips joined. Their bodies touched now, and a secret shiver of delight passed through her. She closed her eyes as desire began to flare in her veins. The music swirled seductively around them, and she didn't care that everyone was looking on with shocked disapproval.

At last he drew back slightly. "We're causing a stir, Lady Marchwood."

"Not as great as the one we'd cause if we did what I want to do right now," she replied.

He laughed and whirled her more and more wildly around the floor. She felt lighter than air. Particular distinction? What a masterpiece of journalistic understatement!

The other dancers glanced uncertainly at one another and then continued to watch as Sir Dane and Lady Marchwood gave themselves to the new dance that many still regarded as shocking. Outwardly, everyone pretended to disapprove, but privately the ladies envied Kathryn the intimacy she shared with one of England's most desirable and notorious men. The gentlemen eyed Kathryn's curvaceous figure approvingly, and wished she was to grace their beds that night instead of her husband's.

Kathryn was lost in the sheer happiness of being with Dane, but then she saw Thomas watching from the edge of the floor. His tormented gaze followed as she danced, and for a moment she couldn't tear her eyes away from him. But at last she did, and looked up at Dane instead.

"Let's go home now," she urged.

"Now! But we've hardly danced at all, and you wished to see the fireworks display."

"I don't want to dance, sir, and I have fireworks of my own in mind," she said softly.

"Do you indeed? I confess you've persuaded me," he murmured, offering her his arm.

They made their way from the floor, and she averted her head from Thomas. Five minutes later their carriage drove smartly out of Cheltenham.

Kathryn's head rested against Dane's shoulder as she gazed back at the disappearing lights of the town. Would she be allowed to spend the rest of the night with him? Would they make love until dawn again? She prayed so, for this was her last chance before his trust was finally shattered tomorrow at the sailing of the *Lady Marchwood*.

As had happened earlier on the bridge with Thomas, she wanted to warn him what was to come. Once again the words refused to come to her lips. Tears filled her eyes and she moved her head in order to look up at him in the darkness. "Love me tonight, Dane," she whispered.

He smiled. "You may count upon it, madam," he murmured, turning to kiss her.

Her mouth trembled needfully against his, and then she sighed as he pushed her gently down to lie on the seat. He pressed his lips to the pale perfection of her throat, and her yearning hands moved eagerly over him.

"When did we last make love in a carriage, my lady?" he whispered, sliding his hand sensuously beneath her gown.

"If you've made love in a carriage, sir, it most certainly wasn't with me."

"No? Then we must correct the omission," he said softly, moving his hand further up her leg to caress her thigh.

"Are you going to take me as if I were a common strumpet, my lord?"

"No, madam, I'm going to take you like the warm-blooded, desirable, fascinating woman you are," he breathed as he drew her gown up to her waist and began to undo his breeches.

His arousal sprang urgently from its confines of silk, and seemed to find its own way between her eager thighs. The heat of him was wonderful as he slid inside with leisurely ease. Her breath caught with intense pleasure as he pushed in as far as he could, gripping her buttocks with his hands to tilt her in order to penetrate further. She felt him quiver with desire inside her, and then her body arched beneath him as he began to move slowly in and out. Acute gratification invaded her entire being. Never let this finish. Never.

# Seventeen

~

It was the morning of Lammas Eve, the day on which Dane
would discover the truth about Rosalind and Thomas Denham, but when Kathryn awoke her only thought was her fear
that she might have been transported back to her own time
again instead of remaining in the past with the man she loved.
She didn't dare open her eyes, but lay there with them tightly
closed. Please let her still be in 1815.

She could hear birdsong outside, but there were birds in the
past and present. What she couldn't hear was anything modern, like traffic noise. Let her be able to slide her hand across
the bed to touch him. She moved her fingers slowly and tentatively over the sheet. He was there! She smiled and opened her
eyes gladly to see the morning sunlight slanting through a
crack in his apartment curtains at Marchwood.

He had yet to stir. His hair was tousled, and his lashes dark
against his cheeks. A sheet covered him to the waist, and a
thin band of morning sun fell across his chest, shining on the
soft curling hairs she'd pressed her lips to during the night.
She leaned up on an elbow and pushed her tangled hair back
from her face in order to gaze at him.

Surely this was what it was like in paradise? Just to wake
next to him made her feel complete. She could hardly credit
how intense her feelings were. It went far beyond simple physical attraction. It was as if she breathed because he breathed.
She was in tune with everything about him, and the sensation
was matchless. This was true love, and if it was only to be
granted for these few hours, she was grateful to have experienced it at all. When the time came for her to go back to her
own time forever, she'd never forget what she'd known with

Sir Dane Marchwood. She'd always worship him. Always.
Bending her head, she put her lips tenderly to his.

"Good morning, sweet sir," she whispered.

He opened his eyes and smiled. "Good morning, my lady,"
he murmured, reaching out to pull her on top of him.

She luxuriated in the delicious feel of his body, and moved
sensuously against his warmth.

"Make love to me again," she breathed.

He rolled her gently on to her back and leaned over her.
"Your request is my command, sweet lady," he breathed, low-
ering his lips to kiss her breasts.

There was no lessening of excitement, no dulling of satisfaction, and renewed passion surged irresistibly through them
both. His strokes were slow and leisurely, as were the rich un-
dulations of delight that spread irresistibly through her. She
did not doubt now that she was in paradise, or that this was the
ultimate ecstasy. If her heart should cease beating at this moment, she'd die knowing the reality of total fulfillment. Flawless, exquisite, unqualified fulfillment . . .

They lay quietly side by side afterward, and several minutes
passed before he spoke. "What fools we were to waste so much
time. It should have been like this before, and I should never
have doubted you, but I always feared this was only a marriage
of convenience to you, entered because your father arranged it."

"Isn't that how it was for you? You'd never have married
again if your father hadn't wanted you to."

"I married again because *I* wanted to."

"But, I thought . . ."

He smiled a little. "I let you think I was merely being duti-
ful, but the truth was rather different."

"What was the truth?"

He smiled wryly. "The truth? I thought you loved Thomas
Denham. If your father hadn't decided I was the better match,
I was sure you'd have rather been Mrs. Denham than Lady
Marchwood."

"And I was sure you were still in love with Elizabeth, and—"
She broke off as she suddenly realized he wasn't wearing the
chain and pendant.

Her reaction wasn't lost on him, and he got up to go to the
window and fling the curtain back so the sunlight streamed
dazzlingly into the room. Then he looked back at her. "I

ceased to love Elizabeth the moment I discovered her infidelity," he said quietly.

Kathryn sat up slowly. "Her infidelity?" she repeated incredulously.

He turned to gaze out at the park. "You're the only person I've ever told this, the only person apart from me to know anything of it. Elizabeth wasn't the paragon everyone thinks, and I've only shielded her reputation because she's the mother of my son. There's no doubt Philip is mine, and so for his sake I've allowed her memory to remain untarnished."

So this was Elizabeth's bitter legacy. Kathryn found it all difficult to take in.

He glanced back at her. "Philip must never know the truth about his mother."

"You know he'll never hear it from me. But I still don't quite understand. If you fell so completely out of love with her, why have you continued to wear her likeness?"

"As a reminder never to love so foolhardily again. I gave my heart to her, and she broke it. I had no intention of permitting that to happen again, especially when I met you and knew how dangerously similar the circumstances would be if I married you."

"Dangerously similar? I don't understand." She got up and went to slip her arms around him from behind. "Please tell me everything, Dane, for I have a right to know."

"Yes, you do, but I find it hard to speak of things I've kept hidden for so long." His hands rested tenderly over hers. "To be painfully honest, until now I would never have conceded you had the right to know anything about my past."

"Why not until now?"

"Because until today I would not have confessed my love to you."

Her heart missed a beat. "Please say that again," she whispered.

"I love you, Rosalind."

At last he'd said the words she longed to hear! She moved swiftly around him and linked her arms around his neck to kiss him fiercely on the mouth. Joy caroled through her, and for a moment she forgot the harsh truth—that later this very Lammas Eve he was going to learn about the affair with Thomas Denham. She forgot too that she was Kathryn Vansomeren, a woman from another time, another life . . .

He drew back first, taking her face in his hands and looking into her eyes. "Rosalind, I couldn't bear it if you failed me as she did . . ."

"I won't, I swear I won't." But the bitter truth was beginning to wash soberingly through her now. Lammas Eve, the duel . . . Time was ebbing away, and she was powerless to change what was going to happen.

His thumbs caressed her. "I'm yours now, Rosalind, your creature, unable to do anything without you, unable to spend a night unless I make love to you. You've made me this way, you've stolen into my heart and enslaved my body. I trust you because when I look in your eyes now I can see my love and need reflected so clearly that I might almost be gazing into a mirror."

"Oh, Dane . . ."

But as she raised her lips to be kissed again, he shook his head and released her. "There's something I have to tell you, Rosalind. I haven't told anyone else, and the only others who knew are dead, but it will explain why I despise Thomas Denham so much."

She leapt to the wrong conclusion. "Are . . . are you going to say he was Elizabeth's lover?" she gasped.

"No, not Thomas, his brother William."

She was shaken. "And that was why you called him out?" she whispered.

"Yes. I've fought three duels. The first was in my hot-headed youth, over the dubious honor of a fashionable courtesan, and the second was when I caught a cardsharp with five aces in his hand. Neither reason was worth dueling over, and now, with hindsight, I can see the third wasn't either. Elizabeth was never the woman I believed her to be. Behind her smiles and glorious beauty, she was cheap and shallow, her only talent being an unequalled ability to seem loving and faithful. She was an adulteress, but she *was* carrying my child, there was no question of that, and for the child's sake I protected the reputation of the mother, which is why I held my tongue over the reason for calling Denham out. He had his own reason for staying silent. As you know, his father was a strict church-going man who believed in the ten commandments. He'd have cut William off without a penny if he found out about Elizabeth."

Kathryn reeled from the shock of what she'd just learned.

No wonder Dane despised the Denhams. She found herself recalling what Jeremiah Pendle had written about the duel. The
banker claimed Dane had tampered with Thomas's pistol, and
went on to suggest the same might have happened when
William died. No, she still couldn't believe it. Dane would
never do anything so contemptible, not even in the face of
such unbelievable provocation. Two wives, both guilty of
adultery with a Denham, and now, to make his anguish even
greater, the second wife carried her lover's child!

He took her trembling hand and drew the palm to his lips.
"Rosalind, that's what I meant earlier about thinking the circumstances would be dangerously similar if I married you. I
knew there'd been something between you and Thomas Denham, and I was afraid you might also deceive me with a member of that cursed family. But I wanted you so much I couldn't
help myself. So I had you, but I wore Elizabeth's likeness as a
reminder never to give my heart completely. Each time I felt
your spell, I looked at her and remembered what she'd done.
That way I was protected from further hurt."

She didn't know what to say. Suddenly everything was so
clear. "What happened to Elizabeth?" she asked.

"The duel took place about a month before she was brought
to bed, and I allowed her every comfort and consideration. I
didn't know what I intended after the birth, but then she died,
and the onus of decision was taken from me." He looked into
her eyes again. "Can you understand how I felt when I returned from the war and found you so cool? And then, when I
heard the rumors . . ."

"Rumors?"

"Your name was linked with his, you'd been seen together,
and—"

"I met him socially, that was all. Oh, and once when I was
out riding I encountered him." What else could she do except
lie? But it was becoming increasingly difficult. She wanted to
tell him the truth, but knew there was no point. Fate would
march relentlessly on. Later today he would find out about
Rosalind and Thomas, and at dawn tomorrow the duel would
be fought.

He smiled gently. "I know now that my suspicions were unfounded, but a man who's been betrayed before sees fresh betrayal at every corner." He ran a fingertip down her cheek.

"You asked me if the *Lady Marchwood* was named after you. Of course she is, for I would never name her after Elizabeth."

She caught his hand urgently. "Dane, you do believe that I love you, don't you?"

"Yes."

"Whatever happens, I'll never stop loving you."

Puzzled, he looked into her eyes. "What is it? Why do you say it like that?"

She couldn't reply, and had to look away.

He turned her face toward him again. "Tell me, Rosalind. Whatever it is that bothers you, I want you to tell me."

She had to dissemble. "There isn't anything," she said, trying to smile.

"Sometimes I find you so changed, that . . ." He didn't finish.

"Yes?"

"That I feel I've fallen in love again with someone new. As if you're my third wife, a different woman entirely from the others."

She gazed at him with silent anguish. I am someone new! I'm Kathryn Vansomeren, and I love you so much my heart's breaking!

He released her then. "Now I've bared my soul at last, I need to blow the final cobwebs away. Would you mind if I go for a ride before breakfast? I believe a wild gallop across the park will be the ideal way to bury the past once and for all."

She didn't want him to leave her, but knew she must. She smiled. "Of course I don't mind. Just come back to me."

"You know I will." He searched her eyes again. "Promise me you'll tell me soon."

"Tell you what?"

"Whatever it is I should know."

"There isn't anything."

He smiled. "Oh, yes, there is, and when the time's right, I know you'll tell me." Bending his head to kiss her on the lips, he turned and went into his dressing room.

When the time was right? The time would *never* be right to tell him a truth like this! She glanced toward the connecting door to her own apartment, and suddenly knew Alice was waiting beyond it. Time was always the master, and was about to dispatch Kathryn Vansomeren back to the future.

# Eighteen

~

Kathryn went through the door and faced the nurse. "I'm finding this more and more difficult," she confessed without preamble.

"I know."

"He's told me about Elizabeth and William Denham."

Alice smiled. "Then you have his love, my dear."

Tears sprang to Kathryn's eyes. "Yes, his love and his *trust!* He believes in me now, Alice, but later today he's going to find out about the real Rosalind and Thomas Denham! I can't bear to think of the pain he'll experience when that happens. Have you any idea how he suffered the last time? He loved Elizabeth, and she failed him. Now he loves me, and he'll think I've done the same thing. It will destroy him."

"You may be able to save him from that."

"How?" Kathryn demanded bluntly. "It seems to me there's absolutely nothing I can do except lie to him, and I'm starting to hate myself for it. I began this for purely selfish reasons; you promised me the sort of pleasure I'd always wanted, and I thought why not? But things have changed. I love him, and can't endure the thought of how he's going to feel a few hours from now. He's going to be so devastated he'll never trust anyone again, and who can blame him?"

Kathryn turned away, trying to blink back the angry tears. Now wasn't the moment to lose her grip, she had to think! Mustering her composure, she faced the nurse again. "I know Rosalind and I have been trading places. Every time I'm here as her, she's in the future as me. And she's pregnant, right?"

"Yes."

"So what's in all this for her?"

"I will tell you later today, when the challenge has been issued and you experience the torment of being rejected by Dane."

Kathryn gazed at her. "Oh, thanks, it's great to know you're on my side!" she said dryly.

"Don't misunderstand me, my dear. It is necessary for you to go through it all, for only then will you be able to make up your mind about something that will change your very existence."

"What are you talking about?"

"I will tell you later," Alice said again.

"To hell with later, I want to know now!" Kathryn cried.

"No."

Kathryn drew a long breath and tried to calm down. "Okay, but will you at least tell me about the duel itself? I've read what's in Pendle's diary, and I don't believe a word of it. So what really happened?"

Alice paused. "I don't know."

Kathryn didn't believe her. "You mean you don't intend to tell me that either?" she accused angrily.

Alice shook her head. "That isn't my reason, my dear. You see, I really don't know anything that happens after midnight tonight. From the first stroke of Lammas Day, my already dwindling powers will be gone forever."

Kathryn stared at her. "Oh, come on, how can that be right? You knew about me, and I was *way* in the future beyond Lammas Day!"

"I can't explain it, Kathryn. I simply knew you when you came to Gloucester. All I can say is that I recognized in you a kindred spirit. That is how it is, as you yourself will discover when your powers are realized."

But Kathryn still wasn't satisfied. "Then how did you know Thomas Denham is going to die tomorrow? Well, answer me that? If you can't see beyond midnight tonight, how could you possibly know? I only found out about it yesterday, when the guide told me at the castle, but when I saw you by Dane's portrait, you already knew."

Alice smiled. "Yes, I knew, because when you were seeing Dane here at Marchwood, Rosalind went into the future and did what you were to do later the same day. She went to the library and read the same things you read. In the few minutes before you and she changed back to your own places again, she told me what she'd discovered."

So *Rosalind* was the person the librarian had logged the things out to earlier that day! She found out all about the duel, went back to the apartment to think and listen to the radio for a while, and then forgot to switch the latter off when she drove back to Marchwood in time to change places again. Kathryn almost wanted to laugh. But then something struck her. "If Rosalind and I are changing places, what's she doing right now?"

"She's trying to speak to your husband."

"Richard?" Kathryn was puzzled. "Why? Why does she keep contacting him and saying all that stuff about going back early?"

Alice drew a long breath. "You must believe me when I say that now isn't the time to tell you everything. But when you do learn all there is, I know you'll understand."

"Well, I'll have to take your word for that, won't I?"

"Yes, and if you wish to see Dane again today, at the sailing of the *Lady Marchwood*, you must continue to take my word for everything."

Kathryn drew back a little. "Be there when he finds out about Rosalind and Thomas? *Be* Rosalind at that moment, is that what you're saying?"

"Yes. It must be so."

"No! I don't want that!"

"Then this must be the end of it all, my dear. I will return you to your own time, and you will never see Sir Dane Marchwood again."

Kathryn closed her eyes. "No, please, I don't want that either . . ."

"I have asked you to trust me, and I ask you again now. I spoke of an audacious plan, and I still believe that plan to be possible. What does your intuition tell you? Should you return to your own time forever? Or will you come back here today to be with Dane when he learns how Rosalind has betrayed him?"

There was no real contest, for Kathryn couldn't contemplate never seeing him again. "I'll come back here," she whispered.

Alice smiled. "Then you must be at the lock gates of Gloucester docks at midday."

"The lock gates at midday," Kathryn repeated, but suddenly she was her modern self again, tying on her robe and hurrying to answer a knock at the apartment door.

It was Jack Elmore. "This was delivered yesterday evening, miss," he said, presenting her with a huge bouquet of her favorite yellow roses.

Startled, and still a little dazed from the suddenness of the change of time, she took the flowers.

He grinned. "I know it's early, miss, but I knew you were up when I saw you draw the curtains back a short while ago. I've an apology to make, for you were out when they came yesterday evening, and I put them in a cool corner to give you on your return, but I clean forgot them. I hope you don't mind too much. Reckon someone back home misses you."

"Are you sure they're for me?" Her wits were so much at sixes and sevens, it was all she could think of saying.

"Well, unless there's another Mrs. Vansomeren staying here . . ." He grinned again. "Go on, take them, for they must have cost your old man a pretty penny to send from Chicago."

"My old man? Oh, you mean my husband." Richard had sent them? She stared at the roses. Yes, they'd be from Richard; he knew how much she adored yellow roses. She'd carried them on their wedding day.

"I didn't exactly sneak a look at the card, it was just easy to see," he explained hastily.

She gave him a quick smile. "I don't mind if you read it, Jack."

"Well, I'll leave you to it then, miss. I'm sorry I didn't give you them yesterday."

"It's okay. Oh, Jack?"

"Miss?"

"What's the quickest way to the docks from here?"

"Oh, it's quite direct, miss. You just follow the signs from the cathedral gates. You'll be there in five minutes."

"Thank you."

She drew back inside and quickly closed the door again. She still felt as if half of her hadn't quite made it back from Marchwood, but as she paused to compose herself properly, she began to feel right again.

She looked at the note tucked into the roses. It was brief and loving. *Can't wait for the weekend and your return. All my love. Richard.*

Her return? New York and Richard Vansomeren seemed part of a different world, a world that didn't matter to her now. Dane mattered. Only Dane. Whatever Rosalind told Richard was of no consequence, because the real Kathryn Vansomeren intended to stay here in England until there was nothing left to stay for, and she couldn't let him go on thinking they were reconciled. She had to call him and set the record straight!

It was the middle of the night in Chicago, but right now she felt it was something urgent, so Richard would have to take the call. But as she put the roses down and went to the phone, suddenly it rang. The moment was so weird that she paused with her hand over the receiver, but then she picked it up.

"Yes?"

"Mrs. Vansomeren?" inquired a female British voice.

"Speaking."

"This is the international operator. I have your Chicago call."

"My call?"

"Yes. Just one moment, I'm connecting you."

Before Kathryn could say anything more, there were some bleeping sounds on the line, and suddenly she heard Richard. "Kathryn? Is that you?"

She couldn't speak. From wanting to have things out with him, suddenly her tongue seemed to be tied in knots.

"Kathryn? Are you there?"

"Er, yes. Hi, there, Richard."

"Hi. I gather you tried to call me a short while ago. Don't think the worst, I wasn't out on the town, it's just so hot I couldn't sleep. I know it's the middle of the night, but I felt so sticky and darned uncomfortable I decided to take a shower. That's when you must have called. Did you get the roses?"

There was a new lightness in his voice, a happiness that almost seemed to reach across the miles. He sounded like he had when they first met, as if all the intervening months hadn't happened.

"Did you get the roses?" he asked again.

"Yes, they're lovely."

"I know you like yellow best."

"I didn't think you remembered." The moment of truth was

slipping inexorably away. She couldn't bring him down, it would be too cruel. But surely it was more cruel to let him go on thinking everything was fine? Oh, God, she just didn't know what to do!

He didn't pick up anything over the line. "Well, I've used my patented Brand Philips pooper-scooper to good effect, and there's no trace of his mess now. Not here in Chicago, anyway. Jeez, that guy makes such elementary mistakes I can't believe he's managed to get where he is. The sooner he retires, the better."

"I couldn't agree more. You've got more talent in your little finger than he's got in his whole body."

"Say it again, it's good for my self-esteem."

She couldn't help smiling, for it was great to be able to speak to him like this again. No atmosphere, no constant gibing, just lighthearted good humor. "Okay, you've got more talent in your little finger than he's got in his whole body."

"Gee, I love it when you talk dirty. I hope you're going to do that when we're together."

"Of course." That wasn't what she was supposed to say! She should be telling him how it really was, not letting him go on thinking it was A-OK again!

"Have you arranged your flight yet?" he asked.

"I'm working on it now."

"I'll be back in New York later today, so when you know what flight you're on, just leave a message at home. I'll be sure to meet you at the airport."

"Okay."

"Honey, I love you so much."

Tears sprang to her eyes. "And I love you, Richard." She did, but not in the way he wanted.

"See you soon."

"Yes, see you soon."

There was a click and the line went dead. Slowly she replaced the receiver. "Nice one, Kathryn," she murmured.

Nice one, indeed. Not only hadn't she done what she knew she should, but she'd aided and abetted Rosalind in whatever stupid game she was playing!

# *Nineteen*

~

Kathryn was nervous as she changed into a fresh shirt to go to the docks. It was half past eleven, and according to Jack it should only take her about five minutes to get there, so she had plenty of time before Alice's midday deadline. She was just dragging a brush through her hair when the phone rang again.

Hesitantly, she picked it up. "Yes?"

"Mrs. Vansomeren?" said another English voice. Male this time.

"Speaking."

"This is Mike Devenish at Waverley Travel. It's about your New York inquiry."

"Yes?" Rosalind *had* been busy.

"Well, I've managed to get you a seat on the flight you wanted. It leaves at nine, and the ticket will be waiting at Heathrow."

Kathryn's mind raced. What flight? When? "Er, nine, did you say?"

"Yes."

"I'm sorry, but I can't quite recall what I asked for now. Which day are we talking about?"

She could feel the surprise at the other end. "Why, tomorrow morning, of course. You were most specific."

"Oh, yes, I remember now." She felt foolish, but there hadn't been any other way of finding out. "Thank you for your help, Mr. Devenish."

"That's quite all right. Have a good flight." He rang off.

Kathryn replaced the receiver and then glanced at the roses. Rosalind was clearly making every arrangement to leave. But why bother? Why go to all these lengths when she knew that in the end she had to return to her own time in the past?

It didn't make sense, but now wasn't the moment to try to think about it too much, not when there was something much more important to be getting on with. Grabbing her shoulder bag, she left for the docks.

As she walked, she glanced through one of the leaflets Jack had given her. Gloucester Docks were being promoted as a great day out, providing leisure trips, museums, restaurants, pubs, shops, and the occasional extra attraction of the tall ships of yesteryear. Jack had told her there was a small fleet of them in the basin now, and Kathryn caught sight of it as she hurried along the sidewalk above the Severn.

The river tide was high and the water muddy as it slid silently past the city, and on the far bank cattle and sheep grazed on the rich flood meadows grass. Directly ahead she could see the lock and its adjacent keeper's cottage, and beyond them the uniform red-brick Victorian warehouses around the dock basin. It was a scene plucked from the last century, its authenticity increased by the masts and rigging of the tall ships.

Crowds of people enjoyed the sunny weather and attractions. There was a fairground, with carousels and a big wheel, and a Scottish pipe band was playing in honor of one of the vessels, a clipper called the *Pride of Edinburgh*. Various small craft glided across the shining water, passing to and fro between the assembled sailing ships, and every quayside mooring was occupied by motor launches or colorful canal barges. Pleasure trips could be enjoyed at a reasonable price, and there was a restaurant in an old ship that had been converted for the purpose. People sat at tables on the deck, shaded from the mid-morning sun by an elegant awning, and there were more people outside the adjacent quayside pub. A traveling company of entertainers, acrobats, mimes, and jugglers drew gasps and applause from onlookers, and children squealed with laughter at a Punch and Judy show.

Flags and bunting fluttered in the light breeze as the town crier's bell rang out for him to announce other forthcoming attractions. For a moment Kathryn's steps faltered. The town crier? Had she returned to 1815? But as she looked at the man in his bright red coat, three-cornered hat, and yellow wig, she realized he was very much from the modern day.

Following Alice's instructions, she made her way to the lock that connected the dock basin and the river. The warehouse to her left had been modernized and converted into the headquarters of the local council, while to her right, across the lock, another was now an antiques center. She could see the tall ships more clearly now. One or two were genuine old vessels, but others were replicas for the movies. She could see Columbus's *Santa Maria*, Drake's *Golden Hind*, Captain Cook's *Endeavor*, and Darwin's *Beagle*, all teeming with visitors.

Two private launches were in the lock waiting for the water to reach river level so they could sail upstream toward the next town of Tewkesbury. Even now, very few dared to attempt the dangerous downstream navigation toward the estuary, for the Severn tides were still as unpredictable and savage as they'd always been.

A small crowd had gathered to watch the launches' progress, and Kathryn glanced at her watch as she joined them. It was almost midday. Her heart began to quicken expectantly as she willed the seconds away. But her excitement this time was tempered with unease, for she knew that what lay ahead today had nothing to do with pleasure. She couldn't do anything but participate in events that were beyond her control, but soon Alice would explain everything. What would that explanation entail? What could the "audacious plan" be? Where Alice was concerned, though, it had to be said that anything was probably possible!

The water in the lock matched that in the river, and the heavy wooden gates were swung slowly open to allow the launches out. Kathryn leaned on a rail to watch, but as she did the launches suddenly seemed to meld into one and increase rapidly in size. Rigging and masts soared above her, and pennants streamed in the air as a schooner was hauled stern-first into the lock ready for the water level to be lowered all over again to that of the river. A brass band was playing sea shanties, and she was still caught up in a crowd of people, but now they were all dressed in early nineteenth century fashions. It was 1815 again, and practically the whole of Gloucester had turned out to see the *Lady Marchwood* leave for the Baltic.

Startled, she stepped back involuntarily, right into the path of one of the sailors hauling the ropes. She gasped, and he apologized. "Beggin' your pardon, my lady," he said, still straining forward with the rope over his shoulder.

"It . . . it was my fault," she replied, getting quickly out of his way and then glancing around. All the trappings of the modern city had vanished again, even the warehouses and lock-keeper's cottage, which were Victorian and therefore built well after 1815. The dock basin was just an open expanse of water edged by a few ramshackle buildings that were clearly only temporary, and some of the embankment was just earth. The unfinished canal being built to bypass the dangerous tidal estuary led away from the south of the basin into untouched countryside, and there was a small timber yard between her and the road that skirted the line of the old city walls. Then Regency Gloucester rose against the skyline, a city barely touched by the industrial revolution that was soon to transform everything.

The *Lady Marchwood* was pristine and elegant, with white decks and gleaming paintwork on her graceful bows and hull, and the press of onlookers on the lockside was really quite alarming as everyone jostled for the best position to watch her departure. There was a decorated dais nearby, from where local dignitaries could observe everything in comfort. She and Dane had been with them a moment or so ago, but now she was on her own on the cobbled quay. She didn't know where Thomas was. But so far all was well between Dane and her, that much she did know. Where was he now? She glanced around again, but still couldn't see him. Her attention was drawn to the small headland where the lock-keeper's cottage was to stand. It was bare now, except for a few willowy bushes, but the Waterloo cannon had been brought from Marchwood to fire a salute when the schooner set sail. Was he among the men standing there in readiness? If he was, she couldn't see him.

The captain cupped his hands to his mouth to shout instructions to the sailors scrambling up the rigging. More crew dashed barefoot along the spotless decks as the vessel was halted for the lockgates behind her to be closed and the water level lowered.

Kathryn watched for a moment, but then a lady and gentleman passed nearby, and she was conscious of the lady's eyes sweeping enviously over her clothes. It was a pleasant feeling to know a real Regency lady of fashion thought she looked good. Kathryn couldn't help a little vanity. This time she wore yellow and white, a tight-waisted daffodil silk pelisse over a striped muslin gown, and her hair was hidden beneath a yellow bonnet from the back of which fluttered a gauzy white scarf.

Suddenly she noticed Jeremiah Pendle, his great bulk laced into a mauve coat and white breeches. He was approaching a thin, nervous man of about thirty, with thick lips and a long nose. The man wasn't rich or poor, a person of business, she thought, glancing at his clothes. Whoever he was, she didn't know him, which meant Rosalind didn't know him either. But Jeremiah Pendle certainly did, for he left the shadow of the dais to go toward him now.

Something urged her to go closer as well. Not too close, for if Pendle should look in her direction, he'd know her straightaway. As she approached, Pendle put a plump hand on the man's shoulder. He whirled about to face the banker, and there was no mistaking his intense dismay. In spite of the occasion and the crowds, Kathryn clearly heard the men's brief exchange.

Jeremiah smiled unpleasantly. "So, *Mr.* Talbot, I've run you to ground at last."

"Run me to ground? I . . . I don't know what you mean, Mr. Pendle."

"Don't attempt to take me for a fool, Talbot. You haven't been paying up, and I'm calling in your debts."

"No! Please! Business has been slack of late, but it's beginning to improve. I can pay what I owe within a week."

"I'm afraid that's not good enough. I've been patient with you, Talbot, but I'm still waiting for that last payment. I don't intend to wait any longer. If the money isn't with me by this time tomorrow, you can say good-bye to your business. Is that clear? And don't think to evade me again, for I mean to send my, er, errand boys, if you take my meaning."

Talbot's eyes widened with dread. "I . . . I'll see you have the money, Mr. Pendle," he said quickly.

"Good."

Kathryn knew the short confrontation was at an end, and she drew hastily away. She felt sorry for Mr. Talbot for having fallen foul of the odious banker, especially when she saw how wretchedly he hurried away toward the city. But then the incident left her thoughts because the crowd gave an excited stir as the water level in the lock neared that of the river. A few moments later everyone surged forward as the river gates began to open.

She was carried with them, and would have been dragged perilously close to the edge of the deep lock if someone's arm hadn't moved protectively around her waist from behind.

"Have a care, for it wouldn't do for one Lady Marchwood to sink just as the other set sail," Dane said.

She turned gladly. He was superbly turned out for the occasion, in a dark blue coat and cream trousers. A gold pin was fixed in his starched neckcloth, and his top hat worn tipped back a little on his thick black hair, but if she hoped to see an answering smile on his lips, she was disappointed. He was cold and remote, and released her the moment he'd drawn her to safety.

Dismay swung over her. Something had happened in the few hours since she'd left him, and he was angry and distrustful again. But what had gone wrong? She knew the confrontation over Thomas hadn't taken place yet, so what was it? Clearly, Rosalind had done something, but for some reason the truth was shut from her. Her intuition didn't come to her aid, and she'd never felt more at a disadvantage than she did now.

Their eyes met and she tried to smile. "Dane, I—"

But he interrupted sarcastically. "Ah, she smiles lovingly. Well, madam, you're wasting your time. I imagine you thought me very much the gull this morning when I believed your tale about having to reply to an urgent message from the ubiquitous Mrs. Fowler. What was it you said? The lady wished to know if you required bows or frills on your new night robe?"

Kathryn's mind raced. "Er, yes, that's right," she said.

"Dear God, I could almost believe you. Well, unfortunately for you, my dear, I've just encountered Mrs. Fowler. Interestingly, she tells me she has no orders from you at present; indeed, she's quite concerned you might not have been satisfied with the ballgown. So much for night robe bows and frills."

More dismay lanced through her, and in that moment she hated Rosalind. "Please, Dane—"

"Have done with all this game-playing, Rosalind, for I've had enough of it. I wish to God I hadn't confided in you this morning, but I did. Now I can only trust you have sufficient regard for Philip not to betray my trust."

"You wrong me, Dane," she whispered, her voice lost in the roar of the crowd as the stern of the *Lady Marchwood* slid out on to the Severn.

"I concede we must speak of this, but later, when we're more private," he said coolly. Then he inclined his head and walked away.

There were tears in her eyes as she watched him go. The chain of events had begun in earnest; she could feel the links slipping inexorably through her fingers, as if dragged by some unseen force. It wouldn't be long now before he was faced with undeniable evidence of Rosalind's adulterous affair.

She tried to blink the tears away as he crossed the narrow footway along the top of the closed lock gates separating the lock channel from the dock basin, and then walked the few yards to the headland to join the men with the Marchwood cannons.

"Rosalind?"

She whirled about in alarm as Thomas addressed her suddenly.

# *Twenty*

~

Thomas removed his top hat, and the breeze ruffled his brown hair. He wore a kingfisher coat and white trousers, and there was ardent warmth in his brown eyes as he smiled at her. "I thought I'd never find you when you left the dais and I lost you in the crowd."

"Please leave me alone, Thomas," was what she said, but what she really wanted to say was "Go away! Don't come near me if you value your life!"

His smile faded, and he looked guardedly around. "What is it? Are you expecting Dane to return at any moment? I thought he was to fire the cannon salute."

"I . . . I just don't want to speak to you," she said lamely, her haunted gaze moving toward the headland. To her relief, Dane was intent upon the cannon. "Please go away, Thomas," she begged, realizing again that she was doing the exact opposite of what the real Rosalind would be doing right now, just as Rosalind was probably doing the opposite to Kathryn Vansomeren in the future. They weren't just trading places, they were changing situations in each other's times as well.

He caught her arm as she tried to walk away. "You can't do this, Rosalind. You sent word you wished to see me here today. I thought that meant everything was right between us again."

What exactly had Rosalind written? She tried to gain an insight, but the blank in the knowledge remained in place, and there was still no flash of intuition to help her either. Panic touched her then, and all she could think of was getting away from him. She tried to pull free without attracting any attention. "Please let me go, Thomas," she begged.

But he held her tightly. "What hold has Dane over you?"

"Hold? There's nothing, Thomas, I just want to stay with him. I realize now that he's the one I love. Let me go, please."

"I don't believe you love him!"

To her dismay she saw they had attracted some attention. "Please, Thomas, people are looking!"

"Then let us go somewhere less public."

Oh, why didn't he save himself by just walking away and forgetting all about her? She looked pleadingly at him. "Why won't you just accept that I wish our intimacy to end?"

"Why? Because you're carrying my child, that's why, and unless you come somewhere private now so we may talk, so help me I'll make a far worse scene than this! The timber yard would seem to offer the necessary shelter from prying eyes. I'll expect you to join me there in a few minutes." He walked away, not going directly to the yard, but taking a circuitous route.

She knew she had no choice but to do as he demanded. She waited a few minutes, and then began to walk toward the yard. The first cannon salute boomed out and the crowds roared as the *Lady Marchwood* shed her ropes and began to move on the river current. All eyes were upon the schooner, as Kathryn slipped unnoticed into the yard.

Thomas came swiftly to meet her. "What's going on, Rosalind? Why do you say one thing one day, and another the next?"

"I didn't set out to hurt you, Thomas, but you *must* believe me when I say I love Dane after all."

"But in your note you swore undying love for me!" he cried, his eyes bright with confusion and disbelief. "If you didn't mean to hurt me, you nevertheless managed it very well! What's more, you continue to do it. Only hours ago you sent a message promising me your undying love; now you insist you love Dane again. You did the same last night at the ball."

"Forgive me," she whispered, her voice almost lost in the cheers of the crowds outside.

"Forgive you? Rosalind, I *love* you, I want to spend the rest of my life with you! And with our child. We belong together, and nothing you say now will convince me you don't feel the same."

Before she realized what was in his mind, he'd taken her in

his arms to kiss her passionately on the lips. He held her so tightly she couldn't even struggle.

Then Dane's icy voice spoke from the entrance to the yard. "So this is your notion of faithfulness, is it, madam?"

Thomas released her and whipped around defensively. "Dane!"

"In the days of our childhood you may have been at liberty to address me familiarly, but those days are long since past, Denham," Dane replied.

At last Kathryn summoned the courage to face him. "Dane, this isn't what it seems," she whispered, but she saw unforgiveness in the bleak gray of his eyes.

"No, of course it isn't, you're merely discussing the price of timber," he replied contemptuously.

"Please believe me!" she cried, taking a halting step toward him.

"I want nothing more of harlots, madam." His manner was arctic cold.

Thomas leapt to her defense. "Take that foul insult back, Marchwood!" He lunged forward, but Dane stepped aside.

Impulsion carried Thomas stumbling out of the yard into full view of the crowds beyond. There was an audible stir as he lost his balance and fell sprawling on the dusty cobbles. Immediately he scrambled to his feet again to fling himself back at Dane.

Kathryn screamed. "No! Please, no!"

Her cries seemed to pierce the air, and a great silence fell as everyone forgot the scene on the river to watch the fight instead. Exclamations rippled through the onlookers as Dane caught Thomas a ferocious blow on the chin, and he staggered as if about to lose consciousness. But then he recovered, and soon forced Dane to trade blow for blow.

The inevitability of it all rendered Kathryn silent. She felt as if she were watching everything in slow motion. When Thomas went down finally, Dane would issue the challenge, and then there would only be the duel itself left. Tears marked her cheeks as the crowd formed a semicircle around the two men and began to cheer and urge them on. The brief but bloody struggle ended when a brutal uppercut sent Thomas sprawling for the last time.

Kathryn pressed her hands to her mouth as he lay dazed for

a moment before hauling himself up to an elbow to wipe the blood from the corner of his mouth. He looked up at Dane. "I demand satisfaction for this, Marchwood! I will defend Rosalind's honor against your insults!"

There were gasps, and Rosalind stared at him. *Thomas* issued the challenge? She'd always assumed it was Dane.

Dane's eyes were like ice. "I'll meet you wherever you choose, Denham, but know his, I am not concerned with my wife's nonexistent honor, more with my own, which has been gravely affronted by her infidelity."

Jeremiah Pendle suddenly pushed to the front of the crowd. "No! I beg of you, Sir Dane. It will be an unequal contest, for Thomas is not a marksman!"

"He was the one who threw down the gauntlet, Pendle, for I most certainly see no reason to face anyone on my wife's account. So know this, I'm not accepting this challenge to defend her, I'm doing it because no man of integrity can decline a challenge without bringing upon himself a charge of cowardice." Dane returned his frozen gaze to Thomas. "Name your seconds."

Pendle spoke up swiftly. "One will suffice, sir. *I* will second my nephew."

Dane nodded. "Then I will name only Dr. Eden, who may not be present at the moment, but who will, I'm sure, stand for me." He continued to look at Thomas. "The choice of weapon, time, and place, should be mine, but I offer it to you. What is your preference?"

Thomas struggled to his feet. "I choose what I know you'd choose, Marchwood. Your dueling pistols, the oak grove on your land, at dawn tomorrow."

More gasps greeted this, for everyone knew William Denham had died in the oak grove, and that Dane's pistols had been used.

Dane affected indifference. "As you wish," he replied, and then turned to walk away, but Kathryn gave a despairing cry and hurried to try to seize his hand. She didn't care that everyone was watching, only that he didn't reject her. "Please, Dane, I beg of you!"

But he caught her wrist, and raised it disdainfully so that for the first time she saw she wasn't wearing her wedding ring.

"You have already ceased to be a wife, madam," he breathed, tossing her arm aside.

"I—I don't know why the ring isn't there," she cried.

"Enough."

"I love you, Dane," she whispered, gazing at him through a haze of tears.

"What would a whore know of love?" He strode away through the crowd, which parted for him to pass.

A terrible numbness settled over her like a shroud. Thomas took an unsteady step toward her, but suddenly his legs seemed to fail him and he slumped to the ground. Jeremiah Pendle gave a cry of concern and knelt to see what he could do, and the crowd closed around them both. She was excluded, condemned as much by the citizens of Gloucester as by Dane.

Suddenly a pony and trap rattled over the cobbles and halted by her. Alice held out a helping hand. "Climb up, my dear, for it is done now, and the time has come for you to decide."

Kathryn accepted the hand and scrambled onto the trap, which soon conveyed her swiftly away from the scene. She was too upset to speak, and was thankful that Alice didn't say anything as the trap drove through the city. There were few people about, for everyone was at the docks, but the sound of the pony and trap brought someone to one of the shop windows. Kathryn caught a glimpse of Mr. Talbot's thin, anxious face, but then he drew hastily back out of sight again. She saw the name written above the shop door. *Frederick Talbot, Gunsmith.*

They'd almost reached Alice's cottage when Kathryn managed to speak at last. "What will happen now?" she asked the nurse.

"The duel will happen. Nothing can prevent it."

There was an unmistakably odd note in the old woman's voice, and Kathryn looked quickly at her. "What is it? What's wrong?"

"Maybe a great deal, maybe nothing."

Kathryn searched her profile as she drove. "Something isn't going according to your plan, is it?" she said suddenly.

Alice maneuvered the pony into the lane to the cottages, and drew the trap to a standstill at her door. A man emerged from a stable that stood where Jack Elmore's apartment was to be in the future, and led the pony away as soon as Alice and

Kathryn had alighted. Kathryn followed the nurse into the cottage, where the ground floor was taken up by a low-beamed kitchen parlor.

Drawing out a chair by a scrubbed table, Alice bade her sit down. "The time has come to tell you all you need to know, my dear, and I hope with all my heart that at the end of it you will make the right decision."

# Twenty-one

~

"Are you really going to explain everything?" Kathryn took off her bonnet and shook her hair from its pins. "Or are you just going to tell me enough to keep me doing what you want?"

"Is that what you think of me?"

"Pretty much." Kathryn lowered her glance then. "No, that's not true. I'm sorry, I don't mean to sound like I do, it's just that what happened just now was pretty grueling."

The old woman sat down as well. "I know, my dear, but you had to endure it."

"Why?"

"So that you would be able to judge *exactly* how you feel about Dane. You had to experience rejection at his hands; otherwise, how could you know the full range of emotion? You'd already tasted ecstasy, the depths of despair had to be sampled as well."

"Well, I guess what I'm feeling right now is pretty much the pits," Kathryn said quietly.

"A quaint expression."

"But appropriate."

"Yes." Alice smiled a little.

"You were about to explain," Kathryn prompted.

The old nurse hesitated before answering. "Yes, I am, but first I must tell you that you are right, things are no longer proceeding as they should."

Alarm leapt through Kathryn. "What things?"

"Rosalind refuses to come back to her own time anymore. She has closed her mind to me and will not do as she must. At this very moment, in your future, she is packing to go back to

New York. She intends to leave Gloucester tonight. She wishes to force you, you see."

"Force me? I don't understand."

"She stands to gain everything she has ever yearned for, my dear. She wishes to be you forever, and relinquish her life in the past to you."

Kathryn was thunderstruck. "Change places permanently, you mean?"

Alice reached over and touched her naked ring finger. "Yes, my dear, and *that* is how determined she is to break with the life she has always known. When Dane placed the ring on her finger, he—"

"Told her he would regard the marriage as over if she ever set the ring aside," Kathryn finished for her, remembering what Alice had said at the very beginning of everything.

"Yes, my dear. She has always been very careful to wear it in front of him, but when she is with Thomas, she takes it off."

"Dane has never deserved to be treated as she treats him," Kathryn said quietly.

"No, but then love is a fierce emotion, and Rosalind loves Thomas very much indeed. I know her, and know exactly why she has removed the ring. It is a gesture of final rebellion against what she has long seen as the injustice of her position. She didn't want to marry Dane, but obeyed her father, and she has regretted it ever since. She knew that if I learned about the ring, I would realize what she intended, so she made certain I remained in ignorance by closing her thoughts from me." Alice smiled a little. "I did not know she could do it, and fear she is stronger and more cunning than I gave her credit for, but then she has a great deal to fight for. However, it has to be by mutual choice. Rosalind fears you may not agree, and so she is doing all she can to prevent you from returning to your own time. She does it because she is desperate to be with your husband."

Kathryn sat back incredulously. "With Richard? But, why on earth would she want to go to him?"

"Answer me truthfully, Kathryn. When you first met Thomas Denham, what did you think of him?"

Kathryn looked at her. "He reminded me of Richard," she admitted.

"Yes, because your husband is Thomas Denham born again.

What was the word you used? Reincarnation? You were right, but it did not apply to you and Rosalind. Thomas's mother was a Larville, which is the family from which Richard Vansomeren's mother came, and Thomas exists again in him."

Kathryn was at a loss for words. Thomas and Richard were one and the same? But, of course, she could see it clearly now. Time and time again Thomas had put her in mind of Richard.

Alice looked wisely at her. "You and Richard are ill matched, my dear, and deep unhappiness awaits you both if you go back to him."

"The divorce court awaits us," Kathryn said flatly.

"But not if the woman who returns to him is Rosalind in your guise. She is his perfect wife, and she carries the child he longs for. His child, my dear, albeit fathered during a previous existence of which he knows nothing. He will think the gods have smiled upon him after all, and for her it is the answer to her prayers. From the moment she conceived, she knew her existence was damned, for Dane would realize the child was not his. She had a premonition that no matter how she and Thomas planned to flee to Jamaica, Thomas was going to meet an untimely end. She didn't know it would be in a duel at Dane's hand, for that information was only discovered when she went to the library in your time. But I've already told you that."

Kathryn nodded. The story was incredible, but she knew it was the truth. Everything was as the old woman said.

Alice went on. "I first realized about Richard Vansomeren when you came here, my dear. From the moment you entered this house, I absorbed everything I needed to know, including your childlessness, your increasing unhappiness in your marriage, and your dissatisfaction with your, er, career." Alice gave a slightly uncomfortable smile. "Forgive me, my dear, but I find it difficult to accept that a lady should be employed at a place of work."

Kathryn glanced away. Work? She hadn't given it so much as a passing thought for some time now. It was as if the TV station and Diane Weinburger had never existed. But then, in 1815, they hadn't!

Alice continued. "I told Rosalind about you, and about Richard, when she came here that night to keep her tryst with Thomas. She remembered I had once spoken of an ancient power, a way to transport people through time and exchange them with those of another age, and she begged me to try to do it for her. She saw it as the solution to everything, the perfect way of being with Thomas forever, and of making his child legitimate, albeit as a Vansomeren, not a Denham. But it wasn't just for her sake I called you back here to this time; I did it for you too, my dear. I feel your unhappiness very keenly indeed, as I do Dane's, for he is not the villain he is widely believed to be. I know that just as Rosalind was Richard's perfect wife, so you are Dane's, and I've brought you together to show you how it could be."

Kathryn ran a fingertip pensively along the grain of the wooden tabletop. "I can see why Rosalind thinks it's all such a great idea, for she has nothing to lose. Thomas is going to die anyway, except he doesn't really die, does he? He's there for the taking as Richard, and all she has to do is whisper sweet nothings to have him eating out of her hand. It's all very neat for her, but the way things are here in the past, it's not going to be so hunky-dory for me, is it? Dane loathes the very sight of me right now, and I can't say I blame him. He's had two wives, and both have betrayed him with a Denham."

"My dear, whatever his rage and hurt right now, nothing will diminish Dane's love for you."

"So you say."

"So I know." Alice leaned across to put a hand over Kathryn's.

"But you *don't* know what happens after midnight tonight, do you?" Kathryn pointed out. "Everything from that moment on is as much a mystery to you as it is to me."

Alice lowered her eyes. "I cannot deny it, my dear. You must weigh everything very clearly, and you must do it for yourself. If you decide to come back here forever, you must do so in the full knowledge that you will never see your family, friends, and colleagues in America again. Everything about your modern life will be lost, never to be regained. You will be Lady Marchwood for the rest of your allotted span, with no guarantee that you will be reunited with Dane. Would that I could reassure you, Kathryn, but to do that would be wrong. I only know what *my* intuition tells me, and that is that you and he will be very happy together. It also tells me that although I do not know exactly what takes place at the duel, you will be able to reveal the truth, and it is that which will bring you and Dane together."

"What do you mean?"

"I don't know," Alice confessed again. "I can only say the words that come to me. You will be able to reveal the truth, and it is that which will bring the two of you together." The old woman sighed. "However, it's all very well for me to tell you that you can rely upon your intuition, quite another for me to advise you to rely upon mine."

Kathryn didn't know what to say. It was as if she were being offered a tantalizing prize that might be snatched away if she reached out to take it.

Alice drew a long breath. "Until midnight, I will still have the power to send you into your own time once more, and then bring you back here forever if you so decide. But there will be no going back after that. Rosalind thinks that if she defies me until midnight, she will be able to escape into the future whether or not you wish to stay in the past. She believes that if she is in your place, you will have to stay in hers, and therefore in the past, but she is wrong. I can send you into the future at the same time she is there. You will both be separate personalities, but in the same time. I intend to do this, my dear, because you *must* be able to make your decision, and that means weighing up everything. You must see your modern life again, and be certain you wish to leave it behind forever. Rosalind's decision is made, but she cannot be allowed to make yours as well."

Kathryn rose slowly to her feet. "Does that mean I'll see her when I go back?"

"Yes, for she's in this house now, albeit in another century."

"And if I decide to keep my modern identity?"

"Then she has no choice but to return to her own time. But if you decide to change places with her, you must do so before midnight. After that it will be too late."

"Will you still be here if I come back?"

"Yes."

"And your intuition tells you Dane and I will be reunited?"

"Yes. Something will happen when you expose the truth about the duel."

"You're only guessing, aren't you? You don't know for sure, you're just trusting your darned intuition."

"Yes, my dear, and that means you have to decide whether or not Sir Dane Marchwood's love is worth the sacrifice you may be making. You could come back here to great and lasting happiness, or to loneliness and permanent rejection."

"Alice—" Kathryn's voice broke off, for the old kitchen parlor had disappeared and she was standing at the foot of the modern staircase leading up to her apartment.

# *Twenty-two*

### ～

For a moment or so she was more disorientated than usual. She held the stair handrail to steady herself, and then glanced down at her clothes. She was Kathryn Vansomeren again, and wearing the things she'd worn for the journey from New York. Some of her hand luggage was on the floor by her feet, and her coat was over the bottom banister. Rosalind was on the point of leaving!

As the realization sank in, she heard a cry of helpless disbelief from the floor above. She knew the English voice well, for it had been hers only a moment before, so she hurried up to push the apartment door open.

Rosalind was standing in the middle of the room in the dainty yellow-striped muslin gown that had so abruptly replaced her jeans, and her hands were visibly shaking as she touched the long telltale blonde curls cascading about her shoulders. Her face went pale as she saw Kathryn. "You!"

"Yes, me." Kathryn closed the door and confronted her. God, what a weird situation this was. Like looking at a sister she never knew she had.

Rosalind backed away a little. "How . . . how are you here at the same time as me?"

"You underestimated Alice, just as she underestimated you. She's sent me back again so I can decide for myself whether or not I want to change places with you," Kathryn replied, unable to keep a certain coldness from her voice.

Rosalind felt it. "You don't like me very much, do you?"

"Why should I after what you just tried?"

"It was wrong of me, I know, but I can't bear the thought of having to stay as my real self, not with things as they are."

"It's your own fault things are as they are," Kathryn replied unfeelingly. All she could think was what this woman had done to Dane.

"I don't deny it's my own fault, but one cannot help falling in love with the wrong man."

"True, but that doesn't make it okay to try to get your own way regardless of the other half of this particular equation. Just how selfish can you get? You know you'll go to Richard and everything will be fine, but you haven't a clue what I might have to endure in your place, and to be honest, I don't think you give a damn!"

Rosalind was stung. "That isn't true! I wasn't doing it entirely out of selfishness, I thought you loved Dane. Obviously you don't."

"Don't presume to judge what I do or don't feel," Kathryn replied heatedly. Just who did this woman think she was?

"Well, do you love him?"

"Yes, as it happens, I do."

"Then why don't you want to stay with him?"

"I didn't say I didn't want to stay with him, I'm just angry with you for trying to *force* a decision on me. You've known about this ultimate choice for a little longer than me, maybe not a lot longer, but still long enough to come to terms with it. But then what's there to come to terms with as far as you're concerned? You get everything you've ever wanted if you become me, but I might not get anything if I become you. Dane despises the very sight of his wife right now, and who can blame him? I might never be able to regain his trust after this, so what sort of existence will I have then?"

"A better one than awaits me if I have to stay as my real self. Have you any idea what it's like in my time to be the mother of an illegitimate baby? It is bad enough to endure the odium of being just a fallen woman, but to have a bastard child as well . . ." Rosalind put her hands to her abdomen, and turned away to hide sudden tears.

Kathryn was unmoved. All she could think of was the way Rosalind had attempted to make her do what she wanted. And the way she'd cheated on Dane. "If you'd been a proper wife to Dane . . ." she began, but Rosalind turned sharply back to her.

"What makes you fit to cast the first stone? How can *you*

find the nerve to stand there with your nose in the air and accuse *me* of being an imperfect wife?"

"What's that supposed to mean?" Kathryn demanded.

"It means I know you're not as immaculate as you'd like to pretend, Kathryn Vansomeren. I've been you, remember, so I know all about Harry Swenson."

Kathryn colored.

Rosalind's green eyes flashed. "Oh, yes, I know how unfaithful you were with him, and as if that were not black mark enough against your supposed sanctity, there is the small matter of how carried away you've been with *my* husband! You've been having an adulterous affair with Dane behind Richard's back. Well, it's the truth, isn't it? Each time you've made love with my husband, you've betrayed your marriage vows to your own!"

Kathryn stared at her. "I . . ." Her lips closed, for it was true. She was as guilty as Rosalind of breaking the seventh commandment, and she had been since Harry Swenson!

Rosalind's chin came up a little victoriously. "Just how superior would you be feeling right now if you knew you had to go back to Richard and tell him you were carrying Dane's child? Well? Answer me that if you can."

Now it was Kathryn's turn to look away and blink back tears. Carry Dane's child? If only it were possible.

Rosalind suddenly realized what she'd said, and put out an apologetic hand. "Forgive me, I wasn't thinking. I didn't mean to hurt you, I just want you to understand how it is for me. Put yourself in my place, reverse everything, and maybe you'll view my conduct with a little more compassion."

Remorse stirred through Kathryn then, but it was still tempered with a little justifiable anger. "Okay, maybe I haven't any business casting stones, but neither should you try making my decisions for me."

"I admit it." Rosalind gave a hesitant smile.

Kathryn met her gaze honestly. "I do want to go back to Dane, but I'm afraid. Maybe if it was as clear-cut for me as it is for you . . ." She went to the window and looked out. Jack had just finished loading the luggage into the rented car, and glanced up to smile at her before going back to his own place.

Rosalind watched her. "I wish I could make happiness as certain for you as it is for me."

"The whole thing is more complicated than you realize." Kathryn glanced back at her. "You see, the hurt Dane feels right now goes much much deeper than it might appear. William Denham was Elizabeth's lover," she said quietly.

Rosalind was shocked. "But, I thought——"

"That the first Lady Marchwood was an angel without tarnish? Yes, so did I. Dane told me the truth this morning. That made it all the worse when he learned about Thomas and you."

"I was convinced Dane wore her portrait because he still loved her."

"So was I. But really, it was a reminder not to be fool enough to fall in love again. Right now he's probably thinking he should have kept Elizabeth in mind a little longer."

"Why didn't he say something at the time of the duel? Why let everyone believe he'd forced an innocent man into a fatal duel?"

"Because of Philip. The boy is definitely his son, and he wished to protect him from knowing his mother had been unfaithful."

"So instead, Philip will always wonder why his father fought what can only ever appear to be an ignoble duel," Rosalind remarked a little dryly.

Kathryn smiled. "That's men for you," she murmured.

Rosalind turned away. "Poor Dane, he didn't deserve my unfaithfulness as well."

"No, he didn't, but then neither did Richard deserve mine," Kathryn admitted ruefully.

Rosalind met her eyes and smiled. "Neither of us are really so very bad, Kathryn. We've strayed maybe, but we aren't out-and-out sinners."

"Richard certainly wouldn't agree, nor would Dane." Tears suddenly sprang to Kathryn's eyes. "And now Dane is going to be damned all over again for murdering a second Denham." Oh, Dane, I want to be with you, to try to make it all right again . . .

Rosalind drew a long breath. "I . . . I never really understood him, you know. He always frightened me a little—oh, I don't mean that I feared he would harm me, it was just that I knew I could never be the woman he really needed. He's so very sensual. Physical lovemaking isn't merely an adjunct of his affection, it's an expression of his whole being. When he loves, it is with every sense, and his wife should be a someone who shares his sensuality. You are just such a woman, Kathryn."

"You don't know anything about me."

"I don't need to, Kathryn, for I've seen how Rosalind is after he's been with you. There's a new happiness in his eyes and touch, and a softness in his voice I've never heard before."

Kathryn had to smile, for wasn't that exactly how Richard sounded after he'd spoken to Rosalind?

"Why do you smile?"

"Oh, I was just thinking of the last conversation I had with Richard. He's changed too, and it's because of you."

Rosalind's eyes warmed. "He's so very like Thomas."

"I can't argue with that."

"None of us are able to change our nature. I could never be like you, Kathryn, and Richard Vansomeren can never be like Dane."

"Yes, I know, but that doesn't mean a straightforward swap between you and me will produce the desired result. Not for me, anyway." Kathryn thought for a long moment. "I wish I knew what really happens at the duel, or should I say happened? I really don't know what tense to use anymore. From here the duel is long since over and done with, but back in 1815, it hasn't yet taken place. It's so confusing."

Rosalind nodded. "I know exactly what you mean—in fact, I'm probably the only other person in creation who understands so well."

"That's true." Kathryn smiled at her, but then the smile faded as her thoughts returned to the duel. "Alice says she feels I'll be able to reveal the truth at the duel, and that that will bring Dane and me together again. But she only feels it, she doesn't know for sure. And she can't shed any light on what that truth might be. I'm in the proverbial dark, and right now I feel I'm likely to remain there, because Alice loses her powers at midnight and after that it will be too late for anything. If I thought I could go back and begin to shine a little in Dane's eyes by clearing his name somehow, then I'd take the risk like a shot."

"You are the only one who can decide if Dane is important enough to you, and thus whether or not to take the chance."

"Yes, I had cottoned on to that," Kathryn replied a little

caustically, and immediately she bit her lip. "I'm sorry, I didn't mean to snap. I just don't know what to do. At least, I know what I *want* to do, but I'm frightened of being back in the past without Dane, and also without all the family and friends I know at present. I'll be alone, except for Alice."

"But if you stay here, you'll never see Dane again."

"I know that too." Kathryn stared down at the courtyard. The scent of roses drifted through the open window, and she could hear the seagulls as they wheeled in the warm air above the cathedral tower.

"I don't believe you can do without Dane, any more than I can do without Thomas," Rosalind said simply. "I know that what I'm saying now probably sounds like another attempt to persuade you to do as I wish, but it isn't, it's a statement of fact. You'll be wretched for the rest of your life if you're parted from him, and that applies as much to staying in the present as returning to the past. Either way, without him you'll be unutterably miserable."

Kathryn knew she was right. "And if I stay here in the present, I'm guaranteed not to see him again, right?" she said, still gazing down into the courtyard.

"Yes, but if you return . . ."

"I stand a chance."

Rosalind fell silent.

Kathryn raised her gaze toward the cathedral, and smiled a little wryly. There wasn't really a choice after all. Hope was only on offer if she returned to the past. "I have to go back," she said quietly.

Rosalind's breath caught. "Are you sure?"

"I'm not *sure* about anything, but I'm going back anyway. I want Dane—no, that's not right, I *need* Dane, I don't think I can live without him." Kathryn turned, and with a start found herself looking at Kathryn Vansomeren! Rosalind and she had changed places again.

# Twenty-three

~

The two women stared at each other, and then Rosalind hugged Kathryn tightly. "Thank you, thank you so much," she whispered.

Kathryn returned the hug, but then felt a perverse desire to laugh. How could anyone explain what had just happened to her? It was an out-of-body, out-of-time experience that was going to last for the rest of her life! She'd just turned her back on everything she'd ever known, and was doing it for a man from another century who might not even want her anymore! It was crazy, but she knew it was the right decision.

Rosalind drew back, and then took her hands. "We'll always remember this moment, no matter how different our centuries."

"I hope so." Then Kathryn remembered something. "Your wedding ring!"

Rosalind looked blank for a moment, and then gasped. "I quite forgot! I was in the drawing room thinking about Thomas, and I took it off, just as I do when I'm with him. Then a maid came in to ask me something, and the ring slipped my mind completely. It must still be on the table by the glass-fronted cabinet."

"So you didn't take it off as some sort of grand gesture that your marriage to Dane was over?" Kathryn asked.

"No, I wouldn't do that, for I know it would only make it even more difficult for you to win Dane's trust again. He'd interpret its absence like you just did. I was guilty of trying to make you stay in the past with him, but not of wanting to make things impossible for you as well! I'm not that selfish."

Kathryn smiled. So Alice had been wrong this time. She

glanced down at the waiting car. "You were about to leave, so I guess there's nothing to keep you now."

"I'm ashamed of how pushy I've been. I just reasoned if I forced the pace, I'd somehow evade all chance of being sent back to the past," Rosalind admitted. "I've even booked a hotel room for tonight, ready for the nine o'clock flight in the morning."

"Well, I'd say remember me to Richard, but I don't really think that would be right," Kathryn said with a smile.

Rosalind smiled too. "Probably not."

Kathryn searched her eyes then. "You know, it's not just Richard you're going to, there's my career as well. You'll have dear Diane Weinburger to deal with."

"No, I won't."

"You won't?"

Rosalind smiled. "I'm going to give it up. I just want to be a wife and mother."

"Well, Richard will be delighted," Kathryn said, "but will you be satisfied?"

Rosalind laughed then. "Why should I not be? Kathryn, you've chosen to go back in time to become Lady Marchwood. What career satisfaction is there in that? It's hardly the role of an emancipated woman, but it's what you want. We've both made our choices because we know in our hearts what's best for us, and that's all that matters."

"I guess you're right, I'm still having trouble getting to grips with all this." Kathryn looked a little wickedly at her then. "Are you really going to give up my career?"

"*My* career. Yes, I am," Rosalind corrected with a grin, but her curiosity was aroused. "What's on your mind? I know there's something, I can tell by your voice."

"Oh, just a small matter of telling Diane Weinburger what she can go do. I've lost count of the times I've wanted to say exactly what I think of her, but I've chickened out. But if you're going to leave anyway . . . ?" Kathryn raised a hopeful eyebrow.

Rosalind grinned. "Nothing would give me greater pleasure. I'll wipe the floor with her."

"In front of everyone! *Please* say you'll do it in front of the entire office!" Kathryn begged mercilessly.

"You have my word on it."

"God, I almost wish I could be there." Kathryn smiled. "Almost, but not quite."

They looked at each other then, and after a moment Rosalind glanced out of the window at the waiting car. "Well, I guess it's good-bye, then."

Kathryn hesitated, and then hugged her a last time. "Take care."

"And you," Rosalind replied, returning the hug.

They held each other for a long moment, both conscious of the uniqueness of their situation. Everything that had happened to them was so wildly improbable that even now it seemed almost like a dream, except they both knew this parting was definitely for real. They'd swapped places, swapped lives, swapped times, and, above all, swapped husbands, but only they knew about it. And Alice, of course.

Then Rosalind had gone. Kathryn heard her light steps on the staircase, and a moment later the car door slammed. She went to the window to watch as it reversed down the lane, and caught a last glimpse of Rosalind's face before she drove off. No, of Kathryn Vansomeren's face before she drove off.

A chill finger suddenly passed down her spine as she realized she'd never see her own face again. Because it wasn't her face any longer, it belonged to Rosalind. She turned from the window. It was done. She'd made the irrevocable decision, but as yet she was neither one thing nor the other. She was in no-man's-land, a helpless limbo of total dependence upon the fading skills of an old woman whose powers would end completely at the first stroke of Lammas Day, 1815!

So, at least she knew the final transition would have to take place before midnight, but that was all she knew. Maybe it would happen within the next few minutes, maybe not until the witching hour itself. So she glanced around the apartment, committing everything modern to memory because she'd never see it again. Never see a TV, a phone, or a refrigerator. Never hear her mother's voice, or enjoy the New York skyline, never drive on a freeway, or go to the movies. And now it would be Rosalind who told Diane Weinburger where to go, because the real Kathryn Vansomeren had opted for the past— for silk and muslin gowns, carriages, servants, and Sir Dane Marchwood. Her pulse had quickened expectantly. Hurry up,

Alice. I'm frightened here on my own, and want to go back
*now!*

But the minutes dragged on, and nothing happened. She remained in the future in her Regency guise. She began to pace
restlessly up and down, glancing frequently at the time and
gradually becoming anxious. What if for some reason Alice
couldn't take her back? What if she was stuck here like this instead? Oh, God, that didn't bear thinking about.

Another hour passed, and still there was nothing. She
couldn't pace any longer, and so lay on the bed. The day was
warm, and the sounds of Gloucester drowsy with summer heat.
She closed her eyes, not expecting to drift into sleep, but she
did, and when she awoke, it was dark.

Her eyes flew open with a start, and for a moment she
hoped she was back in 1815, but then she heard a truck in the
street. She was still in the future! She glanced at the clock
radio. It was a quarter to midnight! What was Alice playing
at? Soon it would be too late! As she lay wondering what to
do, she heard footsteps on the stairs, and then Jack's voice.

"As I was saying, you're very fortunate there's any accommodation free at the moment, let alone at this time of night.
Mrs. Vansomeren had the apartment for a fortnight, and had
only been here a day or so, but all of a sudden she upped and
went home. If you ask me, it was something to do with the
roses her husband sent."

"Oh, really?" a bored male American voice replied.

"Anyway, I'm sure you'll like the rooms. Now then, let me
sort out the keys."

The footsteps halted the other side of the door, and then
Kathryn heard more people on the stairs. Children laughed,
and a woman told them off.

"Can't you make less noise? I have a headache."

A key rattled in the lock, and Kathryn scrambled from the
bed. God, what was she to do? If they saw her in these clothes
they'd think she was some weirdo who fancied herself as Lady
Hamilton or the Empress Josephine! She had to hide—but
where? All she could think of was under the bed, and she dove
beneath it just as the outer door opened and the lights were
switched on.

Jack conducted the newcomers into the apartment. There
was a man and woman and two children, a boy and a younger

girl. Jack stood back for them to admire the accommodation. "It was all done about a year ago, to the highest standards, of course, and like I said, it's available for almost two weeks."

"We can't stay that long, seven days will be just fine. We just need to finish our vacation, but not in the so-called luxury cottage we'd booked," the woman said, running her finger along the window ledge and inspecting it for dust. She was in her early thirties, with long dark hair and a pale, rather pretty face. By her accent, Kathryn guessed she came from somewhere down New Orleans way.

Jack cleared his throat. "Cottage not up to scratch, eh?"

"You could say that. There wasn't a shower, and I *never* take a bath anywhere except my own home," the woman replied emphatically.

"Well, there's a shower here," Jack said quickly.

"What price are we talking?" the man asked. He was a little older than the woman, and *definitely* New Orleans. Something about him told of the workaholic executive who'd come only grudgingly on the annual family vacation. He had brown hair, gray at the temples, and didn't look relaxed in casual clothes.

Jack began to list the charges, but his voice was drowned by the children as they ran noisily from room to room, switching on every light they could find. Their mother called complainingly after them.

"Holly! Patrick! Try to make less noise! Don't you guys listen to anything I say?"

Clearly not, for they shouted excitedly to each other as they investigated every nook and cranny. The woman sighed. "God, will I be glad to hit the sack tonight," she muttered.

The bedroom where Kathryn was hiding had so far escaped the children's attention, but she knew it would only be seconds before one or other of them burst in. She pulled back as far as she could beneath the bed, but was only too aware that even if she somehow escaped detection now, she couldn't stay where she was forever. Sooner or later she had to come out.

"Come on, Alice, do your stuff!" she whispered, then fell silent as the bedroom light was suddenly switched on. The girl ran in, flung herself on the bed, and began to bounce up and down as energetically as she could.

Then the bouncing stopped, and Kathryn turned her head to

watch as the child's feet swung down to the floor again. To her horror she realized a beneath-the-bed inspection was about to commence. Go away, you horrid brat! But the horrid brat got down on all fours and peered under the valance.

The girl's breath caught with shock as she found herself looking at Kathryn, and with a frightened gasp she scrambled away. "Mom! Hey, Mom, there's someone under the bed!" she screamed, and ran from the room.

Kathryn didn't know whether to stay where she was, or get up to face the music. She decided the latter was more dignified, but as she tried to move, she found she couldn't. Her muscles seemed to have lost all their strength, and no matter how hard she tried, they wouldn't obey her.

The girl returned with everyone else, and the room seemed to be filled with feet. The man knelt down and looked under the bed. He stared directly at Kathryn, but didn't seem to see her, for he straightened a little crossly.

"Aw, come on, Holly, there's no one there!"

"But, there was! I saw her!" the girl wailed.

Then Jack knelt down and looked as well. His gaze went through Kathryn, and then he too straightened. "Reckon it was one of our friendly ghosts, my dear," he said reassuringly to Holly.

The boy gave gasp of interest. "Gee, are there ghosts here?" he asked.

"Oh, yes. I especially recall a little old bright-eyed lady with a shawl and a walking stick. Some say she lived here a long time ago. . . ."

Alice! Jack had seen Alice, Kathryn thought, but as she listened to hear more, she realized his voice was becoming more and more distant. Everything began to slowly revolve, and the light in the bedroom seemed to be slipping away, as if she were falling into a deep, dark well. Fear gripped her, for if this was her final journey into the past, it didn't feel at all right.

She continued her endless fall, spinning and tumbling through a frightening darkness that didn't seem to have any end. Why was it so different this time? Had something gone dreadfully wrong?

Suddenly the terrifying fall ended. There was a sickening jolt and then nothing, just silence, and a cocoonlike impenetrable blackness. Her senses reeled so unpleasantly that for a moment or so it was all she could do not to throw up. But then the dizziness began gradually to recede, and her eyes became accustomed to the darkness.

She smiled, for she was standing in the great hall at Marchwood.

# Twenty-four

~

Kathryn was standing next to the fireplace that was under repair, and could smell soot and disturbed stonework. There was dust beneath her feet as she turned to glance around the hall.

Pale moonlight shone across the table down the center of the floor, picking out the arrangement of flowers and making them seem almost ethereal. Her eyes went to the half-landing, but even on canvas Dane now seemed cold and unapproachable. She wished Alice were with her now, but somehow knew the old woman was still in her cottage in Gloucester.

"You're on your own now, honey," she murmured to herself, and a soft echo picked up the sound. *Honey . . . honey . . . honey . . .*

She shivered. How eery it was. There was no sign of anyone, not even a servant slipping quietly about some late task. The castle was silent as the grave. She bit her lip then, for that wasn't a metaphor she much cared for right now. Drawing herself up sharply, she put such thoughts from her mind. She had things to do, starting with retrieving the wedding ring and then trying to speak to Dane, although whether or not he'd be even remotely prepared to listen remained to be seen.

Gathering her skirts, she picked her way over the dust by the fireplace, and then walked toward the staircase. On the half-landing, she paused to touch the portrait, tracing the outline of the painted lips with her fingertip, but then there was a step at the top of the staircase and she looked swiftly up.

Dane stood there. He'd discarded his coat and neckcloth, and his shirt was undone to the waist. His face was as cold as it had been when last she'd seen him, and as he descended slowly toward her she realized that the glass of cognac in his hand was not his first.

He halted a few steps above the landing, his scornful glance sweeping over her disheveled appearance. "So, my lady chooses to return, but where has she been, that is the question? Such disarray suggests she may have been rolling in the hay. With Denham, no doubt. Or wasn't he to hand? Possibly she settled for a groom, or maybe even some rough laborer. Anyone will do, eh, Rosalind?" The echo picked up his words, so his voice seemed to come at her from all sides.

"Don't say such things, Dane, for they aren't true."

"Very well, I take some of it back. Only Denham will do, that's the truth." As he reached the half-landing, he swirled the cognac and then drank it all.

"Is cognac wise if you're to fight a duel?"

"How tender of you to inquire, but I'm sure your interest is born of the hope that I'll be senseless come dawn."

"If that were so, I wouldn't say anything," she replied. His cold loathing touched her like frost, and his eyes were those of a stranger. She wanted to fling herself before him and beg him to believe in her innocence. Then she wanted to hold out her hand and have him draw her to her feet and into his arms. But she knew he'd only spurn her with even more abhorrence than he showed now. He didn't merely *think* she was unfaithful, he knew it. To him, her guilt was proven beyond all shadow of doubt.

He put the empty glass on top of one of the newel posts. "Why have you come here? I would have thought Denham Hall a more appropriate residence from now on."

"This is my home."

"Is it indeed?" He raised a coldly amused eyebrow. "Well, I'm afraid that is no longer so, madam. You're soiled goods now, and Denham soiled you. There's no place for you here, and I expect you to be gone before morning light. Go to your lover. He can take care of you from now on, provided, that is, he lives long enough to carry out his obligations."

"Please don't ask me to go, Dane."

"I'm not asking, Rosalind, I'm ordering. I can no longer bear the sight of your face, and certainly don't want to endure your close proximity. You made your bed, now you can lie in it."

"Yours is the only bed in which I wish to lie, Dane."

"Ah, the softly seductive voice of the injured wife," he mocked. "Dear God, I marvel at your endless capacity to play the martyr. Well, at least you'll never starve, my dear, for if Denham doesn't want you, I'm sure you'll be welcomed at Drury Lane."

"Do you think I was acting last night? Was it all false when I gave myself to you in the carriage, and then again here? Was I deceiving you when I woke you this morning and we made love again?"

"Yes, madam, I believe you were."

"I'm evidently a truly great actress," she said, holding his gaze.

"There's no doubt of it, madam; indeed, I take my hat off to such dazzling talent." He sketched a derisive bow.

"Please don't be like this, Dane," she whispered, feeling the familiar salt sting of tears.

"You surely don't expect me to be affable?"

"I don't *expect* anything, but I *want* you to believe in me, Dane!" she cried. "I love you, only you! Thomas Denham means nothing to me!"

The echo that had whispered their entire conversation so far, now picked up her raised tone almost eagerly, and flung it wildly around the silent hall, as if laughing at her. Nothing to me . . . ! Nothing to me . . . ! Nothing *to me . . . !*

Dane was unmoved. "I suppose that's why I found you in his arms today?" he replied dryly.

"You found me trying to spurn his advances."

He laughed. "Oh, how foolish of me to misunderstand. So you went into the timber yard with him in order to tell him you didn't wish to be with him? How very credible!"

"It's the truth."

"You've forgotten what truth is, Rosalind, I doubt you'd recognize it even if it stood before you with a label around its neck!"

"I want to stay with you, Dane."

"Well, my dear, I don't want you, so we have an impasse, I think," he said acidly.

The tears shimmered in her eyes now. "Is that what you really wish?" she whispered.

"I'll tell you what I really wish, madam. I wish I was monster enough to deal you the appropriate punishment right now!" Suddenly he strode down the final steps and seized her wrist, twisting it savagely behind her back so her body arched painfully against him.

"You're hurting me!" She tried to writhe away, but his grip was like a vise.

Her throat was pale in the faint light of the moon, and he could see the fullness of her breasts, cupped only by the plunging bodice of her flimsy gown, and he gave a low laugh. "Perhaps I should sample you one last time, my dear. You're mine by right—conjugal right!"

He pulled her down to the floor, still twisting her wrist behind her so she couldn't escape, and only letting go when she was pinned helplessly beneath his weight. Then he looked down into her eyes. "Being on your back suits you, my dear; in fact, I'd go so far as to say it was how you were meant to be."

"Take me like this if you wish, it will make no difference to the truth. I love you now, and I always will. Always!" The spiteful echo mocked her. *Always . . . always . . . always . . .*

"Oh, what an unerring touch you have for the dramatic. A veritable *tragédienne*," he breathed. "Well, let's see how convincing you can remain, let's really test your skills."

He wrenched her flimsy muslin skirts up to her waist, and forced her thighs roughly apart. Then he bent his head to kiss her fiercely on the lips. Whether it was anger or hatred that aroused him she didn't know, she only knew that he was far from impotent at that moment. She felt him undo his breeches and take out the rigid shaft through which the bitterness of betrayal pulsed like a heartbeat, then he kissed her again. It was a harsh kiss, but behind its cruel force she could sense his agony. It was within his power to really hurt her physically, but he didn't. He still penetrated her, though, and watched her face as he did. He took his time, pushing in slowly and sensuously until he seemed to have impaled her soul.

Then he remained motionless inside her, and looked contemptuously into her eyes. "What price Denham now, my sweet? You're my wife, mine to do with as I please, and now it pleases me to reject you, for you're not even worth the effort of rape."

With that he pulled out of her and got to his feet. He smiled mockingly down at her as he did his breeches up again. "I swear this is the last time you and I will share any intimacy, and I pray it is also the last time I ever have to look at you. Be gone from this house within the hour. Everything that is yours will be sent to your new protector."

The cruel echo continued to whisper his last word, as if intent upon taunting her to the very end. *Protector . . . protector . . . protector . . .* It was still swirling around the hall as Dane stepped over her, as if over something in a gutter. Then he went up the staircase without a backward glance.

She lay there with tears streaming down her cheeks. If he'd beaten her, or taken his brutal pleasure to the full, she could have borne it more, but instead he'd humiliated her. Nothing could have shown his loathing more than the way he stepped over her, and nothing could have pierced her heart more than the way he hadn't even glanced back.

She wanted to curl up and hide from the world, but then cold facts swept soberingly over her. She couldn't hide, for this was her existence now, and if she gave in to the misery that engulfed her, she might never find the strength to fight for what she wanted. Slowly she sat up, and pulled her gown over her legs. She wouldn't give in because of this, she *wouldn't!*

Renewed determination flooded through her veins, and she got to her feet. Somehow she'd turn Dane's hatred back into love, and she'd begin by wearing his ring again. Gathering her skirts, she hurried up the staircase.

The silence of the castle seemed to intensify as she opened the drawing room door. Everything was ghostly in the moonlight, and a window had been left slightly open, so the night breeze stirred the curtains and the ivy on the wall as she went to the cabinet. The rustling of the ivy made her shiver, just as it had the day she'd met Jeremiah Pendle in this room. She glanced uneasily toward the open window. What was it about that sound that got to her? It had never bothered her before—in fact, she quite liked the rustle of leaves. She certainly didn't like it now, though.

She put the matter from her mind then, to get the ring. It was on table by the cabinet like Rosalind said, and felt cold as Kathryn slipped it onto her finger. She held her hand out in the moonlight, gazing at the golden band. She'd never take it off again, never. Sir Dane Marchwood was her husband, and she wouldn't rest until she was welcome in his arms once more. However much he tried to banish her now, she wouldn't go voluntarily. If he wanted her to go, he'd have to put her out by force!

She turned to leave, but suddenly heard a stealthy sound coming from outside the window. The ivy was shaking from more than just the night breeze—someone was climbing up it! Now she understood why she'd shivered each time she heard those leaves, it was a premonition of some kind!

Smothering a gasp, she drew into one of the deep window embrasures on the opposite side of the room, and her heart quickened as she peeped around the curtain in time to see a furtive figure clamber over the sill and drop softly into the room.

It was a man, his features concealed by his hat and upturned collar as he went to the cabinet. He was slight and wiry, and his fingers were nimble as he opened the drawers to sift hastily through what lay inside. At last he found what he was searching for—the leather case containing Dane's dueling pistols.

Kathryn's eyes widened as he placed it on a table. Suddenly he glanced around, as if sensing he wasn't alone, but although she immediately pulled back out of sight, she was too late. He saw the slight movement and was upon her in a moment. Her lips parted to scream, but his hand clamped over her mouth. The moonlight shone on his other hand as he raised it to strike her. The blow jerked her head back against the embrasure, and the moonlight began to retreat into an inky impenetrable darkness as she sank to the floor. In the split second before she lost consciousness, she saw a scar on the back of the hand that struck her, but that was all.

He froze as he recognized her face in the pale light. Lady Marchwood! For a moment he thought he'd killed her. A numbing fear immobilized him, and he could only stare at her slumped figure, but then he regained his wits. Crouching, he felt for her pulse, and then exhaled with relief. He straightened again and drew the curtains slightly to hide her from view, then he swiftly returned to the table to open the leather case and take out one of the pistols. It was the one Dane always used, its damaged stock distinctive in the moonlight. Taking a small tool from his pocket, he worked swiftly. Within a minute the gun's magazine was cleverly blocked with a bent nail, although this would not be apparent unless the weapon was examined very closely indeed. His task complete, he replaced the pistol in the case and then took the case back to the cabinet, leaving it exactly as he'd found it. A moment later he climbed silently out of the window again.

Kathryn remained unconscious. She was still there several hours later when the moonlight was replaced by the first faint fingers of Lammas Day dawn on the eastern sky, and the hour of the duel approached.

Dane came to the drawing room for the pistols. He wore a charcoal coat and white breeches, and the gilt spurs on his boots jingled as he moved. There was a sapphire pin on his starched neckcloth, and a bunch of seals swung from his fob. He might have been about to sally forth along Bond Street instead of going to face an opponent in a secluded clearing, but the shadow in his eyes and pallor of his face was evidence not only of a sleepless night, but of the torture of knowing his beloved second wife was as adulterous as the first.

He placed the leather pistol case on the table and opened it to examine the weapons, picking up the one the intruder had interfered with so expertly. He detected nothing wrong as he balanced it in his hand for a moment before replacing it with its fellow. Then he picked up the case and went down to the great hall to await George Eden.

Behind the curtain, Kathryn still did not move. And precious time was now trickling away like sand through an hourglass.

# Twenty-five

It was time to leave for the oak grove, but George Eden still hadn't arrived. Dane's spurs rang softly as he paced restlessly up and down in the great hall, and the white of his shirt was startling in the dawn gloom. George had willingly agreed to be his second, so where was he? He paused by the half-repaired fireplace, impatiently grinding some of the stone dust beneath his boot. God, how he loathed this waiting; it wound his nerves up to an almost unendurable pitch.

The echo, which only seemed to come to life during the quiet hours of darkness and dawn, toyed idly with the sound of his pacing. Then a horse trotted into the courtyard, and he breathed out with relief. George, at last. But then there was silence. He waited a minute or so, but there was nothing. Puzzled, he went out to see. The dawn was cold and misty, and he saw a riderless horse wandering aimlessly by the main gatehouse. He hurried across to it, and the mist swirled and parted in the draft of his passing.

For a moment he feared the horse was George's, but almost immediately discounted the notion. George only bought blood animals, this was a modest hack, and the saddle was too old and well worn to be George's. Nothing but the very best would do for an Eden.

He led the animal to the stables, where lanternlight in one of the stalls told him where he'd find the duty groom. But when he reached the door, he saw the man lying fast asleep on the hay. Leaving the horse in the yard, he went to push the groom with his boot. "Is this how you carry out your duties?" he demanded.

The man leapt to his feet. "Sir Dane!" he gasped.

"Well, certainly not his ghost. Not just yet, anyway."

"Sir." The groom lowered his eyes uncomfortably. The

~~whole castle~~ knew about the duel, and feared the outcome, for whatever the rest of the world thought of Sir Dane Marchwood, he was held in high regard by those who worked for him, because they knew he was a fair and reasonable master. He was strict and expected high standards, but he was never harsh or arbitrary. If he died today at Thomas Denham's hands, he would be greatly mourned.

Dane eyed him now. "I trust it isn't your habit to doze on duty?"

"No, sir! It won't happen again, sir!"

"See that it doesn't."

"Sir."

"Very well. Now, do you know whose mount this is?" Dane led the stray horse forward into the light of the lantern.

The groom looked blankly at it. "No, Sir Dane, I've never seen it before. How did you come by it?"

"It arrived in the courtyard without any sign of a rider. Someone must have taken a fall. See that a search is made of the estate as soon as it's light enough."

"Yes, Sir Dane."

Dane thrust the reins into the groom's hand. "Attend to its welfare in the meantime, and take care not to neglect your duties again."

"Yes, sir."

Dane returned to the great hall, and five minutes later he again heard hooves in the courtyard, this time accompanied by the rattle of wheels. He turned relievedly, thinking that this time it had to be George, but once more he was doomed to disappointment, for it wasn't the doctor who entered the hall, but Alice, whose walking stick abruptly ceased tapping as she saw him, although the echo, which faded with each passing minute now, continued to repeat the sound, as if another Alice Longney were walking invisibly across the hall.

Dane's eyes darkened, and he folded his arms. "Good morning, Mistress Longney."

"Good morning, Sir Dane."

"How bright and early you are, to be sure. Have you come to put a hex on me? So that I conveniently expire and leave the way clear for Denham?"

"No one wishes you dead, Sir Dane."

He glanced cynically away. "Except me, perhaps," he murmured.

"You should not think like that, sir."

"There are many things we should not do, mistress." He looked at her again. "Your arrival must mean that my wife has yet to leave. I trust you've come to take her?"

Alice's eyes lightened with relief. "So she's here?"

"Where else? And still claiming to love me!" He gave a mirthless laugh. "Dear God, how amazing she is. I found her actually in Denham's arms, and still she looks at me with those big green eyes and swears I am the only one she loves."

Alice breathed out gladly. It had worked, and Kathryn was the one who'd returned, for only she would vow undying love for Dane. Until this moment there hadn't been any confirmation, and after a lifetime of the power to see so much, the old nurse wasn't accustomed to being as ordinary a mortal as everyone else.

He held her eyes. "I want her out of here without further delay, is that clear?"

"I don't believe you wish her to go, Sir Dane," she said quietly.

"On the contrary, mistress, I wish her as far away from me as possible."

"But she really does love you, sir."

"Do I look like a fool?" he replied icily.

"No, sir."

"Then pray don't treat me like one. She's made her choice, and that's the end of it. She will cease to be Lady Marchwood as soon as the law can oblige me—always assuming, of course, that I live long enough to commence the necessary proceedings.

"You're wrong to condemn her, sir."

"Well, you would say that, wouldn't you?" he replied acidly. "You don't pull the wool over my eyes, Mistress Longney, for I know you'd go to any lengths for Rosalind. Lying to me has never bothered you in the least. I have no doubt that from the outset you've connived at her affair with Denham."

Alice prudently decided to ignore the last statement. "I'm not lying to you, sir. My lady loves you with all her heart, as I believe you love her."

"Don't presume to comment on my feelings, mistress," he snapped.

She drew back a little. "Forgive me, sir."

He turned away, leaning a hand on part of the fireplace mantel. "May I inquire if you saw anything of Dr. Eden on your way here?"

"Yes, sir, I did. I bring a message from him."

Dane faced her quickly. "Well?"

"He rode past me just as I reached Marchwood, and he was stopped by a man who ran across a field calling to him. It seems the man's wife has just been brought to bed of twins, and when the midwife saw the doctor riding to the village, she said it would be best if mother and babes were properly examined. I gather it had been a difficult accouchement. The doctor asked me to tell you he would not be long, and would meet you at the grove."

Dane nodded. "Very well."

At that moment there was an anxious cry from the top of the staircase. It was Josie, and the clamor of her cries stirred the almost slumbering echo into started wakefulness again. "Sir Dane! Sir Dane! It's her ladyship—"

"What's wrong?" he demanded quickly.

"Sir, I . . . I think she's dead!" Josie hid her face in her hands and dissolved into frightened tears.

Alice's face drained of color. "Oh, Kathryn . . ." she whispered.

Dane's spurs rang as he dashed to the staircase. "Where is she?" he asked sharply as he reached the sobbing maid.

"In . . . in the drawing room, sir. I noticed something yellow peeping beneath the curtain, and when I looked, I . . . I saw it was my lady's gown. There's blood on her head, and . . ."

Dane didn't wait to hear more, but ran toward the drawing room. Behind him, Alice struggled up the stairs as quickly as she could, and Josie waited to help her, then they followed to the drawing room.

Dane knelt by Kathryn. "Oh, dear God . . ." he whispered, putting a hand gently to the trickle of blood oozing through the hair at the back of her head. Then he saw the ugly bruise left by the heavy blow that had sent her reeling so forcibly against the wall. He took her wrist. Please let there be a pulse . . .

He closed his eyes with relief as he felt the telltale flutter of life, then he lifted her in his arms just as Alice and Josie reached the door. He told the maid to hurry ahead to her mistress's apartment, then he looked at Alice, whose already pale face became quite ashen when she saw Kathryn's limp figure.

"Your mistress is still alive," he said.

Relief surged visibly through her. "Oh, sir, I . . ."

"Do you know the man who called Dr. Eden away?" he interrupted.

"No, Sir Dane. Let me see her." Alice went closer and looked swiftly at Kathryn's injuries, then she smiled a little. "No doctor is needed, for I can do all that is necessary. She isn't seriously hurt, sir, and with a little attention will soon be all right again. If you would but carry her to her bed, I can attend her."

"How can you be certain of that?"

"You may trust me where my lady is concerned, Sir Dane. If I say I can attend her, then I can."

He felt oddly reassured. Alice knew what she was doing when it came to such things as this. "Then see you do it well," he warned, before carrying Kathryn to her apartment.

As he laid her carefully on the bed, Alice called Josie out into the passage to tell her what was needed from the kitchens and medicine chest.

Alone with Kathryn for a moment or so, Dane leaned over her. "Oh, Rosalind, my love . . ." he breathed, bending to push a loose curl from her forehead. His fingers lingered on the ugly bruise, and then on the congealing blood staining her hair. "If I find the man who did this to you, I swear I'll have his miserable life," he whispered.

She knew nothing of his touch, or the softly uttered words.

He gazed down at the way her golden hair spilled over the pillow, and then raised her hand to his lips. It was then he realized she wore her wedding ring again. He turned the band slowly on her finger. "Why did you have to be as false as Elizabeth? Why, when I loved you more than I ever loved her? Is perfidy always to be my lot in life?" he murmured. Then he lowered her hand to the bed and turned to walk out, pausing in the doorway to address Alice. "Do whatever is necessary for her."

"I will, Sir Dane. Josie has already gone to bring what is required. You may rest assured that her ladyship will soon recover."

Without another word he strode down to the great hall.

Alice rested her walking stick against the foot of the bed and looked helplessly at Kathryn. "What happened, my dear? Did you see someone with the pistols? Is that it? Oh, if only I were more than just a feeble old woman!" She turned as she heard footsteps in the terraced garden beneath the window, and when she went to look out, she saw Dane's tall figure in the misty Lammas Day dawn.

His spurs were faintly audible as he went down the steps toward the level meadows of the meandering River March. He crossed a little wooden footbridge and then followed a barely discernible path across the meadow. The mist stirred as he passed, making him seem to almost glide away from the castle, and Alice watched until the haze enveloped him. He was going to the thick fringe of woodland just under a quarter of a mile away, where the oak grove lay deep among the trees. It was a very secret place, as was necessary for an occasion as illegal and dangerous as a duel. "The gods be with you, Sir Dane," she murmured.

Then Josie returned with a tray on which stood lavender oil, elderflower ointment, chamomile tea, and an infusion of marigold flowers. She put it down on the table by the bed.

Alice brought a fresh towel from the dressing room, and then went to a tallboy in the corner and took out the little vial of sal volatile that was always kept there. She gave the vial to Josie. "Administer this to my lady while I bathe her injuries. Have a care, now, for it is very strong. Hold it to her for a second, and then take it away. Wait a while, then do it again."

Josie did as she was told, and Alice dipped a corner of the towel in the marigold infusion and began to dab the blood away from Kathryn's hair. She worked gently and efficiently, and soon exposed the ugly graze. Then she smeared some elderflower ointment onto it, applying it with a touch so light it would barely have been felt even by someone conscious. Next she turned her attention to the bruise on Kathryn's face, first soothing it with the marigold water, then dabbing it gently with lavender oil.

When she'd finished, she looked at Kathryn's still face and

closed eyes. "Wake up, little one, for now is not the time to slumber."

But there was no response at all. Alice took the vial from Josie and held it to Kathryn's nose for several seconds. "Sir Dane needs you, my dear. Be strong now, and wake up!"

Kathryn's eyes fluttered. "Dane . . . ?" she whispered.

Alice used the vial again. "Come on, sweeting, you're coming back to us, but you must hasten!" she urged.

The smelling salts made Kathryn's breath catch and she began to cough, but Alice was relentless, continuing to hold the vial in place until at last Kathryn's eyes opened. Only then was the vial set aside. Alice smiled. "You are with us again, my dear."

Kathryn stared up at her. "What happened . . . ? I don't remember anything."

"You were found by the window in the drawing room. Someone struck you, my dear," Alice prompted, supporting her head and holding the chamomile tea to her lips. "Drink this, it will help."

Kathryn sipped the refreshing drink, and gradually remembered what had happened. "I . . . I went to get my wedding ring, and I heard someone climbing up the ivy to the window."

Josie gasped and put her hands to her mouth.

Alice frowned at the maid, and then nodded at Kathryn. "Go on, my dear."

"I hid, and saw a man climb in."

"Did you know him?"

"No, it was too dark, but he wasn't very big—quite small and thin, in fact. His hat was pulled low over his forehead, and his coat collar was turned up. I couldn't see anything to recognize him by. He went to the cabinet and took out the pistol case . . ."

"Yes? Go on, my dear."

"Then he seemed to realize he wasn't alone. He looked right at me and I didn't pull back out of sight quickly enough. He saw me and ran over. I didn't have time to scream before he struck me. I . . . I remember seeing his hand . . ."

"But not his face?"

"No." Kathryn closed her eyes, knowing there was something about the man's hand. Suddenly her eyes flew open again. "There was a scar on his hand, right across the back of it. It was the last thing I saw."

Alice straightened and looked at Josie. "Do you know a man with such a scar?"

"No."

"Nor I." The old woman returned her attention to Kathryn. "Is there anything more you can tell?"

"No." Kathryn struggled to sit up, and immediately felt a sharp stab of pain through her head. She gasped and swayed.

Alice steadied her. "You struck your head when you fell, my dear," she explained. "My elderflower balm will soon soothe the pain."

"Where's Dane?"

"He's gone to the oak grove."

Kathryn stared at her. "I . . . I must go to him now."

"But you're not well enough yet to—"

"You don't understand. I *must* go to him," Kathryn insisted, putting her legs gingerly over the edge of the bed and getting to her feet. Her head thudded with pain, but the dizziness began to recede.

"I'll come with you," Alice said promptly.

"No, I'll go alone." Kathryn took the chamomile tea from the nurse's hand and drank it all.

"But—"

"I'll go alone," Kathryn repeated, but more gently. She put a hand on the old woman's arm and smiled. "You told me to use my intuition, and that's what I'm doing. Earlier today you said you felt something would happen at the duel that would bring Dane and me together. Now I feel it too."

"Are you quite sure, my dear?" Alice asked concernedly. "Because if you aren't, then . . ."

"I'm very sure. I'm not going to give up on him. He's my husband now, and I'm going to fight to win him back."

Kathryn kissed the old woman's cheek, and then she hurried from the room.

# Twenty-six

~

Mist drifted between the trees as Dane entered the woods. He still followed the path, narrow and fern-fringed now, and droplets of moisture fell on his dark coat as he brushed past some wild clematis. Birdsong throbbed through the air, and the luminosity in the eastern sky heralded another beautiful day.

The path was marked by the fresh hoofprints of a single horse, and he smiled for it meant George Eden was waiting for him at the grove. Denham and Pendle would come in the banker's two-horse curricle, which couldn't use this route, and any gamekeeper or local poacher would be on foot.

A meander of the river barred the way ahead, and the shallow water was crossed by stepping stones. On the other side, the path continued for a hundred yards through a thick cloak of trees to the oak grove. At the water's edge he noticed how the hitherto steady trail of hoof marks suddenly became a confusion of prints. The horse had clearly resisted when asked to enter the water. Dane smiled again, for now he was certain the trail belonged to George, whose favorite saddle horse was always the very devil when it came to water.

Pausing on the riverbank, he looked up at the increasing radiance beyond the haze. Would he outlive the mist and see the morning sun break through? Or was he taking one risk too many today? He'd already faced three opponents and walked away the victor, could he really expect fortune to favor him a fourth time?

He closed his eyes for a moment, thinking of the woman who'd brought him to this. Rosalind. He should despise her very name, but couldn't. She'd been cold and contrary, but over the past few days she seemed to have changed. He still couldn't help comparing her conduct to that of twins; outwardly identical, but inwardly very different. The old Rosalind had always seemed just beyond his reach, a dream that was never fully realized. The new Rosalind seemed perfection itself. She was his other half, and he'd love her forever, even though, like Elizabeth before her, he now knew she'd betrayed him with another Denham.

He looked down at the water flowing so clearly past his feet. To have loved unwisely once had been a crushing blow, but to have done so twice was a desolating experience. After Elizabeth, he'd sworn to never give his heart again; Rosalind was the price of that broken vow. No, this dawn confrontation was the price of that broken vow ...

He was about to step onto the first stone, when he heard something that made him turn. Beyond the noise of the birds, he was sure he heard a groan. He glanced around, wondering if he'd imagined it, then he looked sharply at the confused hoofprints. Had George's damned horse done more than just balk? Had it bolted and thrown him?

"George?" he called, but there was no response. He called again, and this time was startled as a buck hare bolted from the undergrowth about six feet from where he stood. It bounded away over the ferns and vanished in the mist, which continued to thread eerily between the trees. The cacophany of birdsong threatened to split the air, but there was no repetition of the other sound he'd heard—if sound there'd been.

He was about to call again, just to be certain he was mistaken, when a familiar red-headed figure called from the path the other side of the river. "Where in God's name have you been, Dane?"

It was George. Dane grinned with relief. "Am I glad to see you!"

"And am I glad to see you," George replied. "We've been waiting for some time now."

Dane crossed the stepping stones. "There was a slight, er, problem at the castle."

George looked intently at him. "As your second, it's my duty to try to—"

"Talk me out of this?" Dane finished for him.

"Something of the sort."

"You'll be wasting your breath." Dane pushed the pistol case into George's hands. "Let's get on with it."

"I'm so sorry this has happened, Dane," George said, falling into step beside him as they walked the final yards to the grove.

"Not as sorry as I am," Dane murmured.

"I'd have taken odds that Rosalind was a faithful wife. I talked to her at the ball, and she seemed, well . . ."

"Loving and sincere?" Dane supplied dryly.

"Yes, but at the same time . . ."

"What?" Dane looked at him.

"Well, there was clearly something bothering her, although she insisted there wasn't. I told her that if she wished to confide, I was there for her."

"Confide in my closest friend about her adulterous affair? I think not."

"Possibly. Anyway, she still convinced me it was you and only you that she loved. And when I watched the way you and she danced that damned waltz—well, it was positively indecent!"

Dane glanced away again. "I fear it's just a measure of her deceit. And her undoubted brilliance as an actress."

They reached the oak grove. The mist was thinning all the time now, and the air brightened with each minute. George's mount was tethered to a bush at the far side of the clearing, with his doctor's bag fixed over its saddle. Jeremiah Pendle's curricle stood beneath the wide-spreading trees nearby, and he and Thomas were talking by the offside horse. They walked to the center of the grove as George and Dane appeared.

George put a hand on Dane's arm. "Is an adulterous wife worth it?"

"No, but my pride is. No man puts horns on me and escapes retribution."

"But what if retribution should strike *you* down this time? For God's sake, draw back from the brink, Dane."

"And be branded a coward as well as a cuckold? No."

"Would it matter what was said? The truth would be different."

Dane didn't answer, but walked to join Pendle and Thomas, and after a moment George followed him.

Thomas was very pale and strained, and his chin bore signs

of the fight he and Dane had had at the docks. He wore a maroon coat and light gray breeches, and his neckcloth had been tied rather haphazardly. Pendle, on the other hand, looked almost sleekly relaxed in a russet coat and fawn breeches. The red-spotted handkerchief was tucked neatly into his pocket, and his neckcloth was fussily complicated, as if he'd dressed for a special social function, rather than a secluded meeting at dawn.

George looked at the banker. "As Sir Dane's second, I have to report there is to be no withdrawal from this."

Pendle gave a grim smile. "And as Mr. Denham's second, I report the same."

Dane shrugged. "So be it. Let the duel proceed," he said tersely.

Kathryn's heart was pounding as she ran along the path toward the stepping stones. And, just like Dane, she paused at the water's edge. It wasn't because she noticed the sudden confusion of hoofprints, or because she heard anything untoward, but because she had the strangest feeling of being close to something of vital importance.

Her hand crept to her throat as she glanced slowly around, taking in the river, the ferns, and the misty woods. She saw the hoof marks on the bank, but, unlike Dane, she also saw another trail of them leading sharply away from the water into the woods. Some ferns were broken where the horse had passed, and then there was just the vapor writhing softly between the trees. She looked across the river in the direction of the grove, but then at broken ferns again. Trust her intuition, Alice had said. Okay, her intuition told her to follow the trail into the trees.

The birdsong was almost deafening, and the smell of crushed ferns pricked her nostrils as she went cautiously into the gloom. She'd only gone a few yards when the hairs at the nape of her neck stirred. There was someone close by! Her pulse quickened and she turned sharply, expecting to see a figure draw back behind a tree, but there was no one. The feeling remained, though—indeed, it increased. Someone was definitely there!

"Who's there?" she called nervously, but her voice was inaudible above the clamor of the birds.

Disquieted, she began to back toward the path once more, but again something compelled her to stop. She shivered, her uneasy gaze raking the trees. There still didn't seem to be anything there, but a sixth sense told her there was.

Suddenly she heard a low sound, only just detectable beneath the stridency of the dawn chorus. It was a groan. Yes, she was certain of it. Someone was hurt! But where was he? The groan could have come from almost any direction, except from the path.

"Can you hear me?" she called, but although she strained to hear any response, there was nothing. She began to search, and at last held some particularly dense ferns aside and found herself staring down into the dull, pain-filled eyes of a fatally injured man. It was Frederick Talbot, the unfortunate gunsmith she'd seen being threatened by Jeremiah Pendle at the docks.

In the oak grove, George opened the case of pistols for the duelists to select their weapons.

The handguns gleamed in the luminous dawn light, and Dane looked at Thomas. "I leave the choice to you, Denham, but since I have no desire to be accused of taking an unfair advantage by using a favorite weapon, I suggest you eliminate any chance of such a benefit by taking my pistol yourself."

Pendle stepped hastily forward. "But the advantage would still be with you, Sir Dane," he said quickly.

"Meaning?"

"That the pistol you've used before is probably unbalanced because of the damage to its stock, and although you are accustomed to it, my nephew is not. It would be detrimental to his aim."

"I assure you neither gun is unbalanced. Test them yourself if you wish," Dane offered.

But Thomas prevented further discussion by reaching out to Dane's pistol. "I prefer to rob you of any benefit, Marchwood," he said tersely.

Pendle put a swift hand over his. "No, Thomas, take the other," he urged.

"Have done with it, Uncle." Thomas took the pistol with the damaged stock, and turned away.

"Thomas—"

"The choice is made," Thomas replied.

Pendle stared at him, and then swallowed, returning his attention to Dane. "I suspect you of some sleight of hand, Marchwood!" he accused.

"No sleight of hand, I assure you," Dane replied.

"You made certain of my nephew's choice!"

George cleared his throat uncomfortably. "Come now, that's hardly how it happened, and you know it," he said to the banker.

"I don't know anything, except that your principal deliberately steered mine to the selection of one pistol in particular."

George looked at Thomas. "Are you satisfied with your weapon, sir?"

"Perfectly."

"You have no desire to change?"

"None."

George turned to the banker. "The matter is closed, I think," he said firmly.

"I wish to register my strong objection," Pendle said.

"As you wish, but the decision doesn't lie with you." George nodded at Dane and Thomas. "Very well, gentlemen, if you're ready, please remove your coats, and then take up your positions."

A few moments later they stood back to back, their pistols safely lowered.

"Twelve paces, if you please."

# Twenty-seven

~

In the woods just over a hundred yards away from the duel in the grove, Kathryn tried to think what to do for the dying gunsmith. Her first urge was to run for help, but Talbot's claw-like hand closed convulsively over her wrist.

"No, my lady, I'm done for," he breathed. "My horse took fright at the river and bolted. When I fell I broke my back, I know it as surely as if a doctor told me. I didn't know it was you that I struck; I panicked when I realized someone was there."

*Talbot* was the intruder? She glanced down at the hand that gripped her wrist, and saw the scar she'd glimpsed in the seconds before she'd lost consciousness. Of course! Who better to tinker with a pistol than a gunsmith! But why would he do it? What possible reason could he have? The questions remained unasked as she looked at his ghastly face and knew his life was draining away. "Look, Doctor Eden is only a short distance away in the grove . . ." she began.

He shook his head. "My time's up, my lady, and I don't deserve your help or kindness, for I've carried out the devil's work."

"The devil's work?"

"I've done great wrong to save myself from debtor's jail. My sins have caught up with me now, eh?" He coughed a little, and blood trickled from the corner of his mouth.

"Please let me go for the doctor," she begged.

"It will do no good. I'm a goner." His fingers tightened. "He wanted Sir Dane dead, and, if it came to it, for you to take the blame. Oh, he's clever, and no mistake. He knows how people think."

"Who are you talking about?"

"Why, Jeremiah Pendle, of course. Do this for me, he said, and I'll forget your debts. Refuse, and I'll see you in jail. So I did it. I had to. Now Sir Dane's lucky pistol isn't lucky anymore, and if it's found out, Pendle will see you're the one they'll blame. The unfaithful wife who wants to be free of her husband. That's what they'll say, he'll make sure of it."

She stared down at him. That was what was *supposed* to happen, but it didn't, for Dane wasn't the one who died. . . .

As the two duelists walked their twelve paces, George and Pendle removed to safety at the edge of the clearing. The banker's nerves showed now. He took out his handkerchief and began mopping the perspiration that appeared on his brow. His face had taken on a sickly pallor and his tongue passed nervously over his lips.

He looked at George. "This is badly done, Eden. Marchwood has somehow achieved an unreasonable advantage, I know he has!"

"If you continue in this vein, sir, I might construe it as an attempt to manipulate things in favor of your nephew!"

"Never!"

"Then hold your tongue!"

The banker fell silent, and George returned his attention to the men in the grove. "Turn and cock your pistols, gentlemen," he called.

The clicking sounds carried clearly above the birdsong which still echoed over the woods.

"Take your aim, sirs."

Pendle leaned weakly back against an oak trunk and closed his eyes.

"Fire!"

Both men squeezed the trigger, but only one shot rang out, silencing the birds.

As the report echoed through the woods, Kathryn straightened with a dismayed gasp. It had happened! Thomas Denham had been killed. She glanced down at Talbot, but his lifeless eyes stared back. He was as dead as he'd intended Dane to be, and with him had died any proof of Jeremiah Pendle's guilt. All she had was her word that Talbot had ever confessed to anything. She had no evidence that Dane was the real target, or that she was meant to take the blame. There was nothing to prevent history from damning Dane for everything.

Slowly she backed away toward the path, then she gathered her skirts to step across the stones to go to the grove. Even now she couldn't finally accept that there was nothing she could do to alter the course of things.

Blood welled over the front of Thomas's shirt, and his face had a look of puzzlement as he desperately squeezed the trigger of his pistol several times more, all without effect. The bloodstain spread, and his sudden pallor was dreadful to see. He sank slowly to his knees, staring accusingly at Dane.

George was rooted to the spot, but Pendle lumbered distractedly to his fallen nephew. "Thomas! Oh, Thomas, my boy!" he sobbed.

Dane ran to his stricken opponent as well, but his steps faltered as Thomas's dying words damned him. "My uncle was right! You arranged this, Marchwood . . ."

"Denham, I swear . . ."

"I curse you, Marchwood. May you burn in hell." Thomas's eyes closed and the pistol slipped from his fingers.

Pendle gave a terrible cry, and there were tears on his cheeks as he gathered the dead man in his arms. Dane gazed numbly at them, and then hurled his pistol away as far as he could.

George found his wits at last and ran to get his doctor's bag, before hastening to see if Thomas was really beyond all help, although in his heart he knew by the size of the bloodstain and the swiftness with which it spread, that Thomas Denham was no more. He searched for a pulse, but found none, and slowly he straightened.

"He's gone," he said quietly.

Pendle looked savagely up at Dane. "Murderer!" he breathed.

Kathryn reached the edge of the clearing, but although she parted her lips to cry out that *he* was the murderer, not Dane, her voice wouldn't obey. She couldn't even enter the grove! A concealed barrier barred the way, and she herself seemed to have become invisible. She could only stand on the outside, like a ghostly stranger peering in through a window.

She gazed at Thomas's body on the damp grass. Somehow she couldn't think of him as dead, not knowing what she did. To her he was still alive, albeit in the future. He was Richard Vansomeren, and soon he and the real Rosalind would be together happily ever after. Happily ever after, like all the best fairy tales. But could the same ever apply to their former partners here in the past? She returned her attention to the others in the clearing. Maybe she couldn't say or do anything, but at least the quieting of the birds meant she could hear what was being said.

George was uncomfortable. "You can't accuse anyone of murder, Pendle. Accidents happen, and there's always the chance that a weapon will jam. It was a fair duel."

"Was it? Marchwood foisted that pistol on Thomas! Do you honestly believe its failure was an accident? Examine it, I say!" He grabbed the weapon and thrust it toward George, who took it reluctantly.

There was nothing for it but to do as the banker insisted. Giving Dane an apologetic look, George uncocked the pistol and looked closely at it, then his brows drew together and he bent to search in his bag for something slender enough to poke into the mechanism. He found what he needed, and began to prod the internal workings of the pistol. After a while the cleverly bent nail fell into the grass. George picked it up reluctantly.

Dane stared at the nail. "I—I don't understand . . ."

Pendle scrambled to his feet. "You understand, all right! You fiend, Marchwood! You tampered with the pistol and made sure my nephew used it! You murdered him!"

Kathryn could have wept with frustration as she tried again to go into the grove, but there was nothing she could do; the barrier was complete. Oh, how she despised Pendle! How dared he accuse Dane, when all the time it was *his* actions that had robed Thomas of any means of defense!

Dane still gazed at the nail, but now raised his eyes to Pendle's anguished face. "I swear I didn't interfere with the pistol, Pendle. You have my word I knew nothing of any nail."

"Next you'll claim to have insufficient experience to know exactly how to bend and place such a nail! But who better than Sir Dane Marchwood, eh? He of the valorous exploits on the battlefield, and the three duels at dawn! Oh, you know what to do, all right!" The banker's voice had risen hysterically.

Dane strove to remain calm. "I'm innocent of this, Pendle."

"Liar!" screamed the other, and raised a frenzied hand to strike him, but George caught his wrist.

"No! Don't be a fool, man!"

"He murdered Thomas!" Pendle cried, his voice catching on a sob, but he lowered his hand. Discretion was always the better part of physical valor where he was concerned. Instead, he made another verbal attack, but more levelly now. "Four duels now, Marchwood, and no doubt all won by foul means!"

"My previous opponents all fired back, I assure you," Dane replied coldly. "Pendle, I concede you have reason to despise me, for this is the second nephew I've eliminated, but this is the one and only time anything like this has happened. I didn't do anything to the pistol, and it was pure chance that I said what I did about not wanting any unfair advantage. If the weapon was interfered with, as it clearly was, then I believe *I* was the intended victim, not your nephew."

Kathryn's breath caught eagerly. Yes, Dane! And if anyone was to get the blame for your death, it was me! But the one who really did it all is facing you now! Can't you see the guilt on his face? In his spiteful eyes and mean lips?

But Dane didn't pursue the point, because at that moment something happened that brought the conversation to a sudden halt. Pendle gave a cry of pain and clasped his left arm to his chest. His face contorted with agony, and he pitched forward onto the grass, where he lay gasping for breath.

George knelt by him. "Damn it, man, how long have I been warning you about your heart?" he said, loosening the banker's clothes and in particular his neckcloth. He glanced up at Dane. "There's a clear glass bottle in the corner of my bag, can you get it out for me?"

Dane obeyed, and George held the bottle to the banker's lips. "Take this, it's a herb infusion and will help to calm you. Steady now, just a sip at a time."

Pendle did as he was told, and gradually his color came back. George returned the bottle to Dane, and then fixed the banker with a reproving look. "It's as well for you I took the precaution of bringing that bottle today. I had a notion you'd become overwrought for one reason or another. Look, man, you can't go on like this. You eat too much, drink too much, take too little exercise, and you're the most choleric fellow it's ever been my misfortune to meet. If you don't do something about all four, you're not long for this world. Do I make myself clear?"

"Perfectly, doctor," Pendle replied, wiping his face with his handkerchief. "I'm all right now, it was merely a spasm brought on by grief."

At the edge of the grove, Kathryn took a grim satisfaction from knowing the banker wouldn't live another day. She hoped he died in agony, for that was what he richly deserved. But dead or not, he'd still be able to do irreparable harm to Dane's honor. That wretched diary and all its lies would lay false witness about this dawn confrontation, and even though she knew the truth, there didn't seem to be anything she could do about it.

George helped Pendle to his feet, but the banker shook him away. "Keep your advice and assistance, Eden, for it's clear the only person whose well-being interests you is Marchwood. I suppose you'll contradict anything I say regarding this infamous event?"

George didn't reply, and Dane looked sagely at his friend. "You can't defend me, can you, George?" he said quietly. "You can't, because you aren't sure, nor can you ever be. The pistols are mine, I brought them here, and gave them to you. I then steered Denham, albeit innocently, to the pistol that wouldn't fire, and I made certain of his death by aiming very accurately indeed. I admit to the latter, for it was my intention to kill him, but I didn't murder him. At the moment I fired, I fully expected him to fire back. That is all I can say."

Pendle's sharp eyes remained on the doctor. "Well, sir? I await your comments."

"I cannot and will not say that Sir Dane interfered with the pistol," George said after a moment.

Pendle gave a disgusted snort. "So much for upright, honorable George Eden! But can you say with equal conviction that he *didn't* interfere with the weapon?"

"No, of course I can't, for there's no proof either way," George replied uncomfortably, giving Dane another apologetic glance.

His discomfort offered hope to the banker, who pushed his

face close to Dane's. "Damned by your own second, sir! He cannot say anything one way or the other, but I can! I'm sure of my facts where you're concerned, Sir Dane Fancy Marchwood, and I'm not going to let you get away with murdering two of my kinsmen. I'm going to lay charges against you!"

Kathryn had to turn away from the banker's venomous hatred. You aren't going to be able to bring anything to trial, you maggot! The Grim Reaper's sharpening his scythe for you right now!

George couldn't hide his distaste for Pendle either. "If you take this to court, you'd better be prepared for the worst," he said quietly.

"What do you mean?" the banker demanded.

"I'd have to point out to judge and jury that you are biased against Sir Dane, that you came here today already hating him because of William Denham's death ten years ago, and that your anxiety over the choice of weapons was quite extraordinary, almost as if you knew what had been done to one of them. That might point a few unwelcome fingers at you, sir, for it is not unreasonable for Sir Dane to say that he might have been the intended victim, not Thomas." George held the banker's eyes.

Kathryn was exultant. Go for it, George! You're on the right trail!

Pendle's clever little eyes were sharp. "What's this, Eden? Are you suggesting that *I* was the one who—?"

"I'm not suggesting anything, I'm merely drawing your attention to how things might go at a trial. You had as much motive as anyone to tamper with the pistol, and if you did, it would certainly explain your dismay when Thomas took the wrong gun."

Pendle's unpleasant little eyes narrowed still more. "A neat plot, Eden, I take my hat off to you, but it won't work. Marchwood did it and I won't rest until I've proved it. He should swing for this day's work, and if you refuse to stand up for justice, I'll do all I can on my own. Thomas's death isn't going to be in vain, on that you have my word.'

George met his gaze. "I've said all I'm going to say. Take this to court, and I'll say my piece. On your head be it."

A nerve flickered at the banker's temple, and for a moment he couldn't trust himself to speak, but then he gained control again. "Well, physician, at least show some honor now by assisting me with my nephew's body. I can't carry him to the curricle on my own, and must take him back to Denham Hall."

"Of course."

Dane stepped quickly forward. "Let me help. You can't lift him, Pendle, not with your heart in such—"

"Don't lay your evil hand upon me or my nephew," the banker breathed.

Dane remained where he was as they lifted Thomas from the damp grass and carried him across the grove. Two minutes later the curricle drove out of the grove and vanished into what remained of the dawn mist.

# Twenty-eight

~

Kathryn hoped that with the banker gone, she'd at least be able to enter the grove. Surely events were complete now! But still she couldn't move from her place. There was nothing she could do except continue to watch from the perimeter.

As George returned to pick up his bag, Dane spoke. "What do you really think? Do you secretly wonder if I'm guilty?"

"You surely don't need to ask? I know you to be innocent, but I'd put money on Pendle's guilt."

Kathryn could have kissed the little doctor.

George drew a long breath. "I don't profess to know how he got at the pistols, but I'm sure he did. He came here today certain that you would take the disabled gun, and thus die at Thomas's hand."

"But if mine was the pistol that misfired and the nail was then discovered, surely that would point the finger of suspicion at Thomas Denham?" Dane observed in puzzlement.

Kathryn clenched her fists frustratedly. No, not at Thomas, at *me!* Pendle was going to see to it!

George thought for a moment, and then his eyes cleared. "Would it? There's someone else who might be construed as having good reason to wish you dead."

"Someone else?" Dane stared, then his lips parted. "Rosalind? Is that what you're suggesting?"

"It's not what I'm suggesting at all, but it's what I believe *Pendle* would have suggested if the pistol were examined. When I received your message requesting my services today, and informing me he was Denham's second, I naturally went to see him. He made his opinion of Rosalind very clear indeed. He blamed her for leading his saintly nephew astray. Thomas

Denham, like his brother William before him, was as pure as the driven snow."

"William Denham was far from pure," Dane replied with feeling.

"I believe you, for you wouldn't have called him out without good reason. Anyway, let's consider how events might have unfolded if you had died and Thomas emerged victorious. Pendle would know that the trickery with the nail might not be discovered at all. It's hardly unknown for a handgun to fail, and in this case it was a gun that had already been damaged in the past. So Thomas probably wouldn't question its failure, and Pendle certainly wouldn't. Which would only leave me, and if I discovered the nail, Pendle would instantly prevent any accusation of Thomas by accusing Rosalind instead. He's no fool. Who better than an adulterous wife to want her husband dead? Yes, the more I think of it, the more sure I become. Pendle had it all worked out, but things went gravely wrong. His plan misfired, literally. He didn't reckon on the disabled pistol going to the wrong man, and then he was too craven to save his nephew's life by admitting the truth. Oh, he tried after a fashion, but when it came to it, he let Thomas go to his death. So much for his much-vaunted family loyalty! Now he has to make what capital he can from the situation. His purpose was to destroy you and save Thomas, and even now, with Thomas dead instead, he sees an opportunity to still do you harm."

Dane gave him an admiring smile. "You missed your vocation, George. You have a superb analytical mind, and would have made an excellent barrister."

"As it happens, the law was my first choice, but my father had other notions. Anyway, to return to the matter in hand—the way things have gone today, the facts are very damning for you, but they're equally damning for Pendle. I've warned him what I would be prepared to say at a trial, and when he calms down a little I think he'll see the wisdom of letting the whole thing drop. That's by far the best outcome. Apart from anything else, we all four committed a crime when we met here this morning. I believe he'll realize the hazard of making too much noise. If he lays charges against you, he not only has to admit taking part in a duel, he also runs the risk of being charged himself."

Dane smiled a little. "I hope you're right."

"So do I." George smiled and put a comforting hand on Dane's arm. "As for Denham, don't shed tears on his account. He issued the challenge, and came here knowing one or the other of you, possibly even both, would die." He paused. "Dane, would you take offense if I leave now? I've neglected my duties in order to be here this morning, and really should return to Gloucester to attend my patients."

"Of course I won't take offense, but actually, there's something I'd like you to do first. Another patient, if you like. It's Rosalind." Dane explained briefly what had happened to her.

At first George was concerned, but then smiled when he learned Alice was looking after her. "My dear fellow, if that old witch reassured you all is well, you may take her word for it. Damn it all, Alice Longney probably knows more than I do!"

"I admit to being relieved she was there."

George searched his face. "While you're about it, why don't you also admit you're still in love with Rosalind?" he asked quietly.

Dane said nothing, but George pressed him.

"Damn it, Dane, it's as clear as crystal to me. No matter what she may or may not have done, you can't stop loving her, can you?"

"Very well, I admit it, but it's something that's to remain strictly between you and me," Dane replied at last.

Kathryn closed her eyes. He *did* still love her! There was hope!

George raised an eyebrow. "No word of it will pass my lips, but there's just one thing."

"And that is?"

George looked toward the spot where Thomas died. "Are you sure beyond all shadow of doubt that she and Denham were lovers?"

"Quite sure."

"Since trials have been threatened these past minutes, perhaps a legal comparison might be appropriate. Could you swear in court that your wife was Denham's mistress?"

Dane glanced at him. "Well, short of having caught them actually in the act . . ."

"What *did* you catch them in, Dane?"

"A loving embrace."

"Was it?"

"Yes."

George raised his doctor's bag. "If this bag were a Bible, could you put your hand on it and say on oath that what you saw was a loving embrace?"

Dane looked at the bag, and then at his friend. "I *believe* it was a loving embrace, but she claimed she was trying to get away from him," he conceded.

"Which means she has a different version of what happened. Dane, you owe it to her and to yourself to hear what she has to say."

"I hardly think it's fitting now, do you? Denham's dead, and no matter what, mine was the shot that killed him. It's a little late to ask her for explanations."

"It's never too late."

Dane drew a long breath and looked away. George studied him curiously. "What aren't you telling me?"

"Nothing."

"I don't accept that; I know you too well."

Dane smiled. "Very well. It's foolish, I know, but in the last few days I've almost felt as if . . ."

"Yes?"

"As if Rosalind were two women in one. Twins, with disparate natures, one passionate and truly in love with me, the other cooler, and in love with Denham. Do you understand what I mean?"

George shook his head in bewilderment. "No, dear boy, I don't. I suggest you ask her." He glanced up at the sky as the sun broke through at last. "A fine Lammas Day, I believe," he murmured.

"Lammas Day? Is it?"

George smiled. "Yes, and as such an ideal day for new beginnings. The first corn is cut today, and I believe you should begin cutting back the weeds that spoil your life right now. Well, I'm off then. If you need me, you know where I am, for the time being at least. I've decided definitely to go to America. It's an opportunity too good to miss."

Dane watched him cross the grove to attach his bag to the saddle once more, and then mount. Waving once, George turned the horse and rode away.

It was as he disappeared beyond the trees that the invisible wall between Kathryn and the grove seemed to crumble away too. Suddenly she could step toward Dane and call his name.

He whirled about, and their eyes met. For a long moment he remained where he was, and then he began to walk toward her. Hope surged pitifully through her, but it withered wretchedly away as he walked past without a word.

# Twenty-nine

~

The agony of despair still keened through Kathryn as she hurried after him. "Dane, please let me explain!"

"I want nothing more to do with you," he replied abruptly as he continued swiftly along the path toward the stepping stones.

"You *must* talk to me, Dane!"

"Why?" He paused at the water's edge. "How long had you been at the clearing? Did you calmly observe throughout the confrontation?"

"I . . . I got there just after the shot was fired," was what she said, but she wanted to say she'd been there long enough to hear him admit he loved her.

"And now, I suppose, you wish to add your accusations to Pendle's. Your lover lies dead, murdered because I cravenly feared to face him on equal terms! Well, I salute you, madam, for your infidelity has not only achieved your lover's demise, but my disgrace as well." He sketched an insulting bow, and then crossed the river.

She hurried after him again, almost losing her balance on the stones. "I haven't made sure of anything, Dane, and far from accusing you, I know you to be innocent!"

He halted at a point that was barely ten yards from Frederick Talbot's body. "So you think me innocent? Well, I suppose that's to be expected. After all, with Denham gone, you have to think of yourself, don't you, and it's clearly preferable to endure life here with me than face what might await you if I throw you out."

"I know you're innocent, Dane," she said again.

"And I know you to be guilty, madam, so pray obey my order of last night. I want you off my land, and out of my life!"

He walked on again, and she cried desperately after him. "Jeremiah Pendle coerced Frederick Talbot, the Gloucester gunsmith, into fixing the pistol so it wouldn't fire!"

He turned swiftly. "Talbot?"

"Yes. He was the one who attacked me last night. I was in the drawing room when I saw him climb in through the window. He took the pistol case from the cabinet, but then realized I was there. He panicked and struck me, then he did what he'd come to do, replaced the case in the drawer, and left the way he came. He rode away in this direction, but his mount took fright by the stepping stones and bolted into the woods."

The stray horse at the castle! He glanced along the path toward the river, remembering the hoofprints he'd noticed earlier, and the groan he thought he'd heard. Recalling the latter, he looked sharply at her. "How do you know this?"

"Because Talbot's body is just over there." She pointed into the trees. "He was dying when I found him, and he told me Pendle threatened to put him in jail for debt unless he did as the banker wanted."

"Show me where he is," Dane ordered.

Reluctantly she obeyed, stepping into the gloom of the woods and leading him to the gunsmith's resting place among the crushed ferns. Dane bent swiftly to test for a pulse, but the moment he touched the already cool skin, he knew Frederick Talbot was indeed dead.

Kathryn looked down at the corpse. "He died at almost the same second as Thomas. I heard the shot and stood up, and when I glanced down again, he was dead. I wanted to tell you what I'd learned, so I ran to the grove."

"Intending to clear my name, no doubt," Dane said dryly. He straightened and began to walk back to the path. "I'll have some men come to take him back to Gloucester."

She followed him. "I'm telling the truth, Dane. I *did* come to the grove to tell you what Talbot told me!"

He replied without turning his head. "It's barely a hundred yards from here to the grove, madam, and on your own admission you went there directly you heard the shot. Why, if you knew Talbot and Pendle to be the culprits, did you say nothing in my defense when you arrived? You must have heard every word that damned banker said, but you held your tongue."

She stopped hurrying after him, for the truth was too preposterous. How could she possibly tell him she'd been kept out by some invisible force?

He turned. "You should have thought your lies through a little more carefully, my dear. All you had to say was that you arrived at the clearing the very second you spoke to me, and I might conceivably have credited you with telling a grain of truth, but as it is you admit to having been at the clearing for at least a quarter of an hour before saying anything. Hardly plausible, eh?"

"Dane, I—"

"Just go, Rosalind, before I begin to wonder exactly what your part has been in all this."

"I haven't done anything, Dane."

"No? It seems to me that Pendle's observations about you might have more than a grain of truth. You did indeed have as much reason as he did for wanting me dead, and even if Talbot's was the hand that actually did the deed, you are as capable as Pendle of hiring him."

"I didn't hire him, Dane, nor do I have any motive at all for wishing you dead. I love you, and that is the truth."

"The truth? Deceit is more than just second nature to you, it *is* second nature, and I rue the day I ever set eyes on you, let alone fell in love with you. The two years of our marriage have been the most miserable of my life, more miserable even then the wretchedness I endured after Elizabeth's infidelity, and the last thing I intend to allow now is more of your particularly persuasive brand of lying." He turned to walk on again.

Once more she hurried after him. The wild clematis caught in her hair, and scattered dew over her face, but she hardly noticed. "Maybe most of our marriage has been unhappy, Dane, but can you honestly say that of the past few days?"

Suddenly he whirled about, catching her wrist and forcing her roughly back against a tree trunk. Then he pinned her there, his face only inches from hers. "You know damned well I can't say it of the past few days, and you know it because you listened to everything George and I said! Damn you, Rosalind, what manner of creature are you? A Lorelei? Yes, that must be it, for who but a siren could behave as you do? You lured me with your beauty and sweetly lying voice, and I, poor fool, believed in you." He took her chin roughly between his fingers, ignoring the tears that sprang to her eyes. "I'm still tempted to deal you the punishment you deserve, my lovely. Who would really blame me if I took you here and now? Whore or not, you're still my wife!"

"I'm your wife, but not a whore," she replied, her breath catching with pain as his fingers tightened cruelly.

"Agreed, for one must pay a whore, and you, my darling, give your favors freely!" He thrust her aside and she fell in the long grass beside the path. He stood over her. "I'll find out the truth where Pendle's concerned, of that you may be certain, and if he did indeed put Talbot up to it—"

"There's nothing you can do, nothing either of us can do. Posterity is going to discredit you for having interfered with Thomas's pistol in order to win the duel, and that is the end of it." As the words came out, she felt something almost akin to a jolt that she'd actually been able to say them. She'd just told him something that was *going* to happen!

He didn't seem to realize the significance of her words. "If you imagine I'm going to leave it like this, you're gravely mistaken!" He strode away along the path, toward the edge of the woods and the sunlit meadows beyond.

Suddenly she knew she would now be able to tell him everything. Nothing but the whole fantastic truth would do now. Telling him wouldn't be an attempt to alter history, nor would it interfere with the sequence of recorded events, but it might make every difference to the way he saw her. Maybe he'd think she was completely mad, but maybe, just maybe, he'd believe her. Was this what Alice's fading intuition had predicted? Was this how the yearned for reunion could be achieved?

Sitting up, she called after him. "You likened me to a siren, but do you remember their story?"

He turned with a derisive laugh. "What's this? A lesson in Greek mythology? Yes, madam, I do remember the story."

"So, you recall they were twin sisters, one of whom fell to her death because Odysseus could resist her song?"

"That's one version, yes."

"I will suffer her fate if you resist me now, Dane."

"Oh, come now, isn't that a little melodramatic, even for you? I know you have talent enough for Drury Lane, but you don't have to demonstrate as much to me." His tone mocked.

"I'm not pretending, nor am I being melodramatic. It's how I really feel. Dane, you were right when you said you felt there were twin Rosalinds, one in love with Thomas Denham, the other in love with you."

Slowly he retraced his steps, and stood over her again. "Well?"

"I know you think ill of me for not saying anything all those minutes I was at the grove, but I couldn't say anything. I didn't have any choice."

"A silent siren? A contradiction in terms, surely?" he observed acidly.

"I have a story to tell you, Dane, and, believe me, it's as incredible as any Greek myth."

"Oh, it's bound to be," he murmured dryly.

"Will you promise to hear me out, and not say anything until I finish?"

He searched her eyes. "Very well."

"Thank you."

"Oh, don't thank me, for I'm merely curious to know how far you're prepared to go with regard to self-preservation. As I observed earlier, with Denham gone, you're on your own."

"Just give me the chance to tell you everything, then, and only then, will you be able to judge me, for at the moment you can't even begin to guess the truth."

"You have my undivided attention."

"You'd better sit down, for it will take some time."

He sat on the grass next to her, and she lowered her glance, twisting her hands nervously together. This was it, the moment of ultimate truth. She couldn't even begin to guess what his reaction would be. He was of the early nineteenth century, brought up in the beliefs and principles of an age that regarded the paranormal as the work of the devil, so how could she expect him to absorb the sort of things she was about to divulge? She was from the much more open-minded future, where books and movies about time travel were commonly found, but even that hadn't made it any easier for her to cope when it actually happened. Telling him was a leap in the dark, and she knew it, but it was a chance she felt she had to take. At the end, he'd either have her committed, or believe what she said. Please God, let it be the latter.

Taking a deep breath, Kathryn began to relate everything. "To begin with, I'm not the Rosalind you married, I'm not even from this time, but from a future century."

Her worst fears were instantly realized, as with a gesture of disgust he got up again. "Oh, dear God above, what's this? The outlandish plot from a fourth-rate play? Or are you just plain mad?"

She caught his sleeve desperately. "Please, you promised to hear me out!" she cried.

"Then credit me with a little intelligence. I expected a rational explanation, not a badly adapted Gothic imbroglio!"

"This is no adaptation, and I'm certainly not mad!" She held on to his sleeve. "You promised you'd listen. *Please* observe your word!"

Reluctantly he sat down once more. "Very well, proceed if you must, but I warn you, only a fool would be taken in by the sort of nonsense you've uttered so far, and I'm certainly not a fool!"

"I know you aren't, which is why I pray you'll believe me," she whispered.

"You have my word I won't interrupt again."

# Thirty

~

Kathryn summoned her courage once more. "As . . . as I was saying, I'm from a future century, and my real name is Kathryn Vansomeren. I'm American, and all this started on a hot July day in New York." She paused as he gave an impatient sigh, but he didn't say anything, so she continued. "Richard and I had another argument, one of many, and . . ."

"Richard?" he interrupted sharply.

"My husband in the future, Richard Vansomeren. He's an architect."

"I trust he has sound knowledge on the construction of lunatic asylums?" he observed caustically.

She lowered her eyes, and pressed bravely on. "We had another argument. He wanted to postpone coming to England on vacation. I got angry, and said I'd come on my own. We'd been having all sorts of problems with our marriage, and on top of that I was having trouble at work as well."

"Work?" His brows drew together. "What do you mean?"

"I . . . I was a . . ." Her voice died away. How on earth did she explain what a TV reporter was? "Oh, it doesn't matter what I mean, all that matters is that the argument ended with me saying I was coming to England anyway. So three days ago I left New York for London."

Dane's eyes swung quizzically toward her, and for a moment she thought he was going to question something else, but he decided against it.

She went on. "When I got to Gloucester, I had the oddest feeling of *déjà vu*."

"Already seen?" he said, translating literally from the French.

"Yes, it was like I'd been in Gloucester before, but not quite. Oh, I don't know how to really explain, except it turned out the place I was staying in in the future was Alice Longney's cottage here in 1815."

"I might have known she'd figure in all this," he murmured.

"She figures very much indeed, for it has all been her doing. Anyway, I went to bed that first evening, and something woke me at about midnight. I looked out of the window and saw someone else reflected in the glass instead of me. It was Rosalind. She—she'd been meeting Thomas Denham there while you were dining with George Eden, the bishop, and so on."

A nerve flickered at his temple, but that was all the response he gave.

Kathryn stumbled determinedly on, for she had no choice now she'd gotten this far. "When . . . when I say it was Rosalind I saw in the glass, what I really mean is that it was me, but looking and sounding like Rosalind. To all intents and purposes Kathryn Vansomeren had become her. Thomas was taken in, he didn't detect any changeover, and expected me to behave as warmly toward him as Rosalind would, but I couldn't because all I could think was how much like Richard he was. When he touched me, I felt nothing. Anyway, he left, and Alice promised me a night of excitement and passion with you. Well, I half-thought I was dreaming it all, and so I went along with it. Excitement and passion was something I didn't get from Richard, but I knew somehow that you were everything I'd ever wanted. I felt it from the moment I heard your name, and then, when I actually saw you . . ." She smiled as she remembered.

"Go on, madam, for I vow you have my interest," he prompted wryly.

"I had your interest that night, too, didn't I?" she replied. "When we made love, it was wonderful. I'd always longed for lovemaking like that, and suddenly I had it. When Alice woke me the following morning, I didn't want to go back to my own time, I wanted to stay with you and make love forever. But I didn't have the choice, I was whisked to the future again. Then I started finding odd things. Someone had tidied the place, looked though my things, and called Richard on the phone, saying all sorts of nice things to him. Don't ask me to explain about phones," she begged quickly.

"I have no such intention, any more than I mean to inquire exactly how you managed to be in New York three days ago. The voyage across the Atlantic takes at least three *weeks*, and that is when the winds are fair."

"It doesn't really have any bearing on what I'm saying."

"Why? Because it's a glaring mistake?"

"Could you explain everything about your time to someone medieval?" she countered. "That person would only know of roads like dirt tracks, but you can speak of tarmacadam, swift mail coaches, and so on."

He smiled a little at that. "The point is made, so pray continue."

She looked anxiously at him. "Do you believe any of what I'm saying?"

"What do you think?"

"I think you believe you're humoring a madwoman."

"No, Rosalind, not mad, just clever. I'm put in mind of Scheherazade, who was also mistress of amusing tales."

"Scheherazade told beguiling stories because she wished to earn the love of the man who heard them," Kathryn pointed out quickly.

"Oh, *touché*, my dear. I had no idea you were mistress of the swift riposte as well, but it so happens that Scheherazade saved her life with her cleverness."

"I am intent upon saving our happiness, Dane," she said quietly.

"I could almost believe you, but then I've never really known you, have I?" His tone was harsh.

"How can you know someone you only met for the first time a day or so ago?"

"That's what you'd have me believe. Well, you insisted on saying your piece to the end, so perhaps you should continue."

"All right. The phone call Richard received purported to be from me, and was full of such conciliatory overtures that he called back and left a message for me, saying he longed for me to go back early as I promised. I couldn't understand it, because as far as I was concerned, we'd practically drawn up battle lines the last time we spoke."

"The poor fellow sounds as bemused and misled as I am. He has my sympathy," Dane observed trenchantly.

"The 'poor fellow' as you call him hasn't done badly out of

all this, believe me—in fact, he's done very nicely, although he doesn't know it yet. Anyway, I decided not to think about the messages for the moment, because I wanted to visit Marchwood, and see how much of what I'd dreamed was really there. Right away I noticed things I couldn't have known from the information leaflet, and I got nervous, because until then I was convinced you were a dream."

"Dream? Or nightmare?" He said softly, holding her eyes.

"That remains to be seen, doesn't it?" she replied, and then went on. "When I arrived I lost my nerve a little, I decided to have some coffee, and I met one of the guides. She told me about the duel. I didn't know about it until then. Anyway, I went on the tour of the castle, and saw your portrait in the great hall. I thought how much I wished you'd come to life again so I'd be with you, and suddenly it happened. One moment I was Kathryn Vansomeren, the next I was Rosalind again. You were angry, because you'd found out about the note to Thomas."

"So the note *was* to him, not to Mrs. Fowler?"

"Yes, but I didn't write it, Dane. The real Rosalind did."

"Ah, but you were as glib then as you are now," he pointed out. "Your explanation was swift and believable. It was to my dressmaker, you said, deftly conjuring salvation from nowhere."

"I know, but in my defense I can only say that *I* didn't do anything. I wanted to be the wife you needed, because I was already halfway in love with you. No, more than halfway, I think I loved you from the moment I saw you the night before. Listen, Dane, I know how ridiculous all this must sound, but it *is* the truth, I swear it is."

"It's certainly intriguing, for I cannot imagine how anyone except a writer of lurid novels could invent such a far-fetched tale, not when Bedlam is the usual consequence of such rantings. So, proceed, madam, let us hear it to the bitter end."

"When I heard about Jeremiah Pendle, something told me I had to meet him, that's why I wanted to go with you to the drawing room. I also had a very odd feeling about the open window in the drawing room, it was something about the way the wind rustled through the ivy against the wall. It was a premonition, I guess. Anyway, when Pendle came in, I saw him look at the pistols. You were just putting them away, remember?"

"Yes."

"So he knew where they were kept, which was useful later when he forced Talbot to do his bidding. Anyway, I didn't like him in the least, I could *feel* that he was your enemy."

"He has little cause to like me; after all, I did kill William Denham," Dane pointed out.

"Yes, and Pendle was just waiting for an opportunity to do you harm. He found it useful that Thomas called you out. Anyway, that's to come. I stayed a while, and then went to my apartment, after making you promise to come to me. Do you remember?"

"No man could forget," he murmured.

She felt a warmth enter her cheeks. "Nor any woman," she added softly, and paused to take a deep breath before speaking again. "When you left me, I returned to the portrait in the hall, and Alice was waiting. I tried to get her to tell me what was really going on, why it was happening to me, and so on, but all she'd say was that I'd know everything in good time. She also told me that she had second sight."

He lay back on the grass, gazing up at the branches overhead. "So the old witch is exactly that—a witch," he murmured.

"Something very close to it," Kathryn agreed, glancing swiftly down at him as she thought she detected a change in his attitude toward her. Was he beginning to accept what she said? She pressed on with the story. "At least, Alice *was* something like a witch, but she isn't now. Her powers ended at midnight last night. Anyway, she told me you'd find out about Rosalind and Thomas at the sailing of the *Lady Marchwood*, that nothing could prevent that, but if I wished to see you again before then, at the Waterloo ball, I was to be at a certain place in Cheltenham at a certain time. That was the end of it for the time being; suddenly I was in the future again, and Alice had turned into the guide I'd had coffee with earlier. By now I naturally wanted to find out all I could about what went on in 1815, so she directed me to the main library in Gloucester. I went there and researched the ball, the maiden voyage, and . . . the duel." She was glad he didn't ask questions, for she didn't want to mention Jeremiah Pendle's diary—not just yet, anyway.

She continued. "That night I went to the place Alice said in Cheltenham, and came back to this time again. As Rosalind, I kept an assignation with Thomas Denham. I tried to change things by saying I loved you and was going to stay with you. That's when . . ."

"Yes?"

She looked down at him as he lay on the grass beside her. "That's when he mentioned the baby," she said quietly. How would he take such news? To the deceived husband, surely the only thing worse than the actual betrayal was to learn that it had borne fruit?

He met her gaze, and she could see the trees reflected in his eyes. His face was very still. "Don't stop now," he said softly.

"I . . . I took fright then, and ran back to the hall, where I found you."

"And where you once again gulled me into trusting you, so much so that we made love in the carriage on the way back to Marchwood, and then all through the night after that." Suddenly he pulled her down beside him, and then leaned over her, sliding a knowing hand over her breast and caressing her through the delicate muslin of her gown. "This was how it was then, mm? Sensuous delights until dawn . . ."

He bent his head to kiss her parted lips. He gave her no quarter, employing his considerable skills to tease her into response. The blood began to flow hopefully through her veins and her mouth softened willingly beneath his. Her nipples hardened eagerly at his touch, and her whole body warmed with the swift desire only he could arouse. A sigh escaped her as he moved onto her. He was going to take her right there on the grass! It had to mean he believed her, and that everything was going to be all right!

How wrong she was though, for everything was far from right.

# Thirty-one

≈

There wasn't to be any abandoned lovemaking on the grass, because he hadn't forgiven her, but was merely punishing her again as he had the night before.

For a moment he allowed her to feel the hard shaft pounding at his loins, but he didn't free it to enter her. He simply allowed her to know he could if he chose, then he looked mockingly down into her eyes.

"If I thought you didn't want it now, I'd take you anyway, but you do want it, don't you, my darling? Well, I'm afraid I must leave you panting for more, because nothing on God's earth will ever induce me to sully myself with you again." He sat up as if he'd never touched her.

Tears were wet on her cheeks, but she made no sound, and it was several moments before she at last managed to speak again. "What virtue is there in humiliating me like this, Dane?" she whispered.

"No virtue, madam, but a great deal of satisfaction for the wrongs you've done me. You may claim to be this Kathryn Vansomeren, and say it was beyond your power until now to tell me the so-called truth, but when I look at you now, I see perfidious Rosalind. You've been misleading me, and doing it so successfully I actually trusted you with my closest secret. I told you about Elizabeth and William Denham, and you listened as if butter wouldn't melt in your damned mouth! But all the time you've been carrying Thomas Denham's child!"

Blinking back the tears, she sat up as well, in order to see into his bitter eyes. It was a moment or so before she could make her voice obey her again, but when it did, it trembled with feeling. "No, Dane, I'm not carrying a child. Rosalind is, but not me. And Rosalind wouldn't want your kisses as I do. If you'd taken me a moment ago, I'd have been overjoyed, I freely admit it, but can you really deny that you didn't want me as well, that your arousal had as much to do with desire as punishment? Outwardly you may treat me as if I mean nothing to you, but behind that angry facade . . ." She allowed her voice to trail away.

He looked at the way the sun shone on the golden tangle of her hair, and at the seductive shadows where her breasts curved into her low-cut bodice, then he met her eyes impassively. "There isn't a man alive who couldn't rise to the occasion with you, Rosalind, but whether the act would mean anything to him emotionally is another matter. A few swift thrusts, and I could walk away from you now without a backward glance."

A sad smile played upon her lips. "If you can still say that when I've told you everything, I'll have no option but to accept it. But you gave your word you'd hear me out to the end, and I'm still holding you to that."

"You mean I must endure more of this idiocy?"

She put her hand hesitantly to his cheek. "Dane, I know how hard all this is to believe, and believe me, it's just as hard to say, so hard I've forgotten something vital. You see, when I got back from the library, I discovered someone had been in my apartment again. It was Rosalind, and I realized that every time I came back here in time, she took my place in the future!"

He stared at her, but then shook his head. "This becomes more and more of a fairy tale! Soon there will be giants, wizards, and goblins to add a little *je ne sais quoi* to the plot!"

She tried to compose herself. "I didn't find it easy to believe either, and I was the one it was happening to! I know you think I'm crazy, but the truth is often stranger than fiction. Isn't that what they say?"

"I don't know. Do they?"

"Whether they do or not, it's right. So is what I'm saying to you. When you left me after telling me about Elizabeth and William, I found Alice waiting for me. She told me she'd tell me everything when the challenge was issued at the docks. So I went to the docks, I became Rosalind again, and though I tried my hardest not to let anything happen with Thomas, it did all the same because he threatened to make a scene unless I spoke privately with him. You didn't find us in a loving embrace, you found me trying to get away when he wouldn't believe it when I said I was in love with you. There was nothing I could do, Dane, just as until now there hasn't been anything I could do all along. Events had to take their course, they couldn't be changed, no matter how I tried, and I *did* try, you must believe me." She lowered her glance to the grass.

"Anyway, Alice took me to her cottage after the challenge had been issued, and she told me all I didn't yet know. You see, it wasn't coincidence that Thomas Denham made me think of Richard Vansomeren—he *is* Richard. My modern New York husband is Thomas Denham born again in the future. No, don't stop me now! Somehow Alice's second sight told her about Richard, and she informed Rosalind, who was in love with Thomas and frightened because she was expecting a child that couldn't possibly be yours. Nothing could prevent Thomas's dying today, but if he lived again in the future, Rosalind wanted to go to him. Alice had the power to keep swapping Rosalind and me around, but with one final effort she could see that it took place permanently. That would mean Rosalind's becoming Kathryn Vansomeren forever, and taking her unborn child into the future, to a future Thomas Denham. They'd be perfect together, and, like the best fairy tales, they'd live happily ever after. But it would also mean my agreeing to come back here to you, and I couldn't be so assured of happiness, not when your faith in Rosalind had been so bitterly shattered. Could you ever love me again? That was the risk, but I took it because you mean more to me than anything in the world. I've come back here forever now, and my happiness depends upon you. But so far you've rejected me, and how cruelly."

He glanced away.

She went on. "Last night, when you left me on the staircase, I went to the drawing room for the wedding ring Rosalind told me she left on the cabinet. Yes, she and I did meet, only the once. Anyway, I'd just put the ring on when I heard Frederick Talbot climbing up to the window. The rest you know, more or less. I swear there's never been anything I could say or do. Whenever I've tried to change things or stop them happening, I've come up against some sort of *impasse*. You'll come up against the same thing if you try to face Pendle. Historic facts can't be changed, and those facts are that Pendle's not going to lay charges against you, probably because he fears George's threats; instead, he's going to write a virtriolic and damning version of the duel, accusing you of murdering Thomas Denham by causing the pistol to misfire. Then a heart attack is going to put an end to dear Jeremiah. He'll be dead before tomorrow's dawn."

Dane stared at her. "Dead?"

"The facts are all there in the future." She told him about George's being in America when Pendle's heir discovered the diary, and about no charges ever being actually brought.

He was silent for a moment. "So you're saying I'm obliged to be chronicled as the villain of the piece?"

"Yes." She got to her feet. "The facts can't be changed, you see," she said again. "I don't really know why I've been able to tell you anything now, except I guess it's because I'm not trying to alter the facts. All I'm doing is explaining what's been happening to me. To us." She looked down at him. "I heard you confess to George that you still loved me. What he said was right, Dane, it's never too late."

"You would say that, wouldn't you?" he replied coolly.

She drew a long breath. "If the chill in your voice is a sign of the chill that remains in your heart, then there's little more to be said, except perhaps to repeat that I am indeed Kathryn Vansomeren in Rosalind's body and clothes, I'm not expecting a child, nor have I betrayed you with Thomas Denham. But I *have* been an unfaithful wife, that much I do concede. I took a lover briefly in New York, and every time I made love with you, I broke my vows to Richard again. If that makes me no better than Rosalind or Elizabeth, then so be it. But you also broke your vows, for it wasn't Rosalind you slept with those times, it was me, the siren twin who might be about to fall because Odysseus is able to resist her voice. Or am I Scheherazade, whose amusing stories win the sultan's heart? Which is it to be, Dane?"

He looked up at her. "You offer an impossible choice."

"No, not impossible. Either you believe me, or you don't. It's quite simple, really. I've faced a similar decision, and knew very swiftly what I wanted. I chose you, nothing else would do." She searched his gaze. "What does your heart tell you, Dane? Could you really use me now and then walk away without a backward glance?"

He didn't reply.

She felt the sting of tears, but refused to let them out. "Perhaps I should be the one to walk away then," she said quietly.

He continued to gaze at her, searching her eyes as if there was something about them that struck a chord.

She turned to go, but suddenly he caught her hand. "Don't go. I don't care who you are or where you're from, only that I love you and want you to stay."

Gladness surged ecstatically through her. "Do—do you really mean that?" she whispered.

"Never more so in my life," he breathed, pulling her down to the grass and then leaning over her.

She linked her arms around his neck. "You believe all I've told you?"

"How can I not, when . . ." He paused, looking deep into her eyes. "Tell me, what color eyes does Kathryn Vansomeren have?"

"Hazel. Why?"

"Because I have seen your eyes hazel. Oh, it was fleeting, when our passion was at its height, but I saw green change to hazel. I thought it was a trick of the light, but now . . ."

"Now you know it was no trick, that for a moment you really did see Kathryn," she said softly.

"I know it very well."

"I'm Rosalind forever now, my eyes will never change again."

"I trust you're Rosalind with Kathryn's passionate nature?"

"Oh, you may count upon it, sir. Shall I prove it?" She smiled, pulling his lips down to hers.

It was a long, tender kiss, made complete by the total trust that at last existed between them. There were no secrets anymore, nothing to cast a shadow over their caresses, but there was much to erase. For her, it was the fact that she was no longer Richard's wife, but Dane's. For him, it was the two unhappy years he'd spent with the real Rosalind. They were both beginning anew, and the inevitable and immediate consequence was a need for urgent open-air consummation.

They left the path for the secrecy of some nearby bushes, where soon they lay naked together among the ferns and long grasses. She felt no self-consciousness; indeed, she exulted in the warmth of the sun on her body as they made love. A shiver of delight passed through her as she felt his hot virility push deep inside her, and then her breath caught as he slowly withdrew before plunging in once more. His movements were long and leisurely, and waves of carnal pleasure began to course along her veins. The scent of crushed grass and ferns was all around, and the sun was dazzling through the trees, but she was weightless and ethereal, floating on the joy of his lovemaking.

His skill was matchless. Their shared desire was at fever pitch, and an explosion of sensuality was close as he tempered his thrusts to prolong the gratification. He hardly moved inside her as her body quivered with orgasms of delight so intense they threatened to rob her of consciousness.

At last he took his own pleasure, driving his potent shaft in as far as he could and surrendering to the pounding desire he'd kept at bay in order not to deny her whatever pleasure she sought. His body shuddered, and his skin was damp afterward when at last he gathered her in his arms. Their hearts beat together as he pressed his lips to the pulse at her throat.

She closed her eyes and lifted her face to the sunlight. She held him tenderly, and tears of happiness welled from beneath her lashes. This man made her complete, and the only darkness on the horizon was that he would bear the blame for what had happened to Thomas Denham.

She wished she knew what to do to clear his name. Something was nagging at the back of her mind, something that would solve the problem. Not now, maybe, but in years to come, long after she and Dane were no more. She'd seen something happening now in 1815, and knew it was going to happen again in several centuries' time. It was there, right on the edge of her memory, but infuriatingly beyond reach.

Half an hour later they dressed and returned to the castle. On the way they encountered the search party he'd ordered to look for the rider of the stray horse. The grooms reined in on seeing Sir Dane and Lady Marchwood walking hand-in-hand from the scene of the duel. By now everyone knew how Thomas Denham had met his death, because two gamekeepers had secretly watched everything in the oak grove, and had reported back what Jeremiah Pendle said. Feelings were mixed at the castle. Some said Dane would never do something so base and dishonorable, but others declared they would defend his good name to the end. The grooms therefore tried not to show they knew anything at all.

Dane glanced at them. "You'll find the owner of the horse about ten yards just to the right of the path by the stepping stones. He was thrown and appears to have broken his back."

The groom in charge touched his hat. "Very well, sir."

"It's Frederick Talbot. Does anyone know him?"

"I do, Sir Dane," replied another man, maneuvering his horse forward.

"Does he leave a family?"

"No, sir."

"Then as soon as you've collected his body, have someone ride to Gloucester to inform the authorities."

"Sir."

They rode on, and Dane glanced after them. "Gloucester will ring of this. Two dead bodies emerging from Marchwood on the same day! No doubt I'll be credited with the gunsmith's demise as well."

"There's no reason why you should."

"Gossip needs no reason," he murmured, slipping his arm around her waist as they walked on.

The terraced gardens were sweet with the perfume of roses, and the breeze rustled through the ivy against the castle wall, but it didn't affect Kathryn now. It was just another warm summer sound.

They entered the great hall, where the chip-chip of the stonemasons at work broke the silence. Kathryn's steps faltered and she stared toward the men as her thoughts returned once more to the problem of how to clear Dane's name and see that the real culprits were condemned by the future. The future. With a sudden flash of inspiration she knew what to do, with an excited cry she turned to Dane. "I've thought of a way to see that one day the truth gets out about what happened at the duel!"

He smiled at her flushed face. "Yes," he replied dryly, "we can go into Gloucester and set fire to Pendle's damned coattails. Except we can't do even that small thing, because it would mean altering facts, and that's not allowed."

But nothing could crush her. "Maybe we can't alter the facts that are already recorded, but we can supersede them."

He put a finger to his lips and nodded toward the stonemasons, who might be able to overhear, then he whispered. "Supersede?"

She whispered too. "There's a saying, I forget where it comes from, but it's something about truth being time's daughter. Do you know it?"

"Yes, but—"

"That fireplace will be repaired again in the future, taken apart exactly as it is now. I saw it then, and I've seen it now."

He studied her. "What if it is?"

"If I write the truth about the duel and hide it in the fireplace, it will be discovered again in the future. Maybe it won't help you now, but at least you'll know that one day your name will be vindicated. I'm sure it can be done, for we aren't trying to alter things that have happened, all we're doing is creating things for the future. Isn't that right?"

He ran his fingers through his hair. "Yes, I suppose it is."

"If only I could clear your name now, but . . ."

"It doesn't matter. Sticks and stones break bones, names have yet to succeed. I'm only concerned that you know I didn't do anything to that damned pistol. Oh, and that Philip knows it too."

"He'll believe what we tell him."

"Yes."

"And to hell with the rest of the world!" She smiled.

He put his hand to her cheek, caressing her skin with his thumb. "You came to me through time, so truth is not alone in being time's daughter."

She put her fingers tenderly over his. "I love you, Sir Dane Marchwood, I love you with all my heart and soul."

"And I love you, my sweet lady," he murmured, taking her hand and turning the palm softly to his lips.

The stonemasons exchanged startled glances. Sir Dane Marchwood had just killed a man on account of her ladyship, but that didn't seem to have cooled their ardor in the least! Posh folk were a mystery, and no mistake.

# Thirty-two

~

It was the week before Christmas just over four years later as a car drove into the empty parking lot at Marchwood Castle. Snow drifted in the frozen air, but had yet to settle, and smoke curled from the chimneys in the nearby village.

Rosalind smiled at Richard. "It looks deserted."

"If you ask me it's closed for the winter," he replied, stopping the car close to the shuttered ticket office.

She glanced at the back seat, where a little girl with blonde Shirley Temple curls had fallen asleep with a doll in her arms. "Wake up, pumpkin, we're here."

The child stirred. "Already, Mommy? I'm still tired."

"Darling, you can sleep all you want when we get to Gloucester."

Richard looked curiously at his wife. "Why was it so darned important to come here first?"

"I don't really know. I just wanted to see it again, that's all." Rosalind got out and opened the rear door. "Come on, Alice, let's see if we can take a look at the castle."

Clutching the doll, the child climbed out, shivering as the chill wind blustered freely over the lot.

Richard was glad of their thick winter clothes as he surveyed the towers and battlements rising above the bare trees. "That's some place," he commented.

"Yes, it is," Rosalind murmured. The past was all around her suddenly, and she almost expected to see Dane. She turned her collar up, and shook out her tumbling chestnut curls.

Richard gave her an approving look. "I think your hair looks great like that. I've always liked long curls, and never could stand that bobbed style you used to wear."

"You should have told me."

"You'd probably have taken it as a criticism, and we'd just have had something else to argue about."

"True."

"You know, your coming to England that time was probably the best thing. It gave us both time to think, even if it was only a few days. Still, it's definitely two weeks this time, and we'll have a great time."

"Yes, we will."

He put his hand to her cheek. "Are you still sure you don't regret giving up your career?"

"I've hardly given it another thought, except to gloat now and then about how satisfying it was to make that scene with Diane in front of the entire office. God, was it great! I was in my element."

"I'm told she's been in therapy ever since," he remarked dryly.

"If only."

He searched her face again. "So you swear you're content to just be a wife and mother?"

"What do you mean *just* a wife and mother? It's hard work, and soon to be even harder." She took his hand and placed it against her stomach, where the swelling of another pregnancy was plain beneath her thick clothes.

He kissed her nose. "And to think we believed we'd never have one child, let alone two."

"I have my sights set on more than that, Mr. Vansomeren."

"How many more?"

"How many can you manage?"

He laughed. "Oh, I can manage just fine, I like making babies."

"So I've noticed."

"Are you complaining?"

"No."

"Good." He looked at the castle again. "Well, I'll be surprised if we get inside. It doesn't look like anyone's been here since World War II," he said, bending to swing Alice up on his shoulders. "Okay, sweetheart?"

The little girl squealed with delight as he cavorted around for a moment like a bronco.

Rosalind smiled as she watched. He was the perfect hus-

band, and the perfect father. He adored Alice, treasuring her
more than most men might because he'd never expected to
have her. It had been wonderful to see his joy on discovering
his wife to be pregnant after all. She didn't feel any guilt about
not telling him everything. He didn't need to know. Besides,
she wasn't really foisting another man's child on him, for
Alice was his. At least, she was Thomas's, and that was the
same thing.

This new unborn baby was Richard's in every way, though.
Conceived long after she'd changed places with the real
Kathryn, and conceived in more happiness than Rosalind had
ever dreamed possible. It was weird how like Thomas he
was. Oh, outwardly they weren't in the least alike, but in other
ways . . . She smiled again. Not for a single moment had she
ever regretted what had happened four years previously. She
only prayed the real Kathryn had found similar happiness in
the past.

There was no comfortable woman knitting in the ticket hut,
and nobody on the path leading past the church. It was Sun-
day, and carols were being sung. All very atmospheric, and
very English.

Rosalind shivered with more than just the cold as they
passed the restaurant and souvenir shop, both closed and shuttered like the ticket hut. The Waterloo cannon still stood on
the gravel by the drawbridge and gatehouse, and the steps to
the terraced gardens afforded the same view over the March
meadows toward the woods. She stood on the steps, gazing toward the trees where Thomas Denham had met his death.

"Come on, honey, there's life here after all," Richard called,
and she turned to see he'd managed to bring someone to the
little postern door set into the main gate.

Turning her collar up against the wind, Rosalind hurried to
join him, and with a shock recognized the woman who'd an-
swered Richard's knock. It was the guide the real Kathryn had
had coffee with. "Haven't we met before?" Rosalind asked.

The woman's brows drew together thoughtfully. "I don't
think so . . ."

"Yes, we have. About four years ago. I had coffee with you
in the restaurant and you told me about handsome Sir Dane
Marchwood."

The woman's eyes cleared. "Yes, of course! I remember you well!"

"We were wondering if we could take a look around. I know you're closed and all that, but we've come a long way, and we just want a quick peek."

The woman hesitated. "I'm not supposed to let anyone in until Easter."

Richard's dry humor came to the fore. "We'll be frozen to death by then."

The woman smiled. "We can't have that. All right, come on in, but I'm afraid nothing's aired now, all the rooms are very cold, especially the great hall."

Rosalind stepped through into the courtyard. "I don't care how cold it is," she murmured, gazing around at the remembered scene.

Alice wasn't interested in castles. She was tired and hungry, and sleep was long overdue, which meant she was fractious too, especially when Richard lifted her down from his shoulders so she could walk. She began to cry, holding her arms up to be carried again.

The woman was no novice with children, and smiled at Rosalind. "Will you trust me with her? I have the very thing to amuse her."

"If you're sure . . . ?"

"Quite sure." The woman crouched before Alice. "That's a lovely doll you have there. Would you like to see my dolls?"

"You've got dolls?" Alice stopped crying and looked at her in astonishment. "But you're too old for dolls!"

"Alice!" Richard gave her a disapproving look.

"Well, she is," Alice replied with devastating logic.

The woman smiled again. "Yes, I am, but these are very special dolls. I collect them, you see, and they all have beautiful dresses. They're in my rooms just through that door there, and it's warm inside. I've just baked, too. Do you like cookies?"

"Oh, yes, I love cookies." Alice's eyes brightened. Dolls, cookies, *and* warmth? That beat castles any day!

The woman straightened and held out her hand. "Shall we leave Mummy and Daddy to look around in the cold, while you and I get warm and cozy?"

Alice hesitated, glancing at Rosalind, but on receiving a nod of permission, she gladly accepted the woman's hand, and trotted away at her side.

As they vanished through the doorway, Richard looked at Rosalind. "Well, you've been dying to get here, so we'd better get on with looking around. Which way?"

"That door in the far corner. It leads to the great hall."

"Okay." He put a loving arm around her shoulder, and they walked across the windswept courtyard.

The iron ring handle was like ice to the touch, and it took Richard both hands to turn it, but at last the door swung open, its hinges creaking loudly in the silence beyond. Rosalind walked swiftly toward the hall, and paused expectantly at the entrance to gaze toward the half-landing, and Dane's portrait.

It was like looking at him in the flesh. At any moment he might step down from the canvas and claim her back. Her heartbeats quickened, but then she smiled. He wouldn't want her, not when he had Kathryn!

Richard saw where she was looking. "Who is that guy?"

"Sir Dane Marchwood."

"You mentioned him just now. You seem to find him mighty interesting."

"I do. He's very handsome, don't you think?" she replied, giving him a teasing glance.

"Too damned handsome," Richard muttered.

She smiled and began to walk toward the portrait, but Richard noticed some interesting architectural detail on the arch of the entrance, and didn't go with her. She ascended slowly to the half-landing, and then gazed at the canvas.

"Hello, Dane," she whispered, reaching out to touch the painted face. "Did you forgive me? Did you take Kathryn to your heart like you should? I hope so. God, I hope so . . ."

She stood for a long time looking at the portrait, and remembering her past life.

"Hey, look at this," Richard said from somewhere behind her. The hall took up his voice, making it echo.

She turned. "What is it?"

He was standing by the fireplace. "That guy Sir Dane. Seems he was quite a hothead. He fought four duels, and won them all."

"Yes, he did. How do you know about the duels?" she asked then, going back down the stairs and crossing to join him.

"It says here. There's a document that was found in the fireplace about four years back. Must have been not long after you were here. This Dane feller's wife, Rosalind, wanted to clear her husband's name after he was wrongly accused of some jiggery-pokery with the other guy's pistol at the fourth duel. Not cricket, eh?" Richard chuckled, putting on a mock-British accent.

"Not cricket at all," Rosalind murmured, looking at the framed sheet of ancient, rather soot-stained vellum.

Richard had already read it. "This Rosalind was quite some woman, and certainly loved her husband. It comes over loud and clear in every line."

Rosalind smiled. "Yes, she did love him."

"And she sure points the finger at the real villains, guys called Jeremiah Pendle and Frederick Talbot. God, they sound right out of Dickens."

Rosalind stared at the paper and smiled. Oh, clever Kathryn to have defied history after all!

Richard shrugged. "Why the hell didn't Rosalind speak out at the time? If she knew the truth, why didn't she do something right away?"

"I'm sure there were reasons," Rosalind murmured. Oh, yes, there were reasons all right . . .

Richard looked curiously at her, and then gave a slight start. "God, that was the damnedest thing!"

"What?"

"I thought . . . No, it couldn't be."

"What did you think?"

"Well, for a moment there I could have sworn your eyes were green." He laughed. "Guess I'm more tired than I thought."

She smiled. "Guess so."